AGATHA ZAZA

THE PRETENDERS

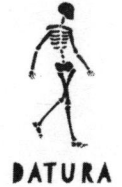

DATURA BOOKS
An imprint of Watkins Media Ltd

Unit 11, Shepperton House
89-93 Shepperton Road
London N1 3DF
UK

daturabooks.com
Secrets and lies

A Datura Books paperback original, 2026

Copyright © Agatha Zaza 2026

Cover by
Set in Meridien

All rights reserved. Agatha Zaza asserts the moral right to be identified as the author of this work. A catalogue record for this book is available from the British Library.

This novel is entirely a work of fiction. Names, characters, places, and incidents are the products of the author's imagination or are used fictitiously. Any resemblance to actual events, locales, organizations or persons, living or dead, is entirely coincidental.

Sales of this book without a front cover may be unauthorized. If this book is coverless, it may have been reported to the publisher as "unsold and destroyed" and neither the author nor the publisher may have received payment for it.

Datura Books and the Datura Books icon are registered trademarks of Watkins Media Ltd.

ISBN 978 1 91741 524 8
Ebook ISBN 978 1 91741 525 5

Printed and bound in the United Kingdom by CPI Group (UK) Ltd, Croydon CR0 4YY

The manufacturer's authorised representative in the EU for product safety is eucomply OÜ – Pärnu mnt 139b-14, 11317 Tallinn, Estonia, hello@eucompliancepartner.com; www.eucompliancepartner.com

9 8 7 6 5 4 3 2 1

For Jo

MORNING

1

The bespoke play den had not been made to blend into the garden setting. It had been built to mimic childhood spontaneity, cleverly lopsided and made of cedar planks, seven feet high and nearly as wide, and painted a grey-blue. It had been designed to be noticed, to appeal to children to come to play in it. Its flat timber roof had been built to hold escaped pirates and rampaging sea monsters. A short flagpole was fixed upon it, made to be captured. Its little door and single window had been framed in white, and two round stumps of wood stood in front of it, serving no real purpose except to be jumped off.

A borrowed sledgehammer smashed into thin wood walls. Edmund butchered the little unoccupied – never occupied – playhouse in a salvo of blows that reverberated throughout the garden and over its walls. A rush of anger freed itself from his lungs through each grunt that came with every blow.

After the assault, he stopped to examine what he'd done. The tiny house held together for a moment, its sides cleaved from one another. Not built to withstand someone desperate to erase it from existence, what was left of the little house swayed and collapsed.

Seeing it fallen, Edmund found himself dissatisfied and continued, splintering the playhouse into the smallest pieces he could. His body was built for this kind of work but was unaccustomed to it. His tall, lanky figure rapidly began to feel the pain. He ignored the beads of sweat that rose in his curly brown hair and stubble. He closed his eyes as his hands gripped the unfamiliar instrument, his skin bruising and manicure quickly damaged. Clods of dirt and debris flew against his pyjamas, and his slippers were ruined.

The sky was not quite dark, but it wasn't yet morning. It was the time of day after the end of parties and the closing of clubs yet before the legions of dogwalkers and early runners took to the pavements and parks. Edmund worked by the dim glow of the streetlamp that stood just outside his garden wall. He battered the playhouse, oblivious to the world around him.

His garden was pristine. The smell of recently mowed grass lingered in the air. Set on a terraced street, the back garden met a park whose trees, verdant with seasonal foliage, spread their limbs over the garden's extreme end where Edmund was splintering now formless planks. He was obscured by shadows cast by its high stone walls embedded with creepers. As he fought, the ground beneath him turned to mud.

Edmund gritted his teeth as he struck the child-sized flag over and over, embedding it in the damp grass.

'Shit!' He winced as he missed and instead struck the concrete border of a flower bed that circled the inside of the wall. The sledgehammer ricocheted, and Edmund slipped with the force, putting out his hand to steady himself, swearing again as he cut his hand on the fallen walls.

The lawn ended in a pale stone terrace, a platform of bland, undistinguished beige masonry. Behind him, four floors of grey-brown brick towered in a silhouette against the city lights in the distance. Edmund felt as if its windows were glaring down at him, as if the house were alive and urging him on, telling him to finish what he'd begun.

He knew the playhouse didn't have to be demolished. It could have been disassembled, sold – passed on to someone with little children who'd play endless games of pirates and cowboys in it. But his rage had needed an outlet, and the playhouse had been here, mocking him day after day, a constant reminder of what he'd lost and would never have again.

Edmund returned to his house on unsteady legs. A swell of relief welled within him as he glanced back at what remained of the playhouse.

He felt closer to the end, able to see the finish line, and he could just about bear looking at his own home. Ahead of him stood a twelve-foot-tall clear glass cube. Attached to the back of the house, a glass extension was framed in black iron, punctuating the garden's Victorian heritage like a slap. With its glass ceiling and walls, the cube stood futuristic in its contrast with the hundred-and-twenty-year-old house. A low light inside it glowed, showing off its contemporary garden furniture. An armchair and two sofas in grey, standing on hexagonal tiling in black and white that hid underfloor heating. A table spoke of drinks and early breakfasts, afternoon barbecues and promises of autumn evenings spent with soft music and books. Its apparent perfection riled him, and Edmund imagined taking a hammer to the glass extension, knowing he couldn't. He wanted desperately to leave this house, sell it – or, preferably, strike it out of existence, erase all traces of the life he'd led here. He wanted to leapfrog past the agents, the potential buyers, the questions and forms to be filled and to escape – to where, he didn't know.

Edmund opened the cube's door noiselessly, and a wall of warm air met him as he stepped inside.

'Finished?' Ovidia asked Edmund as he entered the extension, the sledgehammer abandoned in the garden. She stood lacing a clean pair of running shoes. It was early, even for her. Her eyes were swollen from recent tears and a night spent between crying and tossing and turning in bed. Her worn blue T-shirt and shorts had been washed repeatedly until their colours faded and seams frayed. Her hair was bound in a cheap headscarf and her feet in a pair of lurid purple slippers.

Edmund grunted in response, looking at his ruined nightclothes in the light. He examined his hands and saw that one was bleeding – a cut that immediately began to sting. He rubbed his hands on his shirt, leaving red-brown streaks of blood.

'We could've sold it,' Ovidia said, missing an eyelet. 'We agreed, remember?'

'A month ago,' Edmund replied. 'We've been endlessly putting it off, like everything else.'

'We could have waited a little bit longer,' she insisted, louder, and tossed the shoe onto the floor, her task abandoned.

'What for, a few hundred pounds?' he asked in a quiet, weary voice.

Ovidia picked her shoe up from where it had landed and, sitting down on the closest chair, began to cry. Again. She leaned over, covering her face with her hands and an unlaced shoe. Edmund felt as if it was for the thousandth time that week. He could never have imagined that one day he would run out of empathy, that he'd be unable to reach out to her and comfort her. He was exhausted by her helplessness, her paralysis, her inability to function.

It would soon be over. Edmund steadied himself with the idea that today would close this chapter of his life. He'd finally be able to escape the house and everything in it, even Ovidia.

'Are you going running? Today?' he asked, realising afterwards that it sounded like an accusation.

Ovidia clutched the shoe, her eyes pressed tightly shut.

'It won't change anything if you don't,' he said, and she loosened her grip on the shoe.

Guilt gnawing at him, Edmund watched her cry and finally moved to sit beside her, wrapping her in his arms. He contemplated the contrast between her skin and his skin, something he'd done only in the earliest days of their relationship. He watched the blood seep from his hand into the fabric of her shirt. His thoughts vacillated between knowing the shirt would be thrown away and contemplating how he would survive leaving her.

2

Edmund's personal assistant had given Jasper the wrong address. He'd called her in the morning. She'd answered, her voice groggy with a hint of annoyance. Jasper had tried to compensate for calling her so early by playing up his charm, lowering his voice and dragging the syllables of her name. She'd seemed momentarily flustered, asked after his health, and then asked him to hold while she checked. *'Wait, that's not it,'* he'd thought he'd heard her say to herself, *'this one,'* she'd said.

Jasper had jotted down the Hammersmith address as the PA read it out haltingly, as if it was unfamiliar. It seemed it wasn't often she was asked for her employer's address. Once she'd finished, Jasper thanked her and hung up.

They could have come by Underground – only a short walk away – but Jasper had said he didn't feel like plodding here from the station. But now his hangover had subsided, chased away by more than the recommended dose of painkillers, and Jasper was content. He could imagine having another celebratory drink at his brother's house.

'All right?' the driver had asked when they climbed in.

'Yes, most definitely all right,' Jasper had replied as he reclined in the seat.

On the phone that morning, Edmund's PA had told Jasper that Edmund was in the city, but, she'd said, she didn't know if he was at home or not – those weren't the sort of details he shared with her.

He'd texted his brother the previous night about coming to visit and, upon receiving no reply, had decided to surprise him in the morning. Had Jasper called, he was sure Edmund would have answered, letting him know if he was in a skyscraper in Kuala Lumpur or in his local Waitrose selecting a microwave dinner. The worst that would happen would be their merry little gang would have to find some other place to celebrate.

Jasper knew that he was taking a chance in barging in on him because Edmund, when in London, still spent his Saturday mornings doing nothing but reading newspapers and being happily unproductive. The last Saturday morning he'd ever spent at Edmund's home – the large, gleaming, contemporary flat his brother had owned years ago – Edmund had made a cup of tea and parked himself in a spot by the window in which he could enjoy the sunlight streaming into the room. Edmund had played a form of folksy jazz that Jasper couldn't stand. Edmund had hummed along, quickly and easily finishing a selection of crossword puzzles from an omnibus he'd found in the attic of their parents' house. Later that morning, Jasper had found the omnibus abandoned on a side table, flicked through it, and found inscribed in the inside cover *Ed, 12, Bristol*. He'd chuckled as he scrolled through it, pausing to examine the difference over thirty years made in his brother's handwriting, and finding it fascinating that, at the ages of twelve or forty, Edmund could still find the same pastime fascinating.

Now, Jasper and his companions were arriving in a taxi at exactly 10am, watching the ordinary Saturday morning unfold around them. The road began in a commonplace assortment of houses from various eras of London history – monolithic concrete blocks of flats of the '60s and bland suburban semi-detached houses of the '80s. A third of the way up the street, the left-hand side began to evolve into regal Victorian terraces, while the right remained modest brown brick, though the houses were of the same age.

His brother's house was boldly affluent, like its neighbours. The houses along the terrace were nearly identical, and their inhabitants would call themselves palatable euphemisms for rich – such as 'comfortable' or 'well off'. An agent would say this was in a catchment area for a top school and had excellent access to the city. The row of houses was a few dozen long, each with a stark white ground floor with a bay window beside the front door. The rest of the buildings were brown and grey brick, and each house had six windows set in white porticos and a lower ground floor visible from where it sat low into the ground. Low wrought-iron fences delineated each house, and small front gardens and walkways flung out surprises, such as brightly coloured tiles and plant pots.

Jasper's little group stopped outside the address he'd been given. Edmund's front door was beige. All six windows that faced the street were curtained. The front door was visibly ajar.

3

Edmund got up twice that Saturday morning. At some indefinite time, he'd hauled himself out of a bed in which he'd lain sleepless. After he'd rendered the playhouse into splinters, he'd watched Ovidia leave for her run and, realising there was nothing for him to do, had trudged back up the stairs. Ovidia's alarm for five in the morning had rung in their absence. It rang at that time five or six mornings a week, nearly every week, wherever in the world they were. He'd sat on the bed shutting off the alarm's insistent beeping and, in his soiled night clothes, had fallen into sound yet brief sleep. Then, as usual, at six – even on this morning – he got up himself.

Edmund sat for a moment on the bed he and Ovidia shared most nights. On the housekeeper's days off, he or Ovidia would straighten the sheets and the cover and leave the collection of decorative pillows on the floor where they tossed them each night before bed. Today, it wouldn't be made.

He let his feet rest on the short plush carpet that ended in a rectangle of tiling that bordered the fireplace – the only original feature in the room he'd let remain. He waited, hoping for the strength and motivation to rise. Eventually, he stood, telling himself he had no choice.

Edmund brushed his teeth and washed his face in a bathroom that bore no resemblance to the one he'd had completely gutted and refitted. He had a fondness for long, hot showers, and the shower with a glass enclosure had been his choice but, thinking of Ovidia, he had insisted on the curved white free-standing tub. The two of them had soaked in it together covered in bubbles one evening when it was new, and, in the two years since, it had never been used again.

He struggled down to the kitchen on the lower-ground floor. The journey seemed long and arduous, and he trudged down the stairs, moving slowly. His back hurt. He knew that was from swinging the sledgehammer, but still he felt as if he suddenly and inexplicably weighed twice what he had the night before. He tripped, grabbing the bannister and wincing at the pain in his bruised palms and stiff fingers.

Once in the kitchen, Edmund put the kettle on and sat down on one of four barstools lined up along a large, glossy kitchen peninsula. The kitchen looked almost exactly as it had the day it was completed. He'd listened to the decorator as she'd explained in lengthy, elaborate sentences how she thought they ought to be sympathetic to the house's history. Edmund had no particular interest in old homes. He had several friends who had lovingly restored Victorian, Georgian, and even medieval homes. They'd consulted specialists and spent hours in search of period features to replace those that had been lost. They retained lopsided windows and revelled in creaking floors. To have a new build as he preferred, he'd have had to live further from Ovidia. To him, this house had been an adequate shell in which he and she would build a new life.

He'd ignored the decorator and selected a contemporary design in complete contrast to the building's age, erasing its previous owner's attempt at reinstating its Victorian features. He had little interest in preserving its history, he'd reminded her – he liked its size and location. He didn't tell her it was across the street from Ovidia. Following his instructions, the designer installed sleek, glossy kitchen cabinets in dark blue and had the walls painted in a brilliant white. A dining area followed the peninsula and its stools. Behind the dining table and chairs was an informal living area with nothing except a grey velvet sofa and matching armchair. This was meant to be a family area. The designer had envisioned a mounted flatscreen television and storage for toys, neither of which had been realised.

The kitchen was, the designer had insisted repeatedly, made for entertaining, but Edmund had done that infrequently. A few of his guests had complimented his taste and asked for referrals, to which he said he'd forgotten her name, which happened to be the truth.

Daylight shone in through the glass cube. The light reflected onto the wall above the black dining table, and Edmund could still make out the outlines of the three enormous framed photographs that had been mounted there for a few short months. Still their imprints seemed to linger, though he had examined the wall, checking for physical evidence of their having existed – a subtle change in paint colour perhaps – but found none.

Edmund fried an egg, harder and drier than he wanted, and slid it onto his toast. He reached for the radio standing on the sideboard, heard a strain of classical music only for a second and then turned it off, dreading the sound of any voices that would follow. He sat in silence and chewed his food, his tea untouched beside it. He sat wondering if Ovidia was on a long run, a short run, a tempo run, or the various types of run that she'd explained to him and he'd since mixed up. It was Saturday – which was supposed to mean something in her schedule. As this wasn't a usual Saturday, he guessed she would likely be away for a long while.

He sipped his tea and found it had gone cold. He became aware of how long having breakfast had taken him. He reluctantly returned upstairs. Turning the shower on, still in his pyjamas, he waited first for the water to hit the right temperature, adjusting the handle this way and that, somehow missing the perfect temperature with each manoeuvre. Then he stood beside the glass shower stall and watched the vapour rising, wishing away every drop of water and every joule of heat. Regardless of how awful any day had been before this one, he'd bathed and changed his clothes every single morning. Every morning, regardless of how he may have felt or what challenge was before him, Edmund put on a clean set of clothes. The walk-in wardrobe was equally divided between him and Ovidia.

'I've never met a man who has so many clothes before,' Ovidia had once remarked.

He cocked his head at the sound of her voice – though it was in his own head. Through the fog that was his memory, he remembered the conversation hadn't taken place here but at his previous flat, with its sleek dark wood and masculine leather furnishing. A lifetime ago, it seemed. Ovidia had been looking for a cardigan, shaking her head at his selection of dark blue, grey, and black sweaters before finally settling on one in a shade of grey lighter than the rest. She'd turned towards him as she neatly folded its cuffs to sit perfectly on her petite frame, and she caught the glint in his eye. They'd shared a shower just before, and the aroma of the soap they'd shared still lingered as he put his arms around her again.

He shook his head clear of the memory. This morning, he couldn't muster the energy to shower. His resolve and a lifetime of habit let him down, and he watched the water run until he accepted that he would not be taking a shower nor changing that morning. Tightening the belt on his dressing gown, he went back down the stairs.

He passed through the ground floor and its two reception rooms. He picked up his daily newspapers from beside the front door. As he returned, he was reminded once more of the now nameless interior designer who had talked about this room as becoming 'a tasteful yet welcoming room that extends from here right into the garden'. She'd made an exaggerated sweeping motion with her arms. He stopped at the drinks trolley, picked up a tumbler, and examined an unopened bottle of whiskey that he supposed had been a gift from a guest or work. He took the bottle and tumbler and went down the stairs, through the kitchen, and into the glass extension.

Once there, Edmund sat down and poured himself a drink. He opened one of his papers and folded it neatly and systematically to the crossword page. He sat down in the grey armchair after tossing its cushion onto the floor. He looked at his pencil and then his watch – it was nearly seven. He leaned back into his chair and stared through the glass into the sky.

4

Outside, Ovidia was barely conscious of her surroundings. Her mobile was tucked into her running sleeve and recorded every step she took, every turning, and every detour. As if in a cocoon, she was shielded from the sounds of everyday life on the street on which she lived. She was impervious to the sounds of her feet rhythmically pounding the pavement or a dog barking relentlessly somewhere nearby. Her fluorescent yellow shorts flapped against her thighs and her T-shirt was standard, unassuming, like her speed. She wore a black mesh headscarf that hid her hair in little twists and protected it from a light sweat.

It was a warm morning, a spring day that could turn to rain later. A few clouds floated aimlessly and unthreateningly; a light breeze was in the air. As she ran, all sense of time and distance dissolved. Houses, shops, and the doctor's practice became vague objects in the periphery of her vision. She saw only what was just ahead of her, and then immediately it was behind her, gone. She'd lived on this road for nearly five years; she knew the area surrounding it and every detail of the route on which she ran. She knew where clutches of people gathered and had to be circumvented, she knew where delivery trucks parked and their drivers leered at her, and she knew the dips and trips of the streets and where she had to watch her feet.

The street of elegant homes ended and became a mishmash of modern, dated, and classic buildings. Ovidia ran past parks and boutiques, first heading away from the river. She could have gone further and added hours more if she chose to – she knew where to turn to add a dozen or more miles to her run. She decided against it.

Inside, she felt her emotions simmering as if about to boil over – again. Her temples throbbed, and her eyes felt heavy in their sockets. From the moment she'd woken that morning, she'd been aware of her heart leaden in her chest, every heartbeat counting down to later that day when, she imagined, it would stop beating.

She slowed down as she returned to her street, reluctant to go home and to face Edmund. She wished she could run past the house and never set foot in it again. Then her thoughts wavered as she remembered how she and Edmund had made love the previous night, briefly and tinged with a sense of finality – an unspoken understanding that it would be the last time.

Ovidia glanced towards her own building across the road where her flat took up the third floor of a house of a similar age. She debated where to go. She could go to Edmund, and they could be unhappy together, or she could be on her own in her flat. She could simply lie down and cry without having to be aware of Edmund's look of exhaustion – or was it disgust? There, at least, she could turn the TV on loud to something filled with expletives, sex, and gore to take her mind off the approaching evening.

'How can you not have cable?' It seemed a lifetime ago when the two of them had sat on her sofa, tucked into each other, interrupting TV shows with kisses and opinions, a time when they were still new to each other. She had been holding the remote, dug out from between the sofa cushions.

'Quite clearly because everything is rubbish,' Edmund had replied, as they'd flicked through the endless menu. 'Pirates, Norsemen...' Eventually he'd deferred to her choice. She couldn't remember the show she'd chosen, but she remembered that, minutes into it, he'd put his hand between her thighs and the show was abandoned.

Ovidia had moved to this street before she'd met Edmund. Her flat was indistinguishable from its neighbours in its brown-brick Victorian terrace, her side of the street far less ostentatious than the terrace opposite. It had occurred to her many times that her and Edmund's arrangement was odd. Though it had always seemed like a natural transition, perfectly ordinary, as if, throughout the city, lovers lived across the road from each other. She was proud of her flat, having been forced to save money by bulk-buying noodles and tinned foods for months after having paid a larger deposit than she'd planned. She'd never told Edmund about that brief period of her life, the culmination of an adulthood of independence. She could have easily bought something cheaper that would have caused her less financial stress, but she made the argument that the flat would be worth it for the resale value. In reality, she'd been fulfilling a long-held dream sparked by a picture she'd seen in a magazine many years earlier. It had been a spread on a London abode of someone she'd long forgotten. But what had stayed with her was the difference between the grace of the Victorian building in contrast to the bland '70s and '80s constructions in which she'd been raised. Besides, she told herself at the time, if she had to give it up for financial reasons, it would be of no consequence – more of an inconvenience than anything. Still, something about the flat's old-world grandeur captivated her; it encapsulated her new beginning and decorating it gave her something in which to immerse herself.

When she began to spend most of her time with Edmund, she'd played with the idea of getting someone to rent it, but she couldn't stand the idea of someone else in her home. She'd been considering changing careers and wanted a way to cover her mortgage. Shortly after she'd mentioned her tentative idea to Edmund, she'd found money in her account as she examined her online statement. Each month after that, the same amount appeared – never discussed or negotiated. It always arrived, whether she worked or not. At times, when she was honest with herself, and quite often when disappointed with herself, she felt as if what had been her dream was no longer really hers. Still, she continued caring for the flat, refining its décor, filling its shelves with books almost as if she'd known that one day she'd return to live there.

Ovidia came to a standstill on the pavement, continuing to procrastinate. Usually she knew exactly what she would do next. After three hours of running, she'd have mapped out her day – she knew what she was going to wear, what she was going to eat, and, of course, which home she would go to. Sometimes, if Edmund was away, she'd go to her flat and throw herself on the sofa, still sweating from her run. Today her mind, paralysed by dread, couldn't be made up.

'What do you think about when you're running – you don't listen to music or radio?' Edmund had asked her early on in their relationship, before he'd bought the house, when his car had been parked in front of her building almost every night.

'I just think, I suppose,' Ovidia had responded, thinking it a strange question.

They'd been in bed when he'd asked. It had been on one of those mornings when she wasn't running, and he'd resisted the urge to get out of bed at his usual early hour.

He'd run his hand down her spine and tugged the top of her underwear – grey lace women's briefs, the kind that come in a pack of five at M&S and that she bought on sale.

'What about?' he asked, putting his hands down into them and stroking her backside.

'No one's ever asked me that before,' she replied.

'Don't you get bored – out there with nothing to do, listening to the sound of your feet?'

'Sometimes I solve puzzles, like designing the perfect handbag, or a toaster that will never burn your toast,' she'd spoken quickly, feeling self-conscious. 'But mostly I'm a crew member on the Enterprise, you know, boldly going somewhere. Exploring the universe. That sort of thing.'

Edmund had laughed, his foray through her underwear temporarily suspended. She'd listened to him laugh and was glad to have found him.

Today her usual fantasies had eluded her. She'd run mile after mile, thinking about Edmund, thinking about herself, and about the events that had brought her to this day. She cursed herself, scolded herself, demanded answers to questions she dared not ask herself. She replayed the morning's events again and again. She tried to imagine what she could do for Edmund, tried to conceive of something to show him that she was there for him, but she couldn't imagine anything that would make today any better.

Her mind still churning, Ovidia started running again, taking the first turn that took her to the park behind Edmund's house. There she stopped and walked until she could see the wall that marked the end of the garden. It looked ominous, uninviting – even menacing. Its grey-brown brick loomed like a gothic cathedral and filled her with dread.

She sat down on a bench and inhaled from the depths of her lungs, just like countless online articles she spent ages scrolling through had suggested. She looked around at people making the most of the spring weather: dog walkers, drunks, runners, the elderly, and a group stretching through a yoga session.

A mantra, Ovidia thought.

'I will get through today. Just today,' she said aloud, quickly glancing to all sides ensuring no one could hear her. 'I refuse to think about the future. I will not cry,' she exhaled.

'I refuse,' she began her mantra again, leaning back and closing her eyes and feeling some relief. She visualised herself running in happier times, on a boardwalk near the sea. She imagined the sound of her trainers, the sound of the ocean, but unhappiness intruded once more, and she groaned.

'You all right?' The woman was older with headphones clamped around her neck.

Ovidia gasped in response, as her heart set off racing.

Ovidia glanced at the woman and decided that she'd asked from genuine concern and not because she was being nosey. This passer-by had probably seen a woman sitting, miserable on her own, on a park bench and was worried. By asking Ovidia, a stranger, the woman probably had to defy her instinct to stay away. This was, after all, a city filled with those who stab, punch, and throw acid on strangers.

'Just overdid it. Thanks,' Ovidia mumbled, breathing deeply to calm herself and shocked such a simple interaction had shaken her so completely. She couldn't believe that she'd become one of those people that strangers recognised as being in distress.

Letting the woman walk away, she stood and walked out of the park. 'I will not cry,' she repeated again and again until she found herself outside Edmund's house – which, until that evening at least, was hers as well.

'Not today,' she said, raising one foot onto the top step to the front door.

Ovidia stretched her legs and calves on the front steps. Then she went indoors, barefoot, her shoes abandoned beside the front door. She glanced inside, through the large room that took up half the lower-ground floor where Edmund would normally be on a Saturday morning. She paused in the bathroom and rinsed the sweat from her face, aware of its saltiness drying on her skin. Ovidia saw him when she emerged, sitting in the extension, staring into the distance. Seeing him outdoors in his pyjamas and dressing gown, the enormity of the day ahead overwhelmed her.

She inhaled and marched towards him.

'Edmund,' she said, exiting through the glass doors into the glass cube, 'what are you up to?' She tried to sound spontaneous, but she sensed she'd taken much too long to concoct such a simple question.

Most, or at least many, other couples would have been in each other's arms – or they'd like to think they would be – on a day like this. Soon after she'd met him, Ovidia had learned that Edmund was the kind of man who in public concealed his emotions and even in private was only expressive to those closest to him. She loved him knowing that even his passion was measuredly dispensed, his laugh was never the loudest in a room, and that there would never be a threat of spontaneous dancing or crude jokes at parties. She was glad that he was not one to make a scene or weep in public, or to drink and lose control. She hadn't seen him cry or fly into a rage – ever – not even over these last few months. She knew that now was not the time to berate him for his stoic nature when it was something she once loved about him.

'Oh.' Edmund looked around as if surprised to find himself in the sunroom. Then he tapped the still-folded paper and said, 'Crossword.'

Ovidia gave him a staccato kiss and perched beside him on the thin armrest. His crossword was still blank. 'I can see you've done quite a bit of it.'

'A little stuck, that's all,' he replied. 'Funny, they're usually quite simple.'

'For you, they are.' She lowered her gaze to his feet clad in bedroom slippers. She abruptly changed the subject. 'Can't we wait a little longer, please?'

Edmund looked out into the garden at the splintered remains of the playhouse. 'No, Ovidia. There's nothing to wait for. We have to do this – we agreed.'

'I know,' Ovidia leaned against her partner, resting her head on his shoulder. She shut her eyes tightly and anticipated the tears that would seep through to his pyjama shirt.

She raised her head. 'You're right. I just wish you weren't.' She wiped her eyes, though they were dry. 'Have you had breakfast?' Ovidia asked every morning, and, yes, he'd almost always already had his breakfast. 'But you'll have another cup of tea if I'm making some,' she said, forcing herself to smile.

She was always making a pot of tea, even though some mornings she felt like cocoa or coffee. They very rarely ate breakfast together; either she ran, or he was up too early. The pot of tea after breakfast brought them together, even if briefly. Some weekday mornings when Edmund would be almost out of the door, they'd drink it in only a few minutes, scalding themselves in the process.

In the kitchen, she emptied the kettle of the water he'd used for his first cup and refilled it in the sink. On her own, she'd have microwaved a mug of water, but this way, filling a kettle, waiting for it to boil, bringing out the sugar, and filling a teapot, seemed like some form of expression of affection. Her mother always did it for her father, a quiet ritual Ovidia had thought nothing about before Edmund.

Ovidia fried a piece of bacon and placed it on a slice of toast and ate standing, ignoring the four high stools, stretching her calves and flexing her aching ankle. She turned on the radio – finding a documentary about a classical composer that had already begun. She listened for a few minutes and then switched it off. She opened a kitchen drawer, and her stomach tightened at the sight of a sheath of pamphlets tucked within. She paused with her hand hovering over them, rolled her fingers into a fist and instead pulled out a pair of headphones. She plugged them into her phone and inserted the buds into her ears. She stared at the wall of kitchen units with its concealed fridge and dishwasher, the glossy matching kettle and toaster and a mug with a broken handle that was waiting to be disposed of. She found Cypress Hill, harking back to her teen years, their lyrics replete with expletives, the composers venting their anger at the world as the pot of tea grew cold.

She remained standing, wondering how she could ever have another cup of tea with Edmund or kiss him or make love to him after today. He'd nudged her into making the decision, pushing just a little, again and again, until she was forced to concede. He'd put his arms around her and whispered what they had to do in her ear. She'd pushed him away, but he'd returned again and again, until she had to accept that there were no other options. He'd returned an hour later with a date and a time. The date was today, and the time was drawing closer like an enormous black hole that sucked her in with a force she couldn't escape.

She chewed her breakfast slowly, neither thinking nor tasting, until her food ran out. She glanced at the clock outlined on her phone. It was only nine o'clock.

5

Anne had watched the scenery as the cab purred through the city streets. She felt John's hand resting on her lap. Once or twice, he tapped his fingers on her thigh or traced shapes along the fabric of her clothes. She wondered if he knew he was doing it, or if they'd been together for so long that she was now an extension of his own body and that resting his hand on her was the same as laying it on his own.

The cab held four: two couples. Occasionally they spoke, but Anne could sense their nervousness. She could still feel the effects of the previous night's celebratory drinks coursing through her system, though she'd had less to drink than the others. The rest of them, Jasper's parents included, emptied bottle after bottle of sparkling wine, abandoned bottles of beer half-drunk, and imbibed sherry, remarking on its flavour as if they were connoisseurs. She'd paced herself, floating above the conversation, observing them, fetching glasses and loading the dishwasher.

Holly made some bland observations about where they were going, something about hoping Edmund would like her and really hoping that she'd like him. Anne looked up briefly, but Holly had moved on to whispering something to Jasper. Anne turned back to the window, noting the streetscape, the spring scenery, and the changing architecture. John, who was to be best man, looked thoughtful and relaxed. For the last few years, he'd been not only Jasper's best friend but also his confidant. He'd once told Anne that he was sure he knew everything of importance in Jasper's life, though they'd been friends for only a few years. After the celebration the previous night, all he'd wanted to talk about was the depth of the bond he shared with Jasper.

'I even know how much he earns.' John had woven through the house, incapable of walking in a straight line, and in bed, he whispered to Anne as if it were a secret. 'Let me tell you, guys don't go around telling each other how much they earn.'

Still, Anne thought John's eagerness to accompany Jasper that morning was excessive.

'Oh, come on, it'll be fun!' he'd declared, elbowing her when she'd asked why. 'A bottle of champagne on a spring morning... Well what else are you going to do on a Saturday?' he asked when she again voiced her reluctance.

'Maybe,' he began, and Anne realised he was going to suggest that he go on his own. He was right, she quickly reconsidered, she didn't have anything else planned for the day.

As Anne dressed, John lay on the bed behind her, sighing heavily when she began doing her hair – rubbing in mousse and shaking her head, tousling her short blonde bob. She glared at him when he hummed, examining his nails as she examined her figure in the full-length mirror in their bedroom. She turned to scrutinise her side profile. She checked that her foundation blended into her neck. It gave her skin a hint of a tan, lending colour to her otherwise ivory complexion. She sucked in her stomach and reminded herself that she hadn't lost all the weight she'd gained during her pregnancies. She grimaced at the fullness of her hips and the roundness of her stomach and then pulled off the pair of jeans she'd put on first in favour of a looser pair.

At that point, John lurched off the bed and left through the bedroom door. With him gone, Anne rummaged through her wardrobe again and found a loose floral top, and, this time, the image in the mirror met with her approval. She twirled, telling herself that she was a woman over forty yet still stylish and with, at least some, sophistication. She'd called after John and found him on the landing tidying away their daughters' dollhouse and its occupants.

'You look gorgeous,' John said rising from his knees.

'Thanks for the support,' she replied.

'You don't need my support.' John kissed her on the ear. 'You look perfect every single day.'

He'd put his arm around her waist, and they'd gone down the stairs together.

Anne had come along because she was John's wife – or partner, he occasionally reminded people, since they'd never married – but still she managed to work up her excitement about her friends' impending big day.

Holly had asked Anne to be her to be maid-of-honour less than an hour after Jasper's proposal.

'Don't look so surprised,' Holly joked when Anne's only reaction was that her jaw dropped and she sat arrested in her chair at the dining table.

'You're supposed to start squealing and go on Twitter,' Jasper said, as John laughed.

Holly said she needed someone who was not only a good friend but also had a bit more sense than most of her other friends. Anne said yes, in part because no one else had ever asked her, and she couldn't think of anyone else who ever would.

Anne enjoyed Jasper and Holly's company, but sometimes felt she saw them too much, as if she was meant to keep Holly entertained while John and Jasper watched sport or had long conversations from which their partners were excluded. Countless times the two men sat in John and Anne's garden or lounge, while Anne and Holly found space elsewhere – the kitchen, the conservatory, even the top of the landing while Anne's girls slept. Anne was glad Holly didn't feel the same about her, that Holly didn't regard their relationship as borne from necessity. She genuinely liked Holly – but didn't see her as someone with whom she'd have chosen to spend so much of her time and would never have considered asking her to be her own maid-of-honour. However, Holly also had excellent rapport with Anne and John's daughters, who had been delivered the afternoon before to Anne's mother for the weekend.

'This is nothing like his last place,' Jasper remarked as they disembarked. Holly adjusted the cardigan she was wearing and smoothed down her blue culottes. Anne caught Holly examining her distorted reflection in the blackness of the taxi window as Jasper took off his jacket, revealing a slightly crumpled T-shirt.

Anne glanced around and her gaze landed on a neat metal nameplate fixed to the gate which read 'E Everard'. Jasper turned to pay the taxi driver.

The small patch of shrubbery beyond the wrought-iron gates was neat and manicured – professionally tended. A dark grey Range Rover stood gleaming beside where the taxi had stopped. Jasper pointed out that it was Edmund's. Anne glanced into the car and was taken aback by the pile of magazines, takeaway paper cups, and brochures strewn on the passenger seat and floor. The disorder seemed unlike Jasper's brother, who she knew liked neatness and order, and it ruined the façade – the perfect house and car – that stood in front of the visitors.

They assembled in couples and crossed the minuscule front garden and mounted the steps to the front door.

'Oh, I love this door,' Holly said as they went up. 'I could live here just for the front door.'

Anne also found something to admire, smiling at the paving that ran along the walkway and silently assessing the price of the house.

'Are you thinking about how much this house costs?' John whispered to her.

'Of course,' she replied. 'Aren't we all? I know Edmund has a bit of money, but this…?'

'He used to have a penthouse,' Jasper said, as Anne considered the house's period style. 'Some shiny place with a great view of the Thames. Can't imagine why he'd swap it for this.'

'Maybe its proximity to a few Russian oligarchs,' John chuckled.

The front door was ajar.

'Who leaves a front door unlocked?' Holly asked. 'This is London!'

'Someone asking to be robbed?' John suggested. 'He probably has great insurance. You're not going to just walk in, are you?' he said, as Jasper firmly pushed the door wider and entered.

'Well, the front door is open – it's more of a surprise this way,' Jasper replied, smiling. Anne had seen him check the piece of paper that he'd scribbled the address on several times.

6

Holly followed beside Jasper, watching him moving with longing. Her eyes were bright in anticipation, and she caught up with him and clutched his arm, rubbing it, already having nursed it throughout the journey. This, to her, was a milestone more intimidating than meeting his parents, who, despite the idiosyncrasies of the elderly, she liked. She'd met them several times since she and Jasper had started dating. In their seventies, they were far more youthful than her own parents. Lucinda, Jasper's mother, wore jeans and linen blouses. His father's hair was grey but still retained the headful of curls that Jasper had inherited. The two of them travelled quite often and had a small house in Spain that they insisted she must come to visit. On the first visit, Holly found Lucinda's chatty exterior made her almost impossible to read, let alone get to know. Phil's conversations bordered on interrogation, 'Have you been to Spain? Where in Spain? Did you see this, that, or the other?' He asked about her family – parents, brothers, and sisters – and only seemed to ease off when she mentioned her grandparents had recently passed away, as if he'd just realised that he was being oppressive.

The second time they'd met, there'd been an excitement about Jasper's parents that hadn't been present at their first meeting. Phil's barrage of questions was replaced by a gentle conversation. He spent most of the afternoon leaning back in his armchair discussing gardening and forest walks. Holly was sure that they must have realised that Jasper was serious about her. His mother had pulled out a photo album and shown her pictures of Jasper when he was a teenager.

'He looks…' Holly had hesitated, riveted by one particular photo of Jasper outdoors in dark blue corduroys and a red T-shirt, 'he looks exactly the same, just younger.'

In truth, she'd been shocked by the picture. The image was of someone as far from the Jasper she knew as it was possible to be. In the photo, Jasper wore an enormous smile and a cheer that radiated from his face. His eyes narrowed in the spontaneity of the smile. Even in an old photograph, his skin seemed a warmer hue, and his cheeks were rounded, making him seem healthy and spritely. Slightly ganglier, his hair had been longer with tighter curls, which emphasised his physical resemblance to the older boy who stood beside him, whose smile was more reserved yet still hinting at mischief.

'Did you take it?' Holly asked Lucinda, who nodded. 'What was so funny?' Holly continued when she managed to pull her gaze away.

Lucinda took it back from her and frowned. 'Nothing special. It was summer, I remember, evening. Those two were always larking about.'

'Edmund had probably just told him some dirty joke,' Phil said, glancing at the photo over Holly's shoulder.

'Don't be silly,' Lucinda tapped her husband on the shoulder. 'Edmund doesn't tell dirty jokes.'

To which both Jasper and Phil laughed.

Today, Holly was to finally meet the big brother – she'd heard a lot about Edmund, of course, but somehow, she'd never been to an event at which he was present. Other things seemed to have always been in the way: illness, business trips, or Jasper declaring, 'He's just so boring – we're not going to invite him,' as they made plans to go to a concert or for dinner. 'We have really different ideas of what makes a night out, that's all,' Jasper explained when she pressed him.

Holly would wonder, if Edmund was so boring, why then did Jasper disappear to long lunches or evening drinks with his brother?

'We don't really do anything together. We just talk endlessly,' Jasper defended this contradiction. 'You'd be bored if you came along.'

She knew that she wouldn't get anything more out of him.

Once, after they'd made a firm plan to meet Edmund and he'd called to apologise that he was going to Hong Kong, Holly suggested that maybe the brothers weren't as close as Jasper imagined.

'You're joking, right?' Jasper replied, his eyes wide, offended.

'Then he's avoiding me?'

'He's just busy making money and doing crossword puzzles in airports.' Jasper tried to make light of it. 'Don't take it to heart. He just likes his life.'

'After all this time we've been together, he can't find half an hour for a cup of coffee with me?'

Jasper hadn't answered. He'd simply shrugged, and, that evening, they'd met John and Anne instead.

She'd been certain Edmund was avoiding her. After all, he met Jasper fairly regularly. Jasper would arrive at her flat sometimes tipsy from having consumed wine all afternoon with his brother, to tell her where Edmund had been and what he'd done, and once or twice had shared a tasteless joke that Jasper admitted 'was funnier with booze'.

Holly wondered how alike the two brothers were – physically. She contemplated Jasper's body moving in front of her and thought how much she loved that the man she'd fallen for was strikingly attractive – now. She considered him the perfect physical match. She, an acceptable few inches shorter, was blonde and his hair was a deep brown – nearly black; her hair was straight, thick and heavy and his was a mass of light, springy curls that he often allowed to grow too long. He'd had it cut earlier that week, telling her he had a big event to attend later that week – she hadn't guessed that he'd meant her betrothal. She admired the weight he'd put on since they began dating, as she told him 'in the best possible way'. When they'd met, he'd been gaunt with an anaemic pallor that was accentuated by eyes perpetually ringed in blue that he rubbed frequently. He'd always seemed tired and disinterested. Though she had been attracted to him, even as he was then, watching him now, she wondered if it was she who had turned that troubled, lethargic man into the one in front of her today.

'Mind the body in the library,' Holly said, and she clapped her hand over her mouth when her voice seemed to reverberate through the silence that met them. Jasper's brow furrowed as if to let her know what she'd said wasn't funny. Anne came in last and closed the door firmly behind them. Holly noticed it creep back open but said nothing.

Once inside, Holly paused to look around the contemporary interior that greeted them. The century-old ceilings retained their height, giving the room a modern, angular glamour which, though pleasing, was antithetical to the building's exterior.

The house seemed deserted. The windows must have been double or even triple glazed, ensuring the interior was completely insulated from the noise of the street. Holly was sure they shouldn't have just walked in. She felt a sense of unease, as if something unpleasant was waiting for them.

They lingered too long in the reception. This was a show room, Holly thought, and if Edmund was home, he'd be somewhere comfortable rather than in a space as impersonal as this reception room. She was about to tell Jasper when he darted for a set of stairs and headed down them. John followed. Holly glanced back as she started to descend, seeing Anne pause momentarily to look back at the leather Chesterfield sofa, the grey and blue carpets and light grey armchairs. Apart from a side table that held a few books, the rest of the room seemed as if no one ever used it.

7

'Hello,' Jasper said, glimpsing a figure in the kitchen. It was standing at the kitchen peninsula, a plate empty except for crumbs and a bacon rind. A grey teapot stood beside a tray, two orange mugs, and a bowl of sugar.

The figure didn't react. It was obviously not Edmund. It was female with headphones plugged in her ears. She stood in ankle-high socks and running clothes, upright and rigid, not leaning against the stools or table. Though Jasper could now hear muffled music from the headphones, neither her feet nor fingers tapped in time, nor did she nod her head or acknowledge the music she was playing in any way.

It took Jasper an almost imperceptible moment to recognise her. The moment he did, he felt as if he'd been plunged into a deep, dark pool and was drowning. Breathless, his hands began to shake.

'Ovidia?' Jasper said – his voice too low for the others to hear, his hand of its own volition reaching out and touching her shoulder.

Startled by his touch, Ovidia jolted around, her headphones snapping out of her ears as she turned to face him. The shock was visible on her face.

As his eyes met hers, Jasper felt emotions he believed he'd buried rise like magma bubbling in a volcano, setting his heart pounding and stealing his voice. For an instant, he was afraid, his body seized, and he was unable to move, his face flushed and eyes wide.

But none of his group said anything to indicate they'd noticed his change of posture. Neither John nor the women put a hand on Jasper's shoulder or asked if he was okay. Jasper's back was to them. He couldn't see them, but he was acutely aware of their presence. He knew they would be watching him, perhaps wondering if they were in the wrong house.

Ovidia was standing in the last place she should have been on this particular morning. Why was she here? He couldn't understand.

'Hi,' Jasper hesitated, pulling back from Ovidia and forcing himself to smile. His instinct took over. Without thinking, he launched into an act, pretending he didn't know the woman in front of him. 'I'm looking for Edmund. I'm his brother.'

Jasper saw Ovidia silently colluding with him.

'He's in the extension,' she replied.

The look of astonishment at seeing him could easily be misread as the shock of seeing a stranger in her house. She nodded at the French doors behind them that opened outwards, and his eyes followed her gesture.

Jasper turned immediately, saying nothing else. He'd hoped she'd become upset and say, *'I don't know who you're talking about,'* and demand that they leave the house, perhaps even threaten to call the police. Then they'd leave, quickly, slightly embarrassed, apologising as they went, and they'd laugh about it later, putting it down as a Saturday morning misadventure. He wanted to be wrong. The plaque on the house flashed through his mind. *E Everard* – his brother's name, it had to be his house.

He turned back to his friends. 'Come on,' he said, as they appeared to be hesitating. They glanced uncertainly at Ovidia. Jasper prayed Holly wouldn't try to be polite and speak to her, and, John, please, Jasper begged him silently, don't fancy her and want to chat. Anne opened her mouth, as if she was meant to say something – an apology to Ovidia perhaps. She closed it again.

Glancing back, Jasper caught Ovidia's eye for a moment, and she immediately turned back to her music. She inserted the headphones in her ears, absolving them of all need for formalities and shutting Jasper out. She continued standing despite the row of stools beside her, only now she'd shrunk forward, her spine curved forward as if she was to curl into a ball.

Holly, Anne, and John followed Jasper through the doors and out of the kitchen. Jasper caught Holly furtively looking back and side to side, most likely, Jasper guessed, like he was, repressing questions that were begging for answers. The distance to the seating in the extension couldn't have taken a third of a minute to cover, but that twenty seconds had seemed interminable. Though he marched quickly and determinedly towards where his brother was meant to be, Jasper felt time and distance slow and lengthen, and his stomach began to churn painfully.

Upon seeing Edmund in the glass extension, Jasper was relieved to finally confirm he was at the right house. So relieved, that he briefly ignored the incongruity of his surroundings with what he knew of brother's life. But this disbelief returned and was intensified when he looked down and fully took in his older brother.

What Jasper saw was a man who hadn't moved since he'd first sat down two hours earlier. His newspaper was still turned to the undone crossword, his pen still beside it. The glass still held the alcohol he had yet to drink. He was immobile in pyjamas and a dressing gown that appeared smudged with dirt, and his guests' arrival seemed to have had had no effect on him despite the clattering of Anne's and Holly's heels.

This picture of a man staring into space, unmoving, was how Jasper introduced Holly to her future brother-in-law. He could see her confusion: she pinched the fabric of her culottes and twisted it, like a little girl brought in front of the class. Jasper had promised her a man of almost regal demeanour, with poise and finesse. Their mother constantly lauded the quality of his clothes and the wonders of his posture and personal hygiene.

Yet, today, Jasper's brother was slumped in his seat. Though his pyjamas and slippers were, as with most of his clothes, new and high-end, Edmund himself looked worn down, older than his forty-seven years, his skin pale and the lines around his eyes deeper than they'd ever appeared before. He and Jasper shared their father's nose and a long-dead grandfather's lean silhouette that today looked gangly. Even Edmund's hair lay limp and unkempt, and his fingernails were dirty.

'A bit early for whiskey?' Jasper pretended it was a light-hearted greeting, but he knew something was wrong. He knew that his brother did not sit outdoors in his pyjamas with a glass of whiskey and an undone crossword on a Saturday morning. Jasper tried to fit Ovidia into this scenario but couldn't. Everything was wrong. He clenched his fists in the melange of confusion, the desperation and terror of a small animal caught in a trap.

'Good morning!' Edmund sat upright in his seat, startled. He immediately appeared conscious of his appearance; his hand went to his unshaved chin and then traced its way to his uncombed hair and then ran down the back of his neck. He looked embarrassed and tried to rise from the chair but then lowered himself back down again, his hands on each of the armrests, steadying himself. 'Oh hell,' he said, leaned back into his chair and took a deep breath.

'Hard night?' Jasper asked. 'Hair of the dog?' He pointed at the whiskey, and Edmund looked at it as if it were the first time he'd ever seen the glass.

The last time Jasper and Edmund had seen each other had been for lunch in the city two months earlier on Jasper's invitation or, rather, his insistence. Edmund had arrived exactly on time, impeccably dressed in a tailored suit in contrast to Jasper's blue jeans and casual button-down. Edmund had ordered right away, claiming to be starving and at first eschewing the wine as he was going back to work, then changing his mind and ordering a bottle of red that they shared. Edmund had barely touched his food in the end and had apologised for having recently been so busy that he'd been unable to see Jasper for a while. He'd claimed he'd been constantly rushed off his feet. Edmund had been distracted, repeatedly checking his mobile, looking around himself and abandoning sentences incomplete. Still, he'd stayed with his brother for several hours, talking about Holly, their parents, work, and trivia with no further mention of returning to work.

'I must be coming down with something.'

Seeing Edmund slumped in the seat, Jasper could tell his brother was lying. 'Well, it looks like you have someone to take care of you,' Jasper said, raising an eyebrow, not wanting to be explicit in front of his friends – various possible explanations flicking through his mind, none feasible. Jasper examined his brother's expression, trying to decode the situation from his face. He could see Edmund, in turn, scrutinising his own face but offering no clues as to what was happening that morning.

'Hello.' After a moment, Edmund greeted John, who was standing just behind Jasper, with a visible lack of enthusiasm.

John grinned and gave his characteristically brisk and firm handshake, brushing against Anne to get to where Edmund was sitting.

'And Anne – lovely to see you again.' For her, he forced a smile.

Anne smiled and shook Edmund's hand almost reluctantly, not making eye contact and looking around, perhaps embarrassed by his appearance. Jasper understood; it was as if they'd found their host naked.

'And...'

'This is Holly,' Jasper said with a theatrical flourish of his hand, which landed too firmly and too possessively just below her waist. Holly winced beneath his touch and immediately let go of her culottes and extended her hand towards Edmund.

'Is this a bad time?' Anne began, but Edmund cut in, directing himself at Holly.

'Our mother told me everything – very late at night – in incredible detail and repeatedly.' This time Edmund stood, though it appeared to take considerable effort. He shook Holly's hand but did not give her a kiss on her proffered cheek or embrace her. Jasper had warned Holly ahead of time that Edmund wouldn't. He wasn't given to hugging, back slapping, kissing, or other physical expressions of affection.

'Congratulations, and, please, take a seat. I think I have some champagne in the kitchen,' Edmund continued. 'Let me get it, and we'll toast.'

He fumbled as he turned, appearing to trip on an invisible obstacle. Jasper watched him take a deep breath before he passed through the French doors. Jasper glanced at his little group. Not a single one of them was at ease.

8

'Oh god, why today of all bloody days?' Edmund said as he stood just inside the French doors after closing them behind himself. He realised Ovidia hadn't heard him. Her back faced him, and she was slouched over the kitchen peninsula.

He glanced at the clock on the wall; it was just after ten. He realised how long he'd been outside. He looked at Ovidia, and he once again felt ill. He bit his lower lip, fortifying himself to speak to her when what he really wanted to do was cocoon himself in one of the many barely used rooms in the house and wait.

Edmund quietly took the few strides needed to get to her and gently tugged the earphones from her ears. She reluctantly raised her head.

Edmund coughed to clear his throat of the weight that seemed to constrict it then inhaled deeply. 'What do we do now?' he asked, though he could not see a way to free them of the people outside. He could hardly go back out and tell them he had far more important things on his mind and could they come back another time.

'Maybe I should go to my place? I'll come back when it's time?' Ovidia suggested, stretching as if she'd come out of a long nap. They both faced the French doors side by side, touching – she came to just below his shoulders in her socks.

She wouldn't come back. Edmund was sure of that. He couldn't trust her to keep her word today. He looked momentarily at the pot of tea, remembering that they had intended to drink it more than an hour ago. 'No. Jasper will think you're running away.'

'Aren't I?' Ovidia asked. 'Running away seems like a good idea.'

'No. You belong here, you know that,' Edmund replied. 'This is your home,' he said quietly. 'Besides, he and Holly are getting married – I can't just ask them to leave. Well, I could, but what if Jasper takes it the wrong way'.

'You could say you're not feeling well,' Ovidia suggested. She leaned back, resting her elbows on the peninsula. 'But Anne's a nurse, isn't she?' When Edmund didn't respond she said, 'We'll put on our brave faces; we've certainly had plenty of practice at pretending everything is okay.'

Edmund touched her hand.

Despite her apparent confidence, her voice faltered. 'I think I've felt every second of this morning. It feels like eternity since I got out of bed. I don't know how I'm going to make it through the day.'

He took a deep breath. 'You know Jasper doesn't know anything about us – I've never told him,' he said. He clenched and released his fists.

'It's always made perfect sense not to tell him, but now it doesn't,' Edmund said. 'God knows what he's thinking right now. He looked a little shocked.'

Ovidia replied with a slowness that said she'd had to think hard. 'If he'd told his friends or Holly about me, they'd understand if he wanted to leave, wouldn't they? John's his best friend?'

'Yes, and I can't begrudge him my time, not after everything he's done for Jasper.'

Ovidia was silent, and Edmund took it to mean she understood. Ovidia had once said of herself that silence wasn't something that came naturally to her. *'If I'm not talking, then I'm working or something's wrong,'* she'd said cheerily, but he'd already found that about her. Not so long ago, he'd listen to her conversing, even with a complete stranger, fascinated by her wit, her observations, and her intelligence. Now she'd sit or stand for long periods without speaking, her pen, book, or computer useless in front of her. Her silence had become something to which he'd almost become accustomed.

He looked at her now, still, despite everything, the woman he loved. 'Please – come out and join us. I don't think I can sit with them on my own.' Edmund put his arms around Ovidia and drew her close. He used to joke about the view from above, that he could see the top of her hair. His line of sight followed the outline of her spine down to her feet. He kissed her, faint traces of salt and breakfast obscured by the hours that had passed. He once again was insensible to time as he stood breathing in the familiar scent of her skin and the odour of dried runner's sweat. He exhaled, forcing away the fear of never being able to smell her again.

'I'm here for champagne,' Edmund said, remembering the visitors waiting outside. 'I'm sure we still have some around.'

Ovidia blinked rapidly and craned to look around. 'We do somewhere. It'll be warm, though. It was for that dinner when we found out –' she stopped. 'The glasses are on the top shelf.'

They sought out the glasses and champagne together, as if they were once again entertaining some of the few guests they'd ever invited to this house. Edmund paused to watch Ovidia as she selected wine glasses from a shelf on which they were lined up according to their size and purpose. At the sink, she rinsed off the dust that had settled from disuse and dried each of them with paper towels.

Oxfam would probably sell the glasses for a fraction of what they were worth, he thought. He wouldn't take them with him wherever it was he would move.

Edmund rifled through an upper cabinet filled with assorted bottles of wine and spirits that had never made it to the wine cooler, finding the champagne and flinching when he recalled why it had not been drunk.

The brief task they completed together reminded him of the thrill and anticipation of the life they thought would lead together in this house. Moving in together had been like unwrapping a large gift from the aunt who always got her presents just right. Even when combined, their individual possessions could not have filled this house; everything in Ovidia's flat would have only taken up two of the five bedrooms. This kitchen was cavernous in contrast to the kitchens he'd owned before. This place had been the first time he'd ever visualised himself remaining in a house, not one or two years into the future, but five or ten, not an investment but a life.

He'd never been more insecure of himself than when he chose and prepared the house for him and Ovidia. Only when it was renovated had he brought her to see it. It had not been his intention to ask her to move in with him – he'd been afraid she'd refuse. He'd bought the house on the premise that the proximity to her house would mean it would be almost as if they lived together.

But Ovidia had been a step ahead.

'Are you asking me to move in with you?' she had asked as they'd wandered through the reception rooms and down to the kitchen for the first time together.

'Well... yes,' he'd said. 'No.' It was unlike him to prevaricate. 'I mean the house is here, and I'm in it. If you'd move in, it would make me really happy.'

He'd asked the designer to add a few useful items, and, when he and Ovidia had first moved in, they'd opened drawers in this kitchen to find neatly organised cutlery, crockery, and glassware gleaming with newness. The designer had selected them to match the style of the house – urban and quietly sophisticated.

'It saves us from running around headless trying to find pots and pans that match the place,' Ovidia had said that first morning, pressing the cabinet doors open and shutting them again. The designer had created areas for privacy, for comfort, for entertaining, skilled as she was in anticipating the needs of a contemporary household.

Of course, what they were meant to do was to build upon it with their own taste, but that had happened only sporadically, a few colourful mugs, a few souvenirs from their trips. Ovidia had kept her flat, so most of her decor remained there. The few times he thought about it, their families not knowing about the house robbed it of the sense of permanence it could have had.

Edmund had paused while examining the vase of large silk flowers in muted shades of pink and purple that the designer had left as a gift perched on the peninsula. 'To tell you the truth. It's a bit overwhelming.'

Ovidia had grinned, her teeth showing. 'That's hilarious, you being overwhelmed? By a house?'

'It's not just the house,' he'd replied, not meeting her gaze. 'It's a new life. It's moving in with someone for the first time in my life – at my age.'

Ovidia had looked taken aback. 'Hang on, you didn't tell me that. You've never lived with someone?'

'It's just never happened for me. I moved a suitcase in with…'

'The Lady in Beige,' Ovidia had teased, referring to a woman he'd mentioned he'd dated.

'Not "the Lady in Beige". This one habitually wore linen pants.'

'In beige?'

'Off-white,' he'd replied, handing her a plate for her approval.

'We lasted about two months after that. Our breakup was calm, peaceable, no drama, about as exciting as our relationship.'

He had listened to her giggle.

'So when I've been superseded, what will you call me?' She'd planted her hand on her hips, still grinning.

'The one who wore rainbows.' It'd come out flat. He couldn't joke about the idea of her leaving.

9

Anne had met Edmund three times. The first time, sitting beside him at dinner more than a year and a half previously, she'd found him disinterested in her presence, spending most of the dinner with his back turned towards her, cutting her out of the conversations.

That evening, Anne had already felt slightly brushed aside. She hadn't wanted to go to the evening get-together; she'd wanted to watch the first episode of a new interior-design show that was premiering. Instead, she'd found herself at the end of the table beside Edmund while the others – Jasper, John, Phil, and Lucinda – were chatting animatedly without making an effort to include her, while constantly asking Edmund's opinion on business and economics. He'd replied each time with a brief, succinct response as if refusing to be drawn into the conversation.

John had occasionally leaned across the table to her asking, 'You all right?' And each time she'd replied 'yes', though she wasn't. She'd tried to engage Edmund in conversation, asking about his work and the last location she'd heard he'd visited, but he hadn't answered her third question, instead refilling her glass with wine. Anne had interpreted it as a request for silence, and she was not inclined to beg for his company. Later, she'd described Edmund's behaviour to

Jasper, and Jasper had apologised to her, saying he wasn't always like that, not unpleasant anyhow. Edmund was always at least polite and was an excellent conversationalist.

The next time, Edmund had seemed much more pleasant to her. It had been at a bookshop celebrating how well John's book had been received. There had been perhaps four dozen people at the event. Finger food had been served, and she remembered feeling flattered that he'd chosen to talk to her, especially since there'd been a number of people from the publishing industry who had to be more interesting for Edmund to talk to. Anne decided that he'd been paying attention to her in lieu of an apology – checking if her glass needed refilling and asking insightful questions about her daughters. However, she felt that he wasn't particularly interested in her answers. At the end of that evening, she was sure she knew why Jasper always had an excuse not to invite him to socialise. He was, despite his manners, distant and preoccupied and at times seemed to be disinterested in her company, though he had chosen to remain beside her. There was something about his eyes, as if he had something on his mind, or, as she'd thought at the time, as if he was bored. Despite his efforts, Edmund hadn't been nice enough to overcome the first impression she'd had of him.

The third time, they'd barely spoken. It had been at his parents' house, and, having seemed impatient and distracted, he'd left before dinner without an explanation. His mother and father had briefly discussed what could have made him leave and then shrugged his behaviour away.

Anne knew too little about him to make assumptions about the woman in his kitchen. He hadn't mentioned a partner on the occasions that they'd met, and she was sure

Jasper would have told John and her if he had one. In fact, she was sure Jasper had said, just a few months earlier, Edmund didn't have a partner.

In the short walk through the French doors, she decided the woman couldn't be a prostitute – she scolded herself – sex worker – or a one-night stand. If she were, she wouldn't be in his kitchen wearing workout clothes, at least in Anne's limited knowledge of what sex workers did or didn't do. Then Anne chided herself for thinking that this woman and Edmund were an unlikely pair, that she couldn't be his partner because, Anne acknowledged her own prejudice, the woman was black.

They assembled themselves in the glass extension as Edmund left to fetch the champagne.

'Knowing Edmund, it's probably real-deal champers,' John said. Anne glanced at him, wondering if John really could say he knew Edmund, since he seemed just as confused at the situation as she felt.

Anne followed John's lead and sat beside him on the two-seater outdoor sofa, which was far more comfortable than its modern spindly legs and bucket design suggested. Jasper, with Holly, sat left of Edmund's seat on a matching sofa built for three. Holly pressed herself against Jasper, despite the amount of room remaining on the chair they shared.

John whispered in Anne's ear just as he offered her his cushion, 'This is a little bizarre.'

Anne knew what he meant. Nothing was as it should be. She glanced at her watch – they'd only been there a few minutes – and wondered how long it would be before they could leave. She grimaced in response and took the cushion from John, playfully slapping him with it before putting it behind her and savouring its luxurious softness.

'I wonder what *that* is,' Holly mused, the moment the doors shut. Pointing to the detritus of blue wood in the corner of the garden, a sledgehammer leaning against its one remaining post. 'Looks like one of those little garden rooms.'

They all turned to look at it, but no one answered, and they turned back in their seats.

'This is not what I expected,' John said, craning his neck to see the rest of the garden. 'I thought Edmund's place would be more of a bachelor pad. You know, leather and steel. This is more like a domestic haven. All that's missing is three kids and a trampoline.'

'I was thinking the same thing. Where're the embalmed stag heads and the piles of *Playboy*?' Anne agreed.

'Who has *Playboy* anymore?' Jasper asked. 'It's all online.' Holly smacked his hand playfully, and Anne saw him flinch at her touch.

'Who was the woman in the kitchen?' Holly asked.

Jasper tensed at her question.

'Girlfriend?' Anne suggested, watching Jasper for clues. She couldn't think of a second suggestion.

'No way,' John said, interrupting her.

'Why not?' Holly asked. 'Except… Jasper, you'd have known, wouldn't you?' She turned slightly to face Jasper, who said nothing.

'Well she's too…' John began.

'Young?' Anne proposed. 'Black?' She made the accusation, hoping that someone else, too, would reveal some underlying prejudice.

'I was going to say "cool".' John lowered his voice. 'I think they'd look funny together in public. He's a bit staid and she looks,' he paused, 'exciting. Anyway, I don't think she's that young, probably our age, just better preserved maybe.' He turned sideways from the waist to face Anne. 'And why would her being black be an issue?'

'It isn't,' Anne said, stiffening. She felt embarrassed. 'It was just an observation.'

'This is the twenty-first century. Why should her race be a factor in deciding what she is or isn't?' John said. Anne could hear the annoyance in his voice.

'It isn't a factor,' she said with clenched teeth. She wanted to explain to John that he'd understood her wrong. But then he might ask her what she really meant – and she wasn't sure.

'I never realised how racist my parents were until I brought home an Indian guy when I was at uni,' Holly said cheerfully. 'When he turned out to be a complete bastard it was all, "we told you so, those people this and those people that"… In the meantime, my sister's boyfriend was embezzling money from his boss, but no one said it was "because he was from Cornwall".'

'I didn't know you dated someone Indian,' Jasper said, glancing at her, his eyes leaving the doors that led to the kitchen.

'I've told you all about him – Immanuel,' Holly replied, with a casual air that suggested she'd never mentioned his race.

'Right,' Jasper said, and he dropped the subject.

Anne, too, was surprised, but hid it, quickly turning to look at the rest of the garden behind her. She recalled Holly telling her about a man who left her for an heiress. Perhaps she'd described him as 'dark', but she'd never described him as being of a particular race, and Anne, she admitted to herself, simply assumed he was white. It wasn't particularly important in itself; it just reminded her of how much she didn't know about Holly.

'Maybe she's his assistant – the one you spoke to,' Holly suggested, giggling as she spoke. 'Getting some "overtime" in, maybe?'

'She's not his PA,' Jasper interjected fiercely.

'If your PA is half-dressed in your kitchen on a Saturday morning, then she's not *just* your PA,' John said, following Holly's lead by trying to be funny.

'Well maybe she's not that important to him,' Anne said reassuringly, seeing that Jasper was upset. 'If she was, he'd have told you about her. She could be a houseguest? Or, maybe it's a new thing – too new to have mentioned?'

'Exactly,' Holly said. 'You haven't seen him in a couple of months. Maybe she's been keeping him busy.'

'Who says they're even sleeping together?' John said.

'Yeah – roommates!' Holly continued in a jolly tone. She took Jasper's hand, and he let it lie limp in hers.

'More like a lodger to offset what this place costs,' John said, and both Holly and Anne laughed.

'He probably put an ad on Gumtree,' Holly chuckled.

Their speculation ended with the noise of Edmund returning. He'd taken much too long to have just been fetching a bottle of champagne. His eyes were a little bit brighter, and the heaviness in his step had eased. He had a bottle tucked under one arm and carried six elegant champagne flutes.

'Ovidia will be down in a bit, she's just freshening up after her run,' was his explanation. 'She might take a while.' He said this as if it were an afterthought, or even an apology, indicating that Ovidia would *definitely* take a while. Edmund turned to Jasper and shrugged. 'Well, what do you think? Quite a change from the last place.'

It seemed to Anne that, for a moment, Jasper's shoulders relaxed.

He hiccoughed, but it was probably meant to be a laugh. 'Wow, wait till I tell Mummy: Edmund's got a place in the suburbs, a patio set, a woman…' Jasper waved his hand towards the garden. 'All you need is one of those little lawn mowers that you sit on like in Forrest Gump.'

They all laughed, and Anne felt her own tension ease as well. Edmund had answered both of her burning questions. Yes, it was his home, and, without explicitly saying so, Ovidia was in some way involved with him.

'And a lovely patio set, too,' Holly added. 'The kind of thing Anne would choose. Almost mid-century. Wouldn't you, Anne?'

'Definitely,' she said, distracted from the matter at hand and flattered that Holly would praise her taste to a stranger.

The others glanced at her, briefly, then their collective gaze returned to Edmund.

Edmund put down the champagne glasses. 'She said not to wait for her.' He said it as if confident they knew who 'she' referred to. He picked up the bottle and spoke as he peeled off its foil, and they all stood up in a semi-circle with him at the fore.

'Sorry I couldn't make it for the big announcement. I had something on. If you'd just said, "I'm going to ask Holly to marry me", I'd have dropped everything and come running.' His voice seemed convincing, but, looking at him, Anne was not convinced of his words.

Mid-toast, his gaze drifted towards the horizon, towards the ruined playhouse, then he seemed to snatch his attention back from wherever it had wandered and continued.

'Congratulations to my little brother, Jasper, and to Holly, my soon-to-be sister-in-law,' he said, smiling at Holly. 'Holly, you have brought a great deal of happiness into my brother's life. Thank you.'

Holly smiled back happily.

To Anne, his wording had been too exact. He hadn't said *'you've made my brother a happy man'*, but Holly's face radiated so much joy that Anne knew she hadn't caught the nuance of his phrasing.

A pop sent the cork into the air and effervescence spurted from the bottle, and they held their glasses out to be filled. After congratulating the couple once again, Anne saw Edmund glance back to the kitchen doors and leave Ovidia's glass empty.

10

Edmund was right, Ovidia agreed, he couldn't just ask the guests to leave. Not, at least, without an explanation. She had kissed Edmund again and left, hurrying upstairs to their bedroom, her feet nearly silent on the wood floors. She realised she hadn't told Edmund that she'd return but continued up the stairs, telling herself she'd be as quick as she could. Still, she slowed as she neared the top of the stairs and visualised the safety and silence of her own flat across the road. She could exit unseen through the front door.

She paused with one foot on the top step. Why stop at her flat? She could go somewhere else, visit her parents or even check into a hotel for the night. She could even catch a flight somewhere not too far away – Paris, Berlin, Rome. She toyed with the idea of finding her passport and taking flight. She would come back in a few days' time.

But it wouldn't help anything. It wouldn't stop anything.

The only consequence she could imagine would be that Edmund would trust her less than he already did. She knew Edmund was highly capable of taking on the small group that, with palpable discomfort, had shuffled past her into the glass extension. He was one of the best in his field, a financial expert who was lauded among his peers and paid for his intelligence, confidence, and professionalism. He'd find a way.

But this was most likely the last day they'd be together.

She told herself she wasn't going to abandon him today.

Ovidia peeled off her clothes as she crossed their bedroom.

She couldn't recall the last time she was ready so quickly. After a few minutes of a hot shower, she massaged her skin with lotion and followed with a quick dusting of make-up. She combed through her short hair with mousse. Just as hurriedly, she opened the walk-in wardrobe and faced the rows of clothing, some hanging and some folded, most of which she had ignored for months. She'd made do with the same small pile of running clothes, a few pairs of distended winter tights, sweatshirts, and some now over-washed and worn-out dresses that the housekeeper had taken to placing just inside the wardrobe door where Ovidia could get to them without any effort.

Ovidia held one of those dresses up, examining it, turning it from back to front and back again. For the first time, she noticed that the elasticated waist was slack, the hemline broken, and the blue was fading to grey. It occurred to her that she'd left the house in that dress only a few days earlier – she'd allowed the world to see her in near rags. She'd always liked her clothes and liked to have fun with them, melding her own style with whatever was on trend. She used to shop especially in vintage shops or at eclectic local designers. These past few months had been the only period in her adult life that she'd thrown clothes on without caring about their final effect or how a stranger walking past her would perceive her.

'You're not going outside in that,' Ovidia told herself and threw the dress on the floor. Did it matter now because Jasper was outside? She told herself no, it wasn't to do with him. As she rummaged through her clothes, she asked herself if it mattered that Jasper's fiancée was there beside him. Perhaps? But, she told herself, the person she'd been before would never have greeted her guests in a torn, faded dress. She spun in her underwear slowly in front of a large floor-to-ceiling mirror and thought how she looked older, much older, than the last time she'd honestly looked at her reflection. She traced her fingers along the lines etched beside her mouth that ran downwards, like a sad clown.

She walked back to the bed and sat, reminding herself, *I'll get through today.* She massaged her stomach, trying to ease a knot of unhappiness.

Jasper was out there. She looked at her hands and realised they were trembling. She closed her eyes and studied the blackness.

When her heart stopped racing, she stood, dressed, and left the room.

Ovidia slowed down as she arrived in the kitchen. She waited after she entered, smoothing down her clothes and stretching her calves. She picked up her mobile and checked the time – it wasn't even eleven. It had only been a few minutes since the last time she'd looked. She closed her eyes and inhaled.

She took a few steps towards the French doors and then retreated. She opened a few cabinet doors, not looking for anything in particular.

Perhaps she should offer them tea, she thought, looking at a half packet of biscuits, her favourite type. She picked it up and realised she had no memory of eating them. She bit into one and it was stale.

'Crisps,' she said aloud. She was sure they had crisps somewhere. Ovidia stopped with her hand on a door. She was stalling. 'You belong here,' she repeated Edmund's words. Next, she opened the wine-cooler door and pulled out the first wine bottle that she touched. She gripped it tightly by the neck, steeling herself almost as if were a weapon, not wanting to arrive to battle unarmed.

When Ovidia emerged through the French doors into the glass extension, she stole a glance at Jasper, before diverting her gaze to the rest of the guests. She caught him at that moment breathing deeply and deliberately, surreptitiously – maybe he was hoping that no one else was watching him. He looked tense. Ovidia was hoping that she didn't, though her stomach hurt, and she felt a sense of dread, as if a spectre was bearing down on them all.

Olivia's eyes leapt to Holly, whose smile seemed natural and who seemed at ease. Holly uncrossed her legs and planted them on the floor, as if she was expecting something, maybe a formal introduction. John straightened to attention, also in expectation, brushing his trousers with his fingers. Anne pulled gently away from her partner, a momentary look of annoyance visible on her face.

Edmund stood to meet her, his hand going lightly around her waist and steering her to where he sat. 'You look lovely,' he whispered in her ear. The familiarity of his touch helped her relax and she followed him. With a sweep of his hand, he offered her his seat. She shook her head.

11

The creak of the French doors announced Ovidia's arrival. The garden chairs protested in an angry chorus as the little clutch of people all moved in some way to acknowledge her arrival.

To Jasper, the distance to those doors could have been an entire runway with her on display. He watched Ovidia walking towards them, taking in how much she had changed. Gone was the perfect form preserved in his memory. She was, as she'd been before, the rich dark brown that he had found glorious – he'd once called her a perfect shade of Twix. She'd found it funny and laughed, nudging him gently with her elbow. The event, the date and time, were lost in his memory, but he remembered every detail of her beside him.

In today's incarnation, gone was her softly slender silhouette and the curve of her breasts and hips. In their place was a sinewy, androgynous outline, only a hint of bosom beneath her blouse. She stood and walked with a near-military posture, with the aura of an athlete. Her haircut tapered at the back, almost vanishing at her neck, shaven close along the back of her head and made feminine only by a few inches of afro curls that covered the top of her head to her hairline. For a second, Jasper imagined that it was her near masculinity that appealed to Edmund, but he retracted the thought, embarrassed by his own spite.

Ovidia wore a loose-fitting skirt that ended just above her knees, and, true to the woman Jasper had known before, her top was a flurry of dark blue and orange. She had on discreet make-up, and she wore slippers – two large, round-cheeked grey and white bunny heads encased her feet. To Jasper, she seemed to saunter in, showing no signs of tension or discomfort at his presence. He quietly cleared his throat when Edmund held Ovidia, or did Edmund clutch her? Glancing at Holly, he saw she'd made no response to the sound he'd made. She was, he saw, like the others, fixated on Ovidia.

Jasper smiled at the sight of the slippers flapping against the tiled floor, remembering a pair in the form of smiling purple hippos that she'd once had. He was mesmerised by the colours she wore. Ovidia had always loved colour and contrast. On their first date, she'd worn blue – which he later learned was her favourite colour – a trouser suit whose formality was ruined by a pair of orange and purple socks that screamed from above a pair of three-inch court heels. He'd never thought to ask her about her clothes, what inspired them, because it seemed integral to her personality, like how his brother wore dark colours.

He understood what John meant when he said Edmund and Ovidia would look odd together. Ovidia was splendid in her colours and petite, while Edmund was drab, his clothes conservative and unexciting. Jasper couldn't imagine Edmund putting up with how much Ovidia talked. It had been one of the reasons Jasper was drawn to her, how at ease she was with her own personality, that she felt no reason to modulate her natural tendency to make conversation.

He watched as Edmund's face lit up when he touched Ovidia. Jasper had never seen his brother embrace a woman before. Even though this was a chaste greeting, Jasper could too easily imagine Edmund kissing her, and he had to brace himself as he watched them touch.

Holly's hand touched Jasper's thigh. He ignored it at first, then mechanically put his hand on top of hers, and he felt her snuggle against him as if they were watching something on TV.

Holly had been in pale blue when he asked her to marry him. Anne had taken pictures. This morning they'd scrolled through the photos, and, as Holly had been in the bath, he'd gone through each one of them again, looking at the joy in her face but more so being surprised by the joy in his own.

He tried to recapture that feeling. He scanned his memory of the previous night, trying to seize the emotions on which he'd floated throughout the evening.

'Will you marry me?' he'd asked Holly, unable to remember any of the text he'd written and memorised and stumbling over the simple words.

He'd still been excited until the moment he'd entered Edmund's front door that morning. He visualised the days leading up to his proposal. He tried to recall the anxious anticipation of looking for a ring, of walking past a bridal shop on a high street and stopping to imagine that he would, at some point, be enmeshed in discussions of dresses, suits, and flowers.

He couldn't find those feelings.

Ovidia was holding another bottle – red wine, tucked beneath her arm. 'Hello, everyone!' she said cheerfully, as she let go of Edmund.

How much longer can I last? Jasper thought. His mind blank, he couldn't imagine how he could escape. What would he possibly say to his friends if he ran from this house like he wanted to? The truth was almost farcical.

'Congratulations, Holly. Congratulations, Jasper,' Ovidia said, nodding to each of them; but, like Edmund, she didn't offer a hand or a hug. Was that something she'd learned from Edmund? Jasper wondered. He saw her glance at the space beside Holly on the three-seater sofa, but she took the only other remaining seat – a side table on Edmund's right, moving his glass of whiskey and his newspaper to the floor.

12

'I'm Ovidia,' she announced as she sat down, fighting the urge to run.

Anne and John introduced themselves, though they needn't have. Edmund had described them to her. He'd told her trivia such as Anne being left-handed and that John hated brandy. While Edmund never told her the details of his conversations with his brother, he'd told her of this friendship, saying that he couldn't recall Jasper ever having a friendship as strong as the one with John, and he was glad, though he found John irritating, pompous even. After he'd met Anne, he'd told Ovidia he thought the two of them would get on. Edmund had been to dinner with them after having arrived that morning from a transatlantic trip. 'I could have been nicer to Anne,' he'd said. 'But I was just too tired to make an effort.'

Edmund had never met Holly. Ovidia wasn't sure if he'd been deliberately avoiding her, but she knew that, on at least one occasion, he'd lied to Jasper about having planned an early morning trip, when in fact Edmund had spent the day at home.

Both John and Anne were looking at her with faint, friendly smiles, while Holly's was bright and cheerful. Their expressions confirmed that they knew nothing of her existence. In Anne, she saw the stylish woman she'd expected. The kind who, without expensive labels, could look effortlessly sophisticated. She could see Anne was nervous, discreetly tapping her index finger over and over again, yet her face remained calm and friendly.

Holly kept looking around at everyone as if she was waiting to speak but unsure if she should or unable to think of anything to say.

Starting conversations had once been so easy, but now Ovidia wasn't sure she remembered how. She would have preferred to be indoors, listening to the music that she now couldn't recall. But Edmund needed her with him.

'So, do you live around here?' John asked, clearing his throat.

Ovidia smiled again, wondering how long she would need to keep smiling to make sure they couldn't see through her charade. How strange it was to be in a space with three people whose lives were intertwined with Edmund's, people she should know and yet none of them knew of her existence. Even John, who made a living talking to people, had floundered, coming up with a silly question. He was obviously desperate to know more. If, before she'd come out into the conservatory, Edmund had already told them that he and she were together, he wouldn't have told them much more.

'Ovidia, what a lovely name,' Anne said, gently kicking John's leg. He flinched and rotated his ankle.

'When I was born, our next-door neighbour suggested it. She thought it was from Shakespeare,' Ovidia replied to Anne's question first. 'Turns out her experience of Shakespeare was a high school production of *Romeo and Juliet*. I live across the road,' she said to John, delivering both answers as if they were mere trivia, as if the question of whether she was cohabiting with Edmund was as inconsequential as a neighbour's knowledge of Shakespeare.

'You live across the road?' John echoed, as if he was checking that he'd heard her correctly.

Ovidia ignored his question. She'd been to therapists; she knew he'd want to keep talking until he uncovered an explanation that satisfied him.

She turned to address Holly, while forcing the wine bottle's screw top open. She could feel them all watching her. Even Jasper's eyes seemed to burn into her. She took in details of him in measured glances, repressing the urge to stare. Edmund hadn't mentioned how thin his brother had become. *'He's lost a bit of weight'*, and later, *'Looking much better now that he's put some meat on'* was as much as he'd said.

If this was 'meat', as Edmund had called it, then what had he looked like before? Jasper's fingers were bony and his jaw seemed larger, jutting from his face. His skin had a powdery-white pallor to it, as if he'd recently been ill, and he had dark circles around his eyes. He looked much older than her, though he was a year younger, and he retained only a trace of the good looks she remembered.

'I really should get round to meeting this girl,' Edmund had said about a year ago. 'He seems to be serious about her.' But from then on, he'd mentioned her only in passing. Until the previous night, as they sat in the kitchen silently eating microwave meals and a prepacked salad from its packaging. Beside each of them was tepid tap water in mismatched glasses. They were eating late, as they'd spent the evening each refusing the other's offer of food, both unable to make the effort to eat. The television had been on for a while, but neither had been able to focus. Ovidia had tried a book, trying to fill her time until bedtime when, she hoped, she would sleep for a few hours.

'Jasper just asked Holly to marry him,' Edmund had said.

Ovidia had looked at his hands and then the space around him. His phone had been nowhere near him. This meant it would have already happened. Edmund would have read the messages and only told her now. His face had looked tired but otherwise impassive. Had he shown any happiness at the news, then perhaps Ovidia would have tried to do the same.

'That's nice,' she'd said. She should have felt something at this news, regret or maybe relief, but it did not lift her from the funk in which she was mired. She looked down at her food, a pile of beige, brown, and white sauces with a suggestion of mince, and reminded herself that it was lasagne, though she could taste nothing. She'd shaken more pepper over her food.

'Is it?' Edmund had asked.

She'd tried to think of an appropriate response: a shrug, a joke, something. Edmund had put a forkful of food into his mouth and chewed, his eyes cast to the space behind her shoulder.

'I don't care,' she had replied.

'Holly, you must be so excited.' She made eye contact with Jasper's fiancée, smiling as convincingly as she could muster. 'Edmund told me last night. He was gutted when he realised he should have joined you for dinner.'

If Holly had looked happy before, she was now incandescent, Ovidia thought.

'Really?'

Ovidia looked to the ground, unable to continue her lie. She pulled at her earlobe.

They'd gone back to the glass room after they'd eaten and sat in the same chair Holly was in now. Edmund had occasionally picked up his mobile to answer the texts that continued to come from his mother. Then Edmund had put his arm around her, and they'd stared into the night until finally it was time to go to bed.

'Tell me about your proposal,' she asked, her smile feeling much too tight. She would not ruin Jasper's big day, she told herself, gripping the wine bottle to steady her once again shaking hands.

She kept her back to Edmund as she spoke. 'It's been forever since I had anything to do with a wedding.' She raised the bottle of red wine, now open, to offer it to the others. 'How did you two meet?'

13

Jasper was glad John was with him. When he'd decided to ask Holly to marry him, he knew he wanted John and Anne to be there along with his family: Edmund and their parents. John and Anne had been in his life for four years – less by a summer, longer than Holly. Jasper found them easy to be with; they were both patient – or was it accepting? They were consistent and reliable. John and Anne had entered his life exactly when he needed them.

'Are you okay?' A voice had cut through the grey suffocating mist that enveloped him.

The blonde woman had a confident, reassuring smile. She appeared in front of him as his vision blurred and the feeling of blood churning in his head intensified. He felt his knees weakening.

'Yes,' he breathed.

'No, you're not. You're going to pass out. John!' she'd called, as Jasper crumpled to the ground. The two of them had held him capably, slowing his fall, and, when he'd got to the ground, the woman tried to turn him onto his front.

Jasper had resisted. The concrete was hard against his ribs and cold against his face. He pushed off the ground with all the strength he had, rising only onto his elbow.

A few droplets of water spilled upon them from the leaves above. They were in a park nearly bereft of humans on a chilly and grey Tuesday afternoon. The city's vegetation was still the deep green of summer. Though autumn was approaching, it hadn't arrived yet, and the weather had been miserable for days. Jasper had used it as an excuse to remain indoors, out of contact with the world.

'Do you have any medical conditions? Should I call an ambulance?' the woman asked.

'No, for God's sake, no!' he'd said as loudly as he could, emitting a feeble croak.

'Drugs?' she'd asked.

'No,' he whined and shook his head. He clutched his abdomen as pain shot through his stomach.

'I'm calling an ambulance anyway,' John said.

Jasper struggled to sit up as John pulled a mobile out of his jacket pocket. The rain had stopped hours earlier, but the puddles that remained had soaked through Jasper's trousers and muddied his elbow. His coat was much too warm for an August afternoon, and Jasper had worn it to cover up the fact that his clothes were much too large for him and to hide his near-emaciated body. Jasper realised that he must have looked like a drug addict, at best.

'I'm just...' he began, and the blonde looked at him as if anticipating his answer, '... a bit hungry, I haven't eaten for a while.'

John paused, having not yet dialled. The woman immediately rummaged through her large leather handbag, bringing out a bar of Twix, a tinned espresso, and a half-empty packet of crisps.

He ate three crisps and eyed the chocolate bar, even if it brought back unwanted thoughts.

'A perfect shade of Twix,' he said to himself in a whisper. Dreading the rush of sickly sweet stickiness, he'd declined the bar and continued eating the crisps slowly, fighting the wave of nausea that threatened. He looked to see John put his mobile away, as if relieved.

'Everything all right then?' An older woman stopped. She shook her head at the sight of him. 'I know most of the homeless ones around here. I haven't seen him before.' She talked over Jasper to the woman and John, as if Jasper was irrelevant. 'There's a shelter near here, but they all run off back to their drugs – prescription nowadays.'

'I live just around the corner, thank you.' Jasper had enough in him to be indignant at her suggestion.

'They all say that. Doesn't look like he can afford to live around here, but, then again, looking homeless could be some latest fashion,' she sniffed. 'Best of luck. Call the police if he gets rowdy.' She sauntered off, humming Mamma Mia, her platforms silent against the pavement.

The crisps were a relief. The first sip of lukewarm espresso eased the food's way down his throat, and the shot of caffeine sent a jolt of energy through him. Jasper hadn't eaten in days. The kitchen in the flat he'd recently moved into held frozen convenience foods, putrid fruit on the sideboards, and cereal going stale in open boxes. Every time he bought food, he promised himself he'd eat it. Yet with each microwave meal, every pizza ordered, each Chinese takeaway he opened, a surge of revulsion overcame him. For the last few days, he hadn't even been able to look at food without waves of nausea raging through him. He hadn't seen his parents or Edmund, knowing they might try to force him to eat – how they would, he couldn't guess.

Until those crisps crackled in his mouth, he'd been beginning to believe he'd never eat again.

'Let's get you on to a bench,' the woman suggested.

The two of them helped him up, and he'd staggered to a nearby seat, leaning reluctantly against John until he felt the firmness of the bench beneath him. For a moment, he felt utterly humiliated at having been rescued by two strangers and mistaken for a drug addict by a third. Then he just felt hungry. They sat quietly on the bench, the two strangers watching him slowly nibble and sip as if he was a baby.

'Well, we can't leave you like this,' the woman said. After ten minutes, Jasper had eaten only a quarter of the packet. 'Can we call you a taxi? You'd be better off at home.'

'No, really, I live in the mews just behind here,' Jasper insisted, gesticulating vaguely. 'I'll be fine. I just need to get my strength back.'

The couple looked at each other, their faces saying they were not convinced. 'Well, is there someone we can call?'

'No need. I'll just order a pizza.'

'Seriously.' John narrowed his eyes, 'We'll call someone, or we'll call the police. We're not going to leave you out here.' Jasper had reluctantly given him Edmund's number, stumbling over the digits, though Edmund had had the same number for years.

'Says he'll be here in forty-five minutes.' John had put his mobile back in his pocket after a short call. *Hello, is this Edmund? My name's John. We found your brother collapsed on a pavement. No, he says he doesn't, but we think he does need someone to keep an eye on him.*

The blonde looked at her watch and looked around her as if pressed for time. She ran her hand through her nearly waist-length hair and tugged the belt of her cardigan, tightening it around her lean and petite body.

'Louisa,' John said, 'there's no need for the two of us to stay here. You go on ahead. I'll call you when I've got him somewhere safer than a bench.'

'If you're sure you're all right with him?' Louisa said.

John nodded.

Louisa had kissed him. Jasper noted how her tongue lingered for the briefest of seconds against his lips – a bold yet discreet lick. He looked down at the packet of crisps and only then realised they were salt and vinegar.

John had then taken Jasper to a small café nearby whose décor harked back to the days of empire with pseudo-Victorian furniture and a board outside promising afternoon tea for thirty pounds. John had ordered himself a pot of tea and, for Jasper, freshly squeezed orange juice and plateful of butter biscuits.

'Biscuits,' John said with flourish, 'always do the trick with my girls.'

Jasper ate them with surprising appetite. The biscuits were easy to eat and mildly flavoured. *Had he tried biscuits?* he asked himself. *Perhaps they held a secret.* They crumbled in his mouth, and he felt stronger, tackling the plate with shaking hands. Again, humiliation surged through him as he noticed his nails were ragged and dirty.

John's presence was reassuring, and, to be sociable, Jasper asked what he meant by 'his girls'.

'My daughters, and, well, my wife's pretty fond of biscuits, too.'

When Jasper finished the biscuits he said, 'That's better. I feel rather stupid. Sorry for taking you out of your way.'

'Wasn't doing anything special,' John shrugged. 'You looked like a man in need of biscuits.'

'In need of a psychiatrist, more like,' Jasper said, sipping his orange juice.

'Well, you're in luck. Well, almost...' John said, as Edmund rang to say he was just around the corner.

14

'Yes, please,' Holly said, and Anne too nodded at Ovidia's offer of wine. The men still had traces of their champagne remaining. John gulped his down and said, 'I'll have a bit, too.' They all reused the champagne flutes, Ovidia having forgotten suitable glasses for the red wine.

Holly wondered what Edmund had whispered to Ovidia. Now able to examine Ovidia closer, Holly agreed with John. Ovidia was unexpected. She was cool – for lack of a better word. She could imagine her doing an Ironwoman competition or obstacle race on TV. Holly couldn't see Edmund and Ovidia on a street together. She couldn't imagine where they'd be or what they'd be doing. She had expected Edmund to be with a woman more classically styled, perhaps a slender, older woman with polished blonde hair, muted colours, and discreet jewellery – a bit more like Anne, maybe.

But Holly thought she, like Anne, was putting too much into Ovidia's appearance. In retrospect, she understood what Anne had been trying to say when she mentioned Ovidia's race. She'd been trying to explain the jarring difference between the two: Ovidia's slippers and bright colours and Edmund's muted greys and browns. Ovidia looked far more suited to Holly's own world, to the world of clubs and music and arts journalists – where patrons entered their forties disregarding their own ageing. Holly was sure that Ovidia would be more inclined to that sort of socialising than Anne, and that, since it was now evident that Ovidia was Edmund's partner, they'd go out together sometimes. She wondered if Edmund would come with them. Perhaps to art galleries or things like John's book launch, which she missed and had been disappointed to hear that Edmund had been there.

Holly was really pleased when Ovidia asked her how they met, but she'd have been happier to describe Jasper's proposal. It had taken her by surprise. The night had begun like any other night at his parents' house: they'd arrived, and his mother, as always, had warmly embraced her and stepped back to stand beside her husband, and dinner had followed soon after. Holly was a firm believer that that there was no truer proof of love than marriage. She had resigned herself to cohabiting, happily but not ideally, to being Jasper's partner instead of his wife. Her own parents had been married for forty years. Yet, around her, both men and women appeared content to live together, never making make that ultimate commitment, content to never parade a ring upon a ring finger or wear a white dress in front of enraptured guests.

'We met through work,' Holly said with her glass in her hand, legs crossed, giddy with joy and leaning forward towards Ovidia. 'Well, my friends, his work. I went to a party I really didn't want to go to, and Saskia was like, *"Oh, come on, please meet my friend, make him fall in love with you – I don't think I can stand Mr Misery anymore, he used to be so much fun. And I know he'll love you."'* It didn't occur to Holly to explain Saskia to her audience. 'It was at a new place in Camden; it was pretty awful – it still smelled of paint.'

It had been one of those parties at which minor luminaries starred. The restaurant was dark and industrial – corrugated iron pinned to its walls and exposed ducts painted silver. A DJ played unknown jazz and funk, and guests were expected to queue up at the bar to buy their own drinks. There were whispers that one or two of the celebrities present would possibly make it into the Daily Telegraph since a minor scandal regarding a public slap was fomenting, and that a renowned celebrity journalist would make an appearance at the party. Every other person was in media, communications, or public relations.

When Saskia introduced Jasper, he had been leaning against a varnished wooden post holding a drink he hadn't yet started, surrounded by a clutch of people who all seemed to do exactly what he did for a living. Beside him stood 'Mr Misery', as Saskia had termed him – a work colleague who'd recently emerged from a ten-year relationship, broken. Holly had thought the two men looked ill, and Saskia looked bored.

The first half an hour was miserable for Holly. She and Saskia made polite conversation and endured the men's long pauses and reluctant answers. Eventually Jasper, who seemed unable to stand Mr Misery's company either, said to Holly, 'Look do you want to stand outside or something? You look like you're enjoying this even less than I am.'

Saskia had followed them. 'God, Hector really needs to make an effort,' she'd said once outside, lighting a cigarette and flicking back her shoulder-length box braids. Her dark brown lipstick left a stain on the cigarette. 'I'm really sorry, Holly. I thought meeting someone nice might shake him up a bit.'

'He was with her for ten years,' Jasper had muttered.

'I know, poor guy,' Saskia had replied, 'but I have to share an office with him, and I'm starting to dread coming to work every morning.'

'You can't expect him to just cheer up.' Jasper was louder this time, more assertive.

'I don't. But couldn't he at least try?' Saskia had gulped her beer. 'On top of that, I've got to deal with you. At least I know what's wrong with him. You? You could be on crystal meth for all I know.'

'Saskia,' Jasper had interjected. Holly considered Saskia's reference to drugs. It made sense looking at him.

'No, really. And you know what? I'm the one who gets told "you really must make an effort with your colleagues,"' she'd mimicked their director. '"We're a family, we all need to support each other."' She'd briefly and quietly sucked her teeth.

'You complained about me?' Jasper had asked.

'Yes,' Saskia had replied and looked away.

Holly had watched. It was obvious that Saskia had been accumulating resentment against Jasper and she was finally airing her emotions. Holly had seen the look of indignation on his face, that he'd almost turned to walk away. But she had still been watching him when he'd wordlessly seemed to acknowledge that what Saskia said was true. She'd seen when his chin had dropped, and he'd fixed his gaze to the floor. His face, despite its pallor, had flushed with humiliation.

They'd stood silently for a few minutes, then Saskia had cleared her throat and said, 'Look, I'll see you on Monday, okay?' She'd patted Jasper on his shoulder. 'You coming in, Holly?' Without waiting for an answer, Saskia had extinguished her cigarette and returned indoors.

Holly and Jasper had found themselves alone.

'If you don't mind, I'll just change subject.' Holly had taken charge. 'You said earlier you got food poisoning at a tapas bar – what happened? What on earth did you eat?'

Their conversation had plodded along for half an hour more. Then Jasper had thanked her for her company and gone home. Holly had returned to the party, which now had more patrons, and its celebrity had arrived.

Holly left out most of the details of that evening, mentioning only the club, Mr Misery and Saskia, and the celebrity and his ensuing scandal.

She and Jasper didn't see each other again for a month, Holly explained. Their second meeting was uneventful, a group Saskia organised for drinks at a club re-opening. Her conversations with Jasper were less stilted, and he stood beside her for most of the evening. The third time Holly saw him, she excused herself from her company and went straight to him, knowing by then that he excited her. She'd felt a flutter in her stomach when he walked in the room, and her heart pounded when he'd kissed her on the cheek and put an arm around her gently, as if unsure if he should. That evening they'd been in a well-lit corner in a gallery in which it was impossible to hide from the light. Everything had been a reflective white and powerful lighting had made the room seem impersonal. It had begun to overheat with a swelling number of guests.

'It's great to see you again,' Jasper had said.

She'd opened her mouth to reply, but his eyes were already flitting around the room.

'Do you mean it's genuinely lovely to see me again – or are you just being polite?' Holly had surprised herself at how forceful she sounded.

'Oh,' Jasper had said, and he'd hesitated. 'I'm just being polite.'

Her stomach had sunk, but then their eyes had locked, and she'd caught the spark of humour in his – something she hadn't seen in him before.

'But you knew I was coming.' She'd wanted him to say he was interested in her, not to just infer it. 'You could have called or sent a text – maybe invited me for drinks first?'

He'd smiled. 'I was hoping you'd call me. I'm a bit slow at these things.'

'Bad breakup?' Holly had suggested.

Jasper had looked over her shoulder at an enormous installation behind her and focused on it for a moment. 'Stuff going on in my head.'

'Like depression or something?' she'd asked, her eyes wide in sympathy. Occasionally, she looked back at that moment and asked herself if he had or hadn't nodded. Had the almost imperceptible motion he'd made been in agreement? Or had she simply interpreted it as such? Depression made sense. Perhaps she'd found an explanation that suited her, so she took it.

'So, would you like to go for a drink with me sometime?' Holly had asked, just as Saskia joined in.

'Oh my God! He's smiling, like really smiling!' Saskia had said. 'Holly, you've saved my life!' She'd elbowed her friend. 'I'll just leave you alone then.'

It still had taken another month before they were finally alone together. In that month, always in the presence of others, she'd learned that he could be funny at times, that he would listen as she spoke, exuding concern and interest. She had also learned that he could stare at the ceiling, oblivious to her presence, or snap at her, annoyed at an inconsequential joke or what she thought was an exciting anecdote.

'Then yesterday – a year and half later – he proposed, while we were at his parents'.' Holly smiled at the memory of the hours that came afterwards in the room that had been his since he was a child. His childhood bed had long ago been replaced with a much bigger one, and the room was now decorated for an adult in hues of green and blue, mementos from his youth now on display in a glass-fronted cupboard in the corner.

'On his knees, tears in his eyes, everything – according to the texts from our mother,' Edmund interjected. 'And he asked after dinner.'

Holly was pleased when Edmund spoke. She had been sure he wasn't listening. He looked impassive, responding to the highs of her story with a nod. But she thought, happily, Jasper had probably told him all about her, and who likes to hear a story twice?

'At least if she'd said no, you'd have already eaten. Nothing like rejection to ruin your appetite,' Ovidia continued.

They all laughed except Jasper. Holly hadn't considered refusing. The moment Jasper had lowered himself onto one knee, her heart had begun racing and knees trembling. She'd blushed and felt her stomach begin to churn as she began to understand what he was doing. When he'd taken the ring from his pocket, fumbling with the little box, she'd clasped her hands over her mouth and shrieked, 'Oh!'

It had been simple, nothing forced, nothing contrived, but Holly knew she'd remember it for the rest of her life. The proposal came as an affirmation that, regardless of his silences, his sudden bursts of emotion, and occasional disappearances for which he didn't want her company, Jasper wanted to spend the rest of his life with her.

His parents had watched, their eyes wet with tears, and his mother had fumbled with her phone trying to record the events to send to Edmund.

When he'd risen, she'd leaned against his shoulder and listened to his heart beating, and tears had slid down her face.

'Well, if you're going to cry about it, I can get a refund on the...'

She'd laughed and cried simultaneously, gently smacking him on the shoulder and telling him not to ruin the moment.

'Next stop – babies,' Holly said, looking around at her audience. 'Wedding first, of course.'

'Oh God, Jasper as a father,' John said, and they all laughed along.

'And you two are married?' Ovidia glanced at Anne. Holly was taken aback at how quickly Ovidia changed the subject but then realised she'd been detailing her and Jasper's relationship for quite a while.

'Nine years together.' Anne sipped her wine and asked, 'You?'

Holly watched Anne pre-empt John with the question. She'd known them long enough to see that John was impatient, eager to find out more – the way his eyes flitted from Edmund to Ovidia and back again. Holly watched him take in every detail of them, looking at their shoes, smiling at their words. Right now, Holly guessed, he was waiting for Ovidia to repeat, *'No, I live across the road.'* Then he'd challenge her, he'd joke and say something like, *'You seem very familiar for someone who lives across the road. You won't catch Mrs Bancroft using my shower on a Saturday morning.'*

To Holly's surprise, Ovidia and Edmund looked into each other's eyes.

'Four years?' Edmund said after the briefest of pauses.

Holly, like the others, gasped.

'Just over,' Ovidia replied, with a slight smile that told Holly that she was thinking back to when she and Edmund first met.

After she spoke, Jasper lurched forward in the cushioned sofa, his foot, from where it had been crossed over his right knee, slammed on to the floor. His eyes wide. 'Four years? Four years and you've never said anything to me. Nothing. Ever?'

Holly's hand instinctively went to Jasper's arm as if to restrain him. How could Edmund have been in a relationship for four years? It wasn't possible.

When describing his brother, Jasper said he'd have known if Edmund was in a serious relationship. Jasper had complained on a few occasions that he was the one who bore the brunt of Edmund's ostensibly inactive love life. He was the one always saying no when repeatedly quizzed by their curious and worried mother and by their father, whose latent distaste for homosexuality meant he wanted proof of his son's heterosexuality.

She looked at Jasper, who now appeared frozen, staring at his brother.

'Well of course I didn't say anything.' Edmund offered in way of an explanation and then sipped his wine.

Holly saw as the brothers' eyes locked, and Edmund smiled back faintly – a brief, almost uncertain smile.

Jasper rolled his hands into a fist and then unfurled them, stretching out his fingers. 'So, what, she's married?' he asked, as if Ovidia wasn't right beside Edmund.

'No. She's not, and neither am I, for that matter.'

Holly could see Edmund's response aggravated Jasper even more.

'Why didn't you tell me?' Jasper demanded, louder.

'You know why,' Edmund replied.

Holly would have liked one of them to say why. Instead, the brothers seemed to silently agree that they couldn't discuss it any further in front of the others. Jasper leaned back into his chair and Edmund mirrored his brother's movement, leaning back into his own chair, but more slowly.

Holly shifted in her seat, unsure of what to do next. This wasn't supposed to happen. They were meant to be talking about the future, dresses, children, perhaps a dinner party, so they could celebrate properly with Edmund.

The brothers were no longer locked in a standoff. Jasper's head was down, his fist against his forehead, and Edmund's hands were restless, flying from his face to his thighs, back again, and rubbing against his knees, before he took hold of his glass and only then stopped.

Holly looked quickly at John, who nudged Anne as if passing along the responsibility for continuing the conversation.

'So how did you meet?' Anne intervened. John looked relieved and put his hand on Anne's lap.

'She hit me thinking I was an alien,' Edmund said as Ovidia opened her mouth to begin. He said it without a smile or other hint of humour.

Holly thought she'd heard incorrectly and turned to Jasper, whose brow furrowed as he looked uncomprehendingly at his brother.

'Meaning?' Anne choked as she tried to suppress a laugh. She coughed, and John gently and ineffectively patted her back, his eyes transfixed on Ovidia.

'I'd just finished my first and, I thought at the time, last sixty-mile ultra…' Ovidia began.

'And you've lost me right at the beginning,' John joked, as Holly shook her head in disbelief.

Ovidia continued. 'I'd been running all night, and all I wanted to do was collapse. I was absolutely exhausted. I felt like throwing up. My feet felt as if they'd fall off… But basically, everything seemed perfectly normal until I saw this alien thing walking towards me. And I thought, *oh my God, I'm under attack,* and I got the idea that I was going to save the universe and tried to knock him out.'

Holly chuckled, an odd gurgling sound.

'The alien went *"Ouch!"* in this really annoyed voice,' Ovidia went on. 'I didn't know what would happen next. Would its rocket come down and fetch it? But then I had to lie down, and I didn't notice that there wasn't anywhere to lie down, and I just dropped – onto the ground. Then the alien started turning human, and it was just looking down at me and rubbing its arm. He was probably expecting me to get up and carry on, but there was no way I was standing up. After that, a perfectly normal human being asked if I was okay. I said *yes, fine, and sorry, I was just saving the planet* – and then I threw up all over his trainers.'

'In my opinion, she should have sued the organisers. Absolutely no one in sight,' Edmund said.

'So you were hallucinating?' John asked slowly.

'Forgot to say. Yes,' Ovidia continued, 'I knew nothing about this until I looked it up afterwards. Some ultra-marathoners say they hallucinate on, or after, long runs, and not just the classic desert races or being dehydrated. I'd have thought it was complete nonsense if I hadn't experienced it myself. One woman said how she'd spent half the race talking to someone beside her but there was no one there.'

Holly covered her mouth as she laughed uncontrollably, while Anne and John sniggered. Holly tried to say something about it being the funniest first meeting she'd ever heard of, but she couldn't stop herself from laughing and leaned against Jasper and felt his arm come to rest around her waist.

15

Ovidia told the story just as Edmund first noticed she used to speak: fast, without her hands – her fingers resting on her thighs. She accompanied the story with movements, slumping her head to one side as she 'just dropped' and lurching forward as she 'threw up all over his trainers'.

In fact, that had been their second meeting. Their first having become one of those memories that a couple mutually files away – an inconvenient recollection.

Edmund smiled at the memory of their story. It was the first hint of real joy he'd felt in what felt like never-ending misery. Though he knew that Jasper must be hurt, Edmund allowed himself to savour the warmth that remembering stirred inside him and, feeling stronger, he raised himself in his seat.

He and Ovidia had never planned to hide their relationship from his brother. It had taken years to happen, but it had been inevitable that Jasper would find out. The truth just seemed to escape being told. He and Ovidia socialised, they travelled, they did many things together, but rarely in the context of being partners. It was easier than it seemed. The people with whom they mingled were not the kind to ask without a prompt of some kind. He knew that many looked at them through glasses tinted with prejudice – Ovidia's bright flamboyant clothes, her apparent youth, her colour. Few people made the connection with him, his dark formal clothing, his businesslike demeanour. He'd once asked his PA what she'd meant, when upon realising that Ovidia was his partner she'd blurted, *'I'd have never guessed!'* She'd stammered and said, *'Well, Olivia,'* she'd called her 'Olivia', *'is so, so – colourful.'*

By keeping their relationship away from everyone except a select few, it meant that they rarely talked about how they met. He knew Ovidia had told it in fragments to her family, always keeping them in the dark of the eventual outcome of that day – as if it was a brief encounter of no consequence. Edmund had told no one at all.

He remembered it had been a Saturday – a busy end of a race in Bushy Park with the early spring foliage waking up after winter, the weak rays of the sun keeping the rain away. He'd run his first ten-kilometre race and decided it was his last. His left ankle was throbbing, and he felt ill. It had been part of his new regime: less alcohol and no cigarettes, more exercise and better food. Then he'd noticed a separate clutch of runners trickling in, wearing T-shirts a different colour to his, seeming to have nothing to do with the event he'd attended. He'd been too far off to read their signs, and he'd had no interest in whatever it was they were doing.

He'd never told Ovidia about how, that morning, he'd been sitting on a park bench, raging at his loneliness, berating himself for having no one in his life, and imagining spending the rest of his life alone. He'd never told Ovidia of the conflict that reigned: settle for a woman who was not the love of his life or wait for a woman who he would love unequivocally but, until then, be alone.

He'd been on that bench since the race ended, watching life go on around him. Everyone was in his or her own world or a shared one – celebrations, disappointments, ambivalence, pain. People had talked, embraced, laughed. He'd felt as if a great gulf existed between him and the rest of the world and had been afraid that there, in front of them all, he'd cry.

At that time, his life seemed to revolve around Jasper. His brother's misery permeated every aspect of Edmund's existence – tearful calls in the middle of the night, lost employment, unpaid bills, the way Jasper seemed thinner and sicklier each time they met. Their parents couldn't understand it when Edmund said Jasper needed time. Even his parents, who had always been loving and supporting, faltered in his esteem.

'Is there no one else to take care of him?' his mother had said once when Edmund had arrived to deposit Jasper for a few days, just to make sure someone was watching Jasper while he was away. She'd been unable to hide her exasperation, still convinced that Jasper's condition was not as awful as it seemed. Witnessing his mother's continual denial had made it harder and harder to excite himself at the prospect of spending time in their company.

His mother had taken to baking and flipping through cookbooks, especially those that her librarian convinced her were on trend. She'd packed Jasper plastic lunchboxes of baked goods, of home-pureed hummus and frozen butternut soups, declaring, 'You just need the right food to tempt you.'

Edmund could tell she didn't believe that herself. When she'd asked him to look at her computer that was constantly requesting updates, he'd scrolled through her history: *hyperthyroidism, TB, AIDS, wasting, anorexia, traumatic stress.*

But in Edmund's presence, she'd hummed and smiled more than usual. The music she'd made was tuneless, nothing he could identify or recall. 'You'll snap out of it soon,' she'd said to Jasper.

'How long is this supposed to continue?' His father had at least had the wherewithal to address, in a near shout, his frustrations to Edmund and not Jasper. 'He needs to grow up, that's what he needs to do. It's been nearly a year.' He'd slapped his fist onto the arm of his chair. 'The boy's a ghost. The neighbours asked if he's got cancer. Cancer? What am I supposed to say to that? *"No, he's heartbroken"*? Makes a mockery out of people with real problems.'

Edmund had just rested his head against his fingers and lain back in the sofa, wishing that he could be allowed to rest.

But his father had jabbed his shoulder unpleasantly and uncharacteristically. His tension evident in that act. 'Sorry,' he'd apologised. 'I know it's not your fault.'

'I'm trying to get him to talk to someone, even if it's just a GP.'

'No way. He'll be sectioned.' His father's voice rose again. 'Are you looking at him? He looks like a headcase.'

'Dad, he is a headcase. He's had some kind of a breakdown.' Edmund had shrugged after his father recoiled at the word *breakdown*. 'And there's nothing else I can do to help him.'

'Well, someone has to do something, because I'm about to crack,' his father had hissed in a loud whisper.

It was painful to see his brother fading, withdrawing even further from his life than he had before. Edmund couldn't think of a strategy to help him. Instead, he'd guessed as he went along, taking him to their parents', dropping in on him at home at random hours, taking him out to lunch, and, whenever possible, trying to pretend everything was all right. Sometimes, he'd wanted to shout *pull yourself together*, but he knew it wasn't as simple as that.

He'd made an appointment to see a therapist himself. But when the time came, he'd had a meeting organised, and his PA called to cancel.

Meanwhile, Jasper's pain was seeping into Edmund's life in another insidious way as well. An underlying disquiet that he'd been feeling for years had come to a head. He was at that point where something had to happen. Though he'd imagined that he'd find someone at some stage in his life, Edmund had been content with his bachelor lifestyle. He'd savoured the solitude at the end of a work day, travelling unencumbered by other people, and being able to spend time with his parents and his brother. But finding himself mired in the greatest crisis of his adult life, he'd found his solitude metamorphosed into loneliness. He'd become conscious of the relationships around him, old school friends toasting wedding anniversaries, fathers with children, and aged couples on park benches all sharing moments of intimacy. He'd begun to turn down invitations to social events at the prospect of having to go on his own.

He fought his loneliness. Telling himself that it was just for now – as soon as Jasper was all right, his world would right itself. Then his phone would ring, and he'd hesitate: it was either his family or his work.

His phone's contacts list had its share of women's numbers – women he called for company. However, scrolling through the list iterated the superficiality of his relationships with those women. He'd find himself at dinner with yet another woman in a champagne-coloured shift dress with a diamond bracelet and matching necklace, and he'd be desperate to see behind her veneer. He'd look for clues in what she said, in slips of the tongue and in mobiles left momentarily unattended.

That morning at Bushy Park, Edmund had been steeling himself to stand and then find his car when he'd recognised Ovidia. He'd seen her talking to herself and realised something was wrong. Seeing her, he'd been surprised at his ambivalence towards her. He'd expected to hate her more. Perhaps it was because she'd looked helpless and pathetic as she stumbled. Perhaps because he'd been tired of the fallout she caused. He'd decided he had to check she was all right.

When Ovidia told her version of that morning, it was much more carefree and romantic: two strangers and a funny little event that changed their lives. His memory of that morning was of finding a woman who'd overexerted herself physically and mentally. She'd become separated from those who should have noticed her distress and should have been taking care of her. Both he and Ovidia had been alone.

Four years on, he still hadn't started smoking again and he'd kept his weight constant. But now, he was nearly fifty. His muscle tone was slackening, and, though the scale flashed the same number week after week, he could feel his clothes were a little tighter. Ovidia, on the other hand, had become a resolute runner, occasionally tackling fifty-mile runs. She ran six days a week and, at forty-two, was fit and frequently mistaken for being much younger than she was.

After she'd hit him, only hard enough to make him flinch, she'd vomited on his shoes, and he'd turned her over to make sure she didn't choke. He'd waited for a moment and then helped her up, steering her to a bench and watching her recover. Ovidia had struggled to sit up and then given up and lain on the bench with her feet on the ground and had covered her eyes in the crook of her arm. He could see her silhouette through her leggings and shirt, the nipples of her small breasts, her stomach flat and muscular. He'd turned away, not wanting to stare. He'd felt embarrassed at the immediate sexual attraction he'd felt for her.

'I fell in love on a park bench,' Ovidia explained, glancing at Edmund. 'He sat with me, held my water bottle, and then sent me home in a cab. I got home and slept for twelve hours,' she said. 'When I woke up, there was a message on my phone saying, *"Let me know when you're back from outer space".'*

'And did you?' Holly asked after Ovidia paused.

Edmund's gaze stopped at Anne, who, when her eyes made contact with his, gently, seemingly unconscious of her act, brushed John's hand from her lap.

'No, I was like, *"No, I don't want to get involved with anyone"*. But then I looked on Facebook and there he was, poking me. And I thought, *who still pokes these days?* But I should talk – I'm lousy at Facebook. He asked me how I was with an emoji of an ambulance, and I thought, *funny, he didn't seem like an emoji sort of guy.* So, I was joking, and I said, *"If you want to see me, you'll have to come to my place with food. My legs are aching, and I'm not walking anywhere."* And he showed up after an hour with this huge salad for me and pizza for himself.'

'I thought you'd be into healthy eating,' Edmund interjected.

'I'll skip the next bit.' Ovidia bit her lip, as Jasper shifted uncomfortably in his seat. 'That was a great week though, remember?' She turned to Edmund as she asked.

Edmund didn't need to reply. He remembered every bit of it. Sitting there as Ovidia told their story, pleasant memories flooded back. He recalled feeling a mix of euphoria and terror as he knocked on her door. She'd limped back to the sofa, complaining that the muscles in her legs had seized. He remembered the knot that tightened in his stomach as he watched, and later, as the two of them lay on her carpet, trying to decide what he was supposed to do.

Sex had been almost funny, both of them suffering with various pains from their morning runs, him laughing aloud at her, 'No, you. I can't get on my knees, they hurt like hell.'

'It ended with you losing your job.' She poked Edmund in the chest with an index finger.

'End of story,' Edmund said as he caught the tip of her finger.

'All right then.'

Ovidia and he were flirting. Something they hadn't done for a long time, and somehow it didn't feel inappropriate. Edmund felt his heartbeat accelerating, and he looked in her eyes as if no one was watching, his heart rendered to pieces as he thought of the end of their relationship.

'No,' Holly hooted. 'What happened, Ovidia?'

Edmund was jolted back to where he sat, to his audience listening to him and Ovidia recounting an edited version of how they met, with every inconvenient and unpleasant conversation and event neatly excised from the tale. Ovidia left out the parts where they sat contemplating each other, she telling anecdotes, because she was not one for silence, and he analysing every scenario and every possible outcome of what they were doing in his mind. In Ovidia's retelling, there'd be no mention of how he battled within himself, of the times he caught the image of himself in a mirror on the wall and turned to Ovidia and said, 'I can't do this.'

'I showed up at work a week later,' Edmund said, 'and told my director, "I'm so sorry, but I have no excuse and no explanation for where I've been." She was livid. She'd even reported me missing. She'd roasted my poor PA until she cried. When I finally showed up, she screamed at me with the whole office listening.'

Edmund's colleagues had stopped in their tracks, cups of coffee in hand, mid-conversation. They'd smiled apologetically to their clients or simply ogled at the scene. From their glass enclosures or from open-plan desks, they'd watched. The director was the one person with any seniority over him and the two had worked together for years – but were not friends. She was authoritative and tall enough to stand eye to eye with Edmund.

'I called the police! You could have just bloody answered your phone!' she'd shouted. 'Fired? No, I'm going to have you hanged, drawn, and quartered!' His director had spun around and marched into her glass office, and, in full view of everyone, sunk her face in her hands and screamed into them. Edmund left these details of her distress out of his story – that she'd told him later that she'd thought he was dead, and she'd told him of her embarrassment at being mocked by a board member for having acted like 'such a woman'.

His guests stopped laughing.

He, too, had made it sound simple and fun. He'd felt a shame upon his director's reaction, acknowledging that his decisions had already hurt someone. The shame had been fleeting and had been quickly replaced with the euphoria of his newfound relationship.

'You didn't go to work for a week because you were together?' Anne inadvertently glanced at John. 'No details, please, but where were you?'

'My flat,' Ovidia replied.

'For a week?' Holly asked.

'Discovering the joys of…' Edmund began.

'No need for details, please,' John interrupted.

'… pot noodles and powdered mashed potatoes,' Edmund finished. 'I discovered the one person in this world who makes bulk purchases of dehydrated foods. Then we flew to Paris – much better food – and, God, did she have an appetite after that run.'

Edmund felt as if he'd said too much. But then again, he reminded himself this was their story, and it was a hell of a lot more fun than meeting at a D-lister do.

'It didn't occur to you to call in sick or something?' Jasper demanded.

Edmund had woken up that Monday in Paris. He'd never skipped work without it being planned or without a real reason before. He loved his work, and his effort and dedication resulted in affluence, which he also enjoyed. Not showing up at work would lower his esteem among his colleagues, he worried. He'd imagined he could catch a morning flight and make an excuse.

Then what? he'd thought.

He'd padded to the hotel bathroom and looked at himself in the mirror. The eyes that looked back at him were brighter, and, though he hadn't known it, he was smiling. Two towels were carelessly slung over the towel heater, and Ovidia's make-up had conquered most of the available counter space. Two toothbrushes stood in the glasses and his travel-sized tube of toothpaste had been squeezed almost empty.

He had been happy. But it couldn't last. He was a realist and knew they would wake up to the reality of their situation. In the meantime, he'd decided, he was going to spend every minute that he could with her.

'No. I just said to hell with it and had the time of my life,' Edmund replied to Jasper's question. In reality, he'd worried – about his reputation, his job, and what it was he was getting himself into. But each time he came down to earth, something happened to raise him back into the clouds: Ovidia in a place called Le Musée de Disco trying on orange platforms with a drag queen fawning over her orange and pink polyester blouse, the view over the Seine with a glass of wine after telling Jasper that he was on an emergency trip to Paris and that Jasper would just have to cope until he got back.

He'd revelled in a week of being able to pretend that his life was perfect – and it was – with Ovidia. When they'd returned to London, they'd both assumed it was all over, briefly. He'd gone to his home and she to hers. However, as he'd scrolled through unread texts from his brother and parents, he'd realised that they had survived his absence. No miracles had occurred, Jasper wasn't inexplicably cured, but he was still holding on. The worst had not happened.

He'd sat alone in his flat and realised he didn't dread calling them back. Yes, he'd dawdled, making a cup of tea, emptying his case, and making a note of things he needed in the fridge. But when he did, he'd discovered he had a newfound strength: he'd told his father that, whether he liked it or not, Jasper would see someone, and he'd firmly told his mother that her newest pizza recipe was not going to sort out Jasper's insides. He'd listened to his brother, nodding, reassuring Jasper that they would get through this crisis together.

He and Ovidia could have stopped there, no one would have ever known. Their week would have remained in nothing but the hundreds of photos they'd taken. But he'd dialled her number. He loved her, he'd told himself, and he was allowed to love her.

His director had held his escapade against him for weeks, repeating that his madness was company money forgone. He'd heard her muttering to her assistant that what annoyed her most was that someone who had been exemplary in his behaviour for years had turned out to be a fool, and that it must be because of a woman or man.

'Drugs?' her assistant had suggested, but the director had shaken her head and returned to her office.

Edmund had almost told his brother everything once. He'd stood outside a restaurant on a cool day a couple of months earlier in a light jacket that hadn't been warm enough. He'd scratched his head as he waited to meet Jasper, chasing an itch that refused to remain still. He'd scratched behind his ears, the top of his head, and at the base of his neck over and over again. He'd told himself that Jasper was the only person he could tell. Constantly maintaining the façade of normalcy was a crushing weight on his shoulders, and he'd had to admit he was floundering.

Completely against his nature, he'd found himself snapping at his work colleagues. His PA found herself constantly put upon and repeatedly reprimanded, and that morning she'd appeared, her eyes red and her face etched with fatigue. He'd scolded her the previous evening. He could barely recall what he'd said, accusing her of laziness and of not performing her best.

He would confess to Jasper, about Ovidia and how he'd found himself at this point. Perhaps Jasper would forgive him.

How would he begin? Because he was so much older, their childhoods had barely overlapped. When Jasper said his first words and took his first steps, it had been at Edmund's urging. Jasper had been someone he cared for, entertained, and educated. Of course he loved his brother, but their relationship was unlike those of brothers who were two or three years apart.

When Edmund was fifteen, Jasper had been nine, much too young to confide in as Edmund had navigated his teenage years. As a teenager, Edmund had taken his brother on adventures, tramping through mud and up hills, and instigated pranks against their parents, grandparents, and neighbours with his little brother in tow; but the joy had not been in the activity but in the sound of Jasper squealing in laughter or hopping up and down with joy as he tried to recount his latest exploits.

Edmund's first girlfriend, their fumbled first night, the awkward holding of cold clammy hands; feeling ill each morning when, for the first time in his life, he found himself failing in academia – yet refusing to give it up because he would not accept his own failure; looking at himself in a mirror at his adolescent face and body and cursing what he saw as ugly and thin; and making the tactical decision to be 'the guy who always buys you a drink' so that he'd be invited out by the in-crowd at the office, knowing that he didn't have looks or a sense of style that he could rely on to attract people towards him. These were things he'd never told Jasper. What Jasper had seen was the stellar A-levels and university distinctions, the skyward trajectory of his career beginning with his first job – not Edmund teaching himself to dress well from a cache of magazine-page cut-outs or saving money to have his teeth straightened.

Edmund had opened the restaurant door exactly on time and looked around. He'd seen Jasper. He'd watched

Jasper's silhouette as he tapped on his phone. Despite how his breakup with Ovidia had ravaged his body, he was still a handsome man. He was still young and had shown remarkable resilience, but had he recovered enough to deal with a new shock?

Jasper had looked up and smiled, relaxed. Edmund had strolled towards him, grunted hello, and sat down.

'What's up?' Jasper had asked, as a waiter arrived beside him.

'Nothing much,' Edmund had replied spontaneously, his voice stronger. 'Work, mostly.'

16

Ovidia remembered that first week with a flutter in her stomach. It had been a long time since she'd thought about that period. She'd lain on a bench watching him through the gap between her face and her elbow. She'd turned a few times, craning her neck, watching the race organisers dismantle their banners and water tables, and pack their uncollected goodie bags. She'd thought about the last twelve hours that she'd spent running and a thought occurred to her – how would she train for such long periods if she had a partner?

The thought had caused her to flinch. It wasn't the first time in that year that she'd wondered how she would ever date again or what kind of man would have her, but, as she smiled apologetically as her foot hit his knee, a man no longer seemed an impossibility.

Ovidia found Edmund's resemblance to Jasper in his hair and skin colour, his nose and his eyes, but, she decided, it wasn't strong enough to explain her attraction to him. She evaluated him physically and remembered that he was not that much older than her. When she was younger, five years would have seemed like an immense gap, but then, at thirty-eight, it didn't seem as much. Edmund's clothes told her that he'd bought them all at once, probably following a list of what he wanted and needed. Sombre colours, every item from a single brand ensuring that everything matched and was of equal quality. Ovidia deduced that Edmund was the type who planned and executed tasks with precision. As she'd lain on the bench, she'd waited for him to leave, even claiming she had recovered when she quite clearly hadn't.

She'd spent that week vacillating between the euphoria of what looked like love and a niggling dissatisfaction caused by lying to herself, repeating to herself that history didn't matter. Did she have the right to be as happy as she was in the mornings that she woke beside him?

She'd found herself singing in the bathroom, and she'd stopped, uncertain. Her voice sounded odd to her own ears. How long had it been since she laughed or sang uninhibited? A moment later, as she'd folded her towel, she began singing again, and this time she didn't stop herself.

Edmund's phone had beeped at intervals with angry messages, missed calls, and unanswered emails reminding them of his life, whereas hers stayed silent except for a few messages congratulating her on her run. She'd discovered that parts of him were the antithesis of his dark clothes and restrained demeanour. He would happily help her pick out an orange vintage dress, even though he himself rejected any attempt to add colour to his wardrobe. He could make her laugh uncontrollably with only the slightest of smiles on his own face. As they'd sat in a café in Paris, a man in pale chinos with freckled skin and red hair appeared, greeting them with a firm handshake and unable to keep his eyes from repeatedly flitting from Edmund to Ovidia and back again as if he was hoping for more information than just 'this is Ovidia'.

He'd left after talking to Edmund for a few minutes, drilling him on the latest news from the industry. They'd had a brief but intense discussion, but Edmund had ended it with a firm, 'I'm off work for now, so I'm not quite up to speed. Catch up with you when I'm back at work.'

'When will that be?' The man had pulled out his phone, probably to key in the date.

'I've no idea,' Edmund had replied, and the man had looked nothing short of shocked.

'Well, call when you can,' he'd stammered, then he'd seized Ovidia's hand and shook it saying, 'Yellow. If you can get this man away from work, you can get him to wear yellow.'

They'd watched him leave, and Edmund had said, 'The two have nothing to do with each other.'

When Edmund had returned to work, he'd phoned her up after his director had apologised for saying he was fired and the question Ovidia had been asking herself – What are you doing with this man? – was answered. Somewhere underneath his demeanour was an underlying silliness, a man who was up for an escapade, an adventure – a man who had his passions but kept them obscured in greys and dark blues.

'Got my job back after half an hour of unemployment.' She could hear the laughter in his voice when he'd called her after the dressing down from his director.

'Edmund, you could have said you had to go back to work,' Ovidia had said quietly.

'I didn't have to do anything of the sort,' he'd replied, chuckling. 'I worked hard to get to where I can skive off work when I want.'

Ovidia hadn't replied. Holding her mobile, her breathing had become heavy and laden with anxiety.

'We need to talk, don't we?' Edmund had said.

She'd nodded, though they were on the phone.

'I think I'm serious about you. But, I guess you're not sure about me,' he'd continued.

'I've been thinking about it all morning,' Ovidia had replied. 'We're pretending everything is all right. We have to be honest with ourselves... I think.'

'I'm perfectly happy lying to myself,' he'd replied, his voice taut. 'If it means getting to stay with you.'

'But what if I...' she'd asked.

'I won't let you,' he'd cut her off. 'You won't have to worry as long as you're with me.'

'It's not about letting me. What about...' she'd hesitated; Jasper's name hadn't been used all that week. 'What will we tell him?'

'Nothing.' From his tone, Ovidia had known he'd already made a decision. 'This has nothing to do with him. The two of you can never be together again; he knows that.' Edmund had paused. 'Are you still there?' he'd asked when she was silent. 'In the worst-possible-case scenario, we'll run away. New York, Singapore, Cape Town...'

'I can't run away from myself,' she'd replied. She'd searched for excuses. 'And what about my family, what about my career?'

'What about me?' Edmund had pressed the word 'me'. 'I know I must sound like a wet blanket right now, but I'm not willing to lose you just to keep everyone else happy. I'm a decent man, aren't I? I take care of my family. I make money for my company. I've never broken a law in my life. I am as entitled to love as anyone else.' He'd sworn. 'And now I seem pathetic and desperate.'

'I should have got you on tape. I could play it back to our kids,' she'd stopped, realising the idea had slipped out too easily.

'Maybe you're right,' Edmund had said quietly. 'What if we just break up, take the safe option, like choosing the colour of my next suit?'

Ovidia had smiled, though he couldn't see her. 'Grey, navy, or charcoal?'

'Foolproof system. Every item in my wardrobe matches,' he'd replied, and Ovidia had giggled. 'But all we'll have to look forward to is life in shades of grey.'

His voice had lowered almost to a whisper. 'We have a choice. We can rush headlong into a really stupid idea or go back to being alone. You make me sick with happiness. I'll never find anyone like you again.'

'And you have to understand that I never want to go through that again,' Ovidia had replied, clamping her eyes shut and reaching out for support and finding nothing there. 'I'd rather be alone.'

'I'll take care of you,' Edmund had replied. 'I promise, we'll be fine.'

AFTERNOON

17

John smiled when Holly said, 'Strange, that's not how Jasper... I mean, from what I knew about you...' She'd stopped, probably realising that she shouldn't have pursued that train of thought. 'I thought you were...'

'Boring,' Edmund suggested. John watched him snuggle further into his chair and look up through the glass ceiling in contemplation. 'I am very boring.'

John had watched Edmund and Ovidia tell their story but was also fascinated by the interplay between Edmund and Jasper. Jasper was tense, on edge. His brother was much better at concealing his emotions. John knew that his own work as a psychologist gave him a certain perspective on humanity. He knew it was perfectly possible to be two disparate characters at once. Some people had distinct faces for different aspects of their lives – they could be one person at work and another at home or at their children's school. It was possible that Jasper had never in his life seen this side of his brother – a side that skipped work to spend a week in a flat of a woman he'd only just met.

Nonetheless, John didn't expect to meet such people in his everyday life. He too was stuck, unsure of what to make of this version of Edmund. This was not the man he'd spent weekends with at the brothers' childhood home. This was not the man who'd arrive in a grey suit on a Friday evening with a briefcase in one hand and swinging a grey cashmere scarf in the other.

One particular weekend – he supposed it had been nearly two years earlier – John had been invited to stay for the weekend at Jasper and Edmund's parents' house with Edmund present. He'd seemed off-colour, objecting to the music that was played and the walks that were taken.

John calculated that Edmund must have already been with Ovidia for two years at that point. He supposed that Edmund could just have been eager to get back to Ovidia. John, despite his expertise, would never have guessed that Edmund could have been hiding a relationship from his family. Most men he knew – friends, families, colleagues – would have been incapable of hiding the existence of their partners. They would have left clues or dropped hints, taken on some of the traits of their partners: peculiarities of speech, reading certain books, or preferring some subjects of conversation. John couldn't recall ever seeing Edmund with anything of a bright colour, nor had he ever discussed running or holidays in Paris.

John felt slightly cheated. He wished he could assign Edmund to some kind of abnormal category of behaviour, but he corrected himself. It was he who had taken Edmund at face value and upon Jasper's descriptions. He'd missed a fascinating subject, or, rather, he had run away from one.

On the Saturday evening of that weekend, while Edmund had been in the kitchen with his mother, John, Jasper, and Phil had begun discussing Edmund. Comfortably ensconced in the conservatory overlooking a neat garden, it had seemed to John that, for Jasper and Phil, speculating on Edmund's sexuality, a topic which he was apparently secretive about, was not unusual.

'I've decided he's asexual,' Jasper had stated, crossing his legs. It was hard to tell if he was teasing. 'I read an article about it recently. Apparently it's gaining recognition as a sexual orientation.'

'That would be too exciting, in my opinion,' John had said, looking back at his day in Edmund's company. 'Whatever Edmund does or is, it will be so uninteresting that you'll wonder why you spent so much time talking about it.'

'So, we'll agree he's gay,' Jasper had said. 'That's horribly boring. In the closet and not wanting to come out because it might be too "exciting"?' He was laughing at his brother; he liked to.

'He's not gay,' Phil had said abruptly.

The discussion had ended, but not for John. He'd heard what he wanted to hear. When John had grown out of his teens, like many men, he realised that sexual desire was about far more than physical perfection – if it were, a vast swathe of humanity would be excluded from those who interact sexually. He knew it wasn't looks – of the two brothers, Jasper was by far more conventionally better looking, and yet, John felt an intense physical attraction to Edmund.

The last time he'd slept with a woman other than Anne, she'd been strikingly curvaceous – dark haired with fire-engine-red lipstick. She exuded burlesque, she teased nineteenth century courtesan, she was risqué, daring, bold. Her thighs were dimpled, and her waist had an overhang of fat, markers of having given birth naturally to three children. Without her clothes and make-up, she could have been one of the many clients who came into his office. But with her billowing skirt and nipped-in waist, she was a figure from his fantasies. Edmund now was the subject of his fantasies – assertive, physically imperfect, and emotionally inaccessible – and that Edmund was male only made it so much more exciting.

John told himself sometimes that Anne had to be stupid. Anne had caught him out only once – she'd said nothing and done nothing except slap him – so hard that his face was left red and stinging.

Sexual repression was a term bandied about in his profession. It was a convenient explanation – he wanted another life, of sorts. He wanted the kind of sex that he couldn't ask of Anne. He wanted acts and sensations that he couldn't articulate. He had sexual desires that couldn't be satiated in a marital bed – the longing for, and the pursuit of, someone other than Anne was part of what made the sex so exciting.

John had been surprised the first time he cheated. It was not as difficult as some people claimed. He was an average – some days he called himself less-than-average – man. Shorter than most men he knew, with hair that was perhaps too voluminous and curled viciously. Anne was just that little bit taller than him, tall enough to be considered a tall woman but short enough that, as long as she didn't wear heels, he didn't think they looked ridiculous together.

John liked to think that his craving for sex wasn't about self-esteem. He saw it as the thrill of having secrets. What greater secrets existed, he asked himself, than those with sex at their core? None that he could think of, none that existed in the realm of ordinary people. He decided the people around him who were having the most fun were those having surreptitious meetings, encountering strangers in restaurants, and having uninhibited sex without anyone else knowing. Affairs were complex; they involved emotion and the risks were much greater. They took more effort – and if all one wanted was sex, then an affair had no added value.

He was successful in his field, respected, invited to conferences, and asked to give talks and lead panels. He'd written a book and, as his publisher said, it had become a self-help sensation. He was looking forward to his next book tour and more celebrity and acclaim. He'd be away from Anne for days at a time. Of course, he'd miss her and his daughters. He always did. To him, there was no more precious sound than the shrieks of his two little girls on a Saturday morning, followed by Anne bellowing at them to quieten down. But, on the road, he didn't have to watch the time, making sure he was home before the girls went to bed or to inspect himself in the mirror to make sure no trace of his adventure remained.

John remembered each meeting with Edmund; each time they'd part, he'd be left savouring memories of Edmund's aftershave or his crisply laundered clothes. John would replay Edmund's voice and marvel at the ease with which intelligent conversation came to him.

Each time they met, John added one more thing he admired about Edmund to his list. His obsession was becoming uncomfortable. The idea that he wanted anything more than a pure physical encounter with him was starting to intrude into his fantasies – ideas about waking up together, having breakfast, laughing over a cup of coffee.

'Our father is not-so-secretly homophobic,' Jasper had said, once Phil had gone to get more beer. 'He knows his opinions are unpopular, so he never says it directly, just things like *"oh, who does that person think he is?"*, or *"they've let another one of them on TV"*.'

'And you think Edmund knows this, so he doesn't say,' John had suggested, using the gentle tone he used on clients.

'God knows. Edmund and I are seven years apart. We are close but… only so close. By the time I was teenager, he was off at uni. We talked about girls but not in intimate detail. I'd tell him stuff, he'd tell me about some girl he'd met. And when the age gap mattered less, there was always a reason not to talk about women. You know – discretion and stuff. He'll talk about them in general or ask me about mine. I do know that he desperately wants someone in his life, in an old-fashioned way – I'm pretty sure with a woman.'

'But come on, you're his brother – you'd know?' John had asked.

'I'm sure if he was really serious about someone, he'd tell me.' Jasper had looked pensive. 'But brothers can keep pretty big secrets from each other.'

'You don't think he's carrying around a broken heart type of thing?' John had asked, making sure to sound casual.

Jasper had cocked his head to one side. 'No,' he'd said brutally. 'I'll go with the no luck with women – easier to believe. Look at him, he's hardly sexy. Does the guy even own a pair of trainers?' Jasper had paused. 'No wait, he does. He took up running a couple of years back. Said he hated it.'

'When you're raking in whatever he makes a year, I'm sure a lot of women would quite happily deal with boring,' John had suggested.

'But Edmund wouldn't spend a second with those women. I know Edmund,' Jasper had declared. 'Him, give away his hard-earned cash to a gold digger? No way.'

'Anyway, dinner smells marvellous – I'm starving.' John had been careful not to show too much interest. There were things you didn't tell friends. Jasper knew that John was unfaithful to Anne – that this was the real reason he didn't want to marry her. He didn't want to make a vow of fidelity in front of witnesses, a vow that he couldn't, and didn't want to, keep.

John had found Edmund alone a little later that evening. Dinner had been announced as nearly ready, and Jasper had disappeared with his mobile just as Edmund had sat down with a glass of water.

'So, what do you get up to when you're not travelling the world?' John had begun.

'Nothing exciting,' Edmund had replied.

'Golf, sky-diving?' John had asked, pressing on.

'Definitely not sky-diving,' Edmund had replied.

'Sorry, I'm just being friendly,' John had said in response to Edmund's brusqueness. 'We could also just sit in silence till Jasper gets back.'

'Reading, crosswords, and, very occasionally, chess,' Edmund had replied. 'I used to be very good at it. I really can't stand it now.'

'Excellent, now we're getting somewhere. Are you worth betting on?'

Surprisingly, Edmund had laughed and John watched. Jasper had said Edmund had his teeth fixed in his twenties, and, to John, they were perfect.

'Ever go down to your local? Cafés, nice restaurant ever?'

'I like good restaurants,' Edmund had said. 'I can recommend some excellent ones.'

'I don't suppose you'd like to try one – one of these nights?' John had said, emphasising *nights*.

John had sensed Edmund's gaze lingering. He'd guessed Edmund was assessing him, trying to ascertain his motives.

'No thanks,' Edmund had replied, his tone unchanged.

'Nothing formal or anything.' John had to try again. 'Just you and me?'

'No,' Edmund had said, still holding eye contact.

John left it there. Disappointed. 'Sorry. Forget I asked.'

'Does your wife know that you chat up men?' Edmund had asked, looking amused.

'It's not something I do,' John had said, glancing towards a blank wall.

'I'd say it's something you do quite a lot,' Edmund had replied, his hand lightly touching his chin, his index finger resting above his top lip. 'Or do you generally stick to women?'

'Anne and I have an understanding,' John had replied, knowing that no such understanding existed between him and Anne.

'What do you suppose she'd do if she knew?' Edmund had asked.

'What's there to know?' John had bristled, knowing he'd made a serious mistake. 'Look. Sorry, I shouldn't have come on to you.' John had tried to end the conversation.

'Oh, don't be sorry,' Edmund had said, once again looking amused. 'Jasper and my dad love discussing my sex life. Maybe if I go on a few escapades it would make things more exciting for them.'

John had sensed that Edmund was teasing him. He'd forced a chuckle.

Edmund had leaned against his armrest. 'John has a secret life. Who'd have known?'

Now, Edmund's words took on a new meaning to John, as he sat watching Edmund flirt with a woman he'd been with in a secret relationship with for four years.

18

They were discussing running. Anne had run half marathons before, but not since she'd had children, which she realised now was a long time ago. Now she occasionally did five or ten kilometres, which didn't need as much training time, and in which she still could feel some pride, but did nothing to help her lose weight. She felt overtaken by Ovidia's ultramarathon running and asked how Ovidia found the time.

'A patient partner,' Ovidia replied. 'Someone happy, or who at least seems happy, to drive you to the back of beyond, and deal with blisters, and can stomach black toenails.'

Anne's eyes were immediately drawn to Ovidia's slippers and thereafter to Edmund's traditional, brown men's slippers. The contrast made her smile, but she was warming to their relationship and beginning to see Edmund in a new light. In the four years they'd been together, Anne assumed, he'd made no attempt to restrain this colourful and bubbly individual, to rein in her bold plush slippers, or early morning runs. Ovidia's clothes and mannerisms were an expression not just of her personality but of Edmund's, too – an aspect of him that they'd somehow all missed.

'When you have kids, there are some things that you give up,' Anne said.

'Why run an ultramarathon if you know you might not finish it? And, even if you did, you still wouldn't win?' Holly asked. 'It doesn't look like fun, and well, you were even hallucinating.'

'I came second once,' Ovidia replied. 'There were six women, and one of the front runners tripped and another got a stomach bug. It's amazing when you cross the finish line. I can't imagine life without it.'

'What's the motivation? Why? I don't get it,' Holly insisted, waggling her wine glass.

'It's like drugs,' Ovidia replied, gazing upwards. 'It blocks out the rest of the world, and it becomes you and the pavement. Even if there are other people around me, in the end, it's my feet – my body – taking me to the finish line. I learned my own physical and emotional strength. It changed me.'

John's mobile rang, interrupting her. 'Sorry,' he said, standing. 'It's your mum,' he said to Anne, as he put his hand on the door handle to exit the extension. 'Your tooth fell out! That's wonderful, sweetheart,' he said and stopped, still in the cube. 'Of course the tooth fairy can find you at Gran's. Well, why don't you leave him a note? Tell him sorry he can't have your tooth today, but to look for it at home on Sunday.' He paused, listening. 'Yes, sometimes the tooth fairy's a boy – remember we can be anything we want, even a tooth fairy. Love you, sweetie. See you tomorrow.'

As he returned to join them, Ovidia stood, opened her mouth as if to say something, but then pushed past John into the kitchen. The moment she opened the door, she lowered her head and put her hands to her face. Anne couldn't tell if she was crying. She heard Ovidia's slippers slapping against the floors as she went.

Anne was shocked by Edmund's lack of response. His posture remained unchanged, though it shouldn't have. *If your partner runs out of a room, don't you rush to help?* she thought. The guests waited for a cue, but he neither explained nor apologised for her escape and didn't even try to cover it up with *'more wine anyone?'*.

Anne watched Ovidia leave, puzzled, repressing the urge to chase after her. She saw John smirk. Like her, just when she was warming to them, he must have been reminded how odd Edmund and Ovidia seemed together.

With Ovidia gone, the subject of running seemed moot.

Jasper remained as he was. Anne was really hoping he'd suggest leaving. He must have been able to see that they were intruding upon something. Perhaps Ovidia, or even Edmund, was having some sort of episode – a bout of depression?

'The wedding. Have you thought about it?' Anne said the first thing that came to mind to break the silence. 'If you want it this summer, then you have to get to it pretty quickly. Or just accept that the weather will be crap and go for a stylish autumn one. I've heard that they're cheaper.' She glanced at John for help.

'It has to be summer. I want to wear something off the shoulder, maybe a low back. Something sexy. It'll be too cold for it in autumn,' Holly said. She gestured about her neck area as if tracing the shape of a neckline of an imagined dress.

'Oh, no,' Anne said. 'Stick to something more traditional, something you won't regret. The last thing you want is to spend all day fighting with sliding bras and tripping over bits of your dress.'

Anne was glad to return to an easier subject – the reason they were here. Though, without Ovidia, and with Edmund silent, it felt as if they were talking among themselves and they could have been in a pub. Anne could see Jasper's attention waning. He was examining his shoes, checking his mobile, trying not to appear as if he was tinkering on it – he'd often said how he thought it was rude to mess about with a phone when in company. Anne knew Jasper wasn't interested in the details of the wedding – it had come up the previous evening. He'd asked about budgets and locations and whether it would be a Christian or secular service – saying he really would prefer a secular one.

But Jasper's eyes were searching, troubled, resting on Holly for a minute and then gone again. Anne expected that, on the day after his engagement, Jasper would be completely wrapped up with his future wife, as he'd been the previous night. She was a little disappointed in Jasper, recalling how he'd been fawning over Holly the previous night. She was more critical of him than her husband: she expected him to be civil and decent to the people around him, not so self-absorbed. Even though she put up with John's unpredictable moods and disappearances, she was less inclined than him to be silent when he pushed the boundaries of her patience.

'You knew.' She'd elbowed John the previous night as Holly and Jasper had kissed after Holly had dried her tears.

'Helped him pick out a ring,' John had said proudly. 'God, do you remember the state he was in when he first came to visit.' His face was suddenly serious.

'I try not to,' she'd replied. 'You've been a good friend; he's lucky to have you.' She'd rubbed his shoulder reassuringly, and he'd put his arm around her waist and plucked the elastic on her waistband.

They'd watched Jasper as he took Holly's hand and explained the ring. Holly had turned to show it to her, and

Anne had to admit that it was incredibly pretty. The ring made of three slim bands attached by fine filigree fitted perfectly on Holly's ring finger.

'I can't believe this. I can't. I can't,' Holly had repeated. 'I've got to call my mum and dad.' She'd fanned herself with her free hand, her eyes fixed upon her ring.

'They watched the whole thing.' Jasper had pulled his mobile off the shelf where it had been partially obscured and on a tripod. Her parents were now furiously waving.

Holly had seized the phone. 'Hi, Mum,' she'd begun and headed for the kitchen, asking if they could believe what had just happened.

Anne and John had hugged Jasper in turn, congratulating him again.

Looking at Jasper, today, she thought, *for God's sake, make an effort for poor Holly.*

'Well, I suppose there are some sexy traditional designs,' Holly suggested, appearing surprised at Anne's conflicting idea about the wedding.

Edmund had lapsed into that unpleasant – or was it unhappy? – silence again. Why didn't he go to Ovidia when something was so obviously wrong? Anne tried not to stare at him but found it difficult. He looked haggard, not like the man she'd met before. Looking at him now, she could believe he was as dull and work-obsessed as Jasper claimed. But, even the first time she'd met him, the cut and quality of his clothes had hinted at a contradiction to her. His clothes told her that he cared about the way he looked and, on several occasions, she recognised the restaurants Jasper mentioned the two of them visiting from the urbane tastemakers she followed in magazines and blogs. She wished she'd probed more into his interests, perhaps discussed décor and design;

she felt she may have learned more. The house they were in, though disappointingly stripped of its Victorian heritage, had been decorated by someone with some taste, though it lacked individualism. Perhaps, she thought, it said something about Ovidia. Was she as colourful as she seemed?

'Mind if I?' Anne began, pointing to the French doors. 'There's one just after the kitchen and a few upstairs – take your pick,' Edmund replied.

Anne went in search of the toilet downstairs, thinking how it was a perfect opportunity to look around, if just a little. She left the kitchen, the dark wood flooring continued along a corridor. But she decided, as she needed to be discreet, she would stick to the lower floors, recalling how impersonal the ground floor had been. Edmund and Ovidia were an enigma, and she felt she wasn't learning enough about them. An itch to rifle through everything she could burned inside her, and having to pass bedrooms and studies would be too much of a temptation.

Anne had seen houses like this in magazines and on blogs. She'd once been on a design house tour, joining queue after queue across London for a chance to walk through houses that everyone nodded and whispered in approval of their beauty and style. The tour group all understood that it was, to an extent, artificially staged, possessions edited or hidden to show the world.

But this was the home of someone she knew, if only a little. Yet it was like those homes on show – the feeling that the owner was away. The details or imperfections that differentiate a house from a home – muddy boots, overdue library books, and carelessly tossed backpacks – were missing.

In the minutes she had to find the toilet, she imagined what items Edmund could source on his travels – authentic kilims or kimonos, hand-stamped batiks, if he wanted to. She walked along the corridor, imagining how she'd tweak the décor, making it more personal, and then nodded when, in her imagination, her job was done.

'Oh, wow,' she said as she opened the bathroom door.

The downstairs bathroom was spacious enough to have a large claw-foot tub as its centrepiece. Its skirting was painted white, offsetting the black walls that made up the top half. It was well thought out, designed for show – not like her own bathroom renovation, which was all about utility, about being able to withstand a family of four.

As soon as she closed the door behind her, she opened the medicine cabinet. She found only spare soap, toothpaste, and toothbrushes still in their packages. She inspected the room, the hand towels appeared new and were completely unmarked, the floor tiles seemed pristine, the room appeared to be cleaned more often than it was used.

'Stop it, nosey,' Anne told herself, wondering what she was looking for but disappointed that she couldn't find it. She finished with the toilet, and washing her hands, checked her face and inspected her teeth.

Looking in the mirror, Anne, for a second, was distracted by the sight of her face: the heaviness under her eyes that her make-up could not obscure. She picked up a towel, and, as she rubbed her hands dry, the musky smell of unused linen hit her.

Surprised, she put the towel back on the rail where, from a distance, it had seemed clean and fresh. She sniffed the other towel and it smelled the same. The towels must have been there long enough to begin to reek, unchanged because they hadn't been used, she thought. She shuddered as she left the room.

Walking back through the corridor, Anne could not resist the urge to snoop. She saw the house with a new perspective. Whoever cleaned only did so superficially. Someone didn't care, the cleaner or the owner. The cleaner was no longer held accountable or was unsupervised. The floor was obviously cleaned, but as she looked in corners, she could see where the mop had not gone all the way to the wall on a regular basis and muck had accumulated along the skirting. She noted a fine layer of dust on the console table, which, when its drawers were opened, revealed unopened mail and brochures unsorted and disordered.

The housekeeper was certain there would be no guests – that no one would use the towels or wander along the corridors. Jasper hadn't even known the address.

Something was very wrong in Edmund's life. Anne paused when the thought hit her.

Him sitting outdoors in that condition was part of something much bigger. Everything she'd seen or heard about Edmund said that his home would be pristine. Yet he was paying a housekeeper who didn't do their job, who was so sure they wouldn't be reprimanded that he or she had become complacent.

She entered the kitchen and moved quietly to the sitting area behind it, which, like the cooking space, appeared clean at first glance. She lifted a sofa cushion and, when she saw the mess of crumbs and pencil sharpenings wedged between the cushions, she thought, *they can't really be paying someone for this*. Though she was sure they must be, the house was much too big for the two of them to be cleaning it themselves.

Anne exited through the kitchen doors, stopping to look at the large soulless kitchen behind her, and sat back beside

John. A man as meticulous as the Edmund she'd met before would not stand for the filth she'd found today, but this crumpled man in front of her just might.

She exhaled and smiled briefly at her husband. *The house is just dirty, she told herself, why is that so important? So they're between housekeepers.*

But it was more than that, Anne thought, and looked at Jasper. If Jasper knew anything about his brother's personal life, if he had an explanation for Edmund's pyjamas and dirty house, he would not have brought them here unannounced.

'Anne's going to be my maid-of-honour,' Holly was saying to Edmund. 'Aren't you?' She glanced at Anne.

'Of course I am,' Anne replied quickly, falling into the conversation, desperate to cover up for obtruding into their home. 'And the guys are all going to wear morning suits. We can put Edmund in charge of that.'

'I don't think so,' Edmund said. 'I'm sure you can sort everything out. I'll just show up.'

Once again, he smiled, a forced smile. He had to be thinking of Ovidia, maybe considering going after her, but he, like his brother, seemed compelled to stay.

'No way – you'll be in it from beginning to end,' Holly insisted. 'Everyone will have a task to carry out. That way everyone feels involved.'

'You should draw up a master plan,' John said. 'A spreadsheet with everyone's names, deliverables, and date of completion.'

'I know you're joking, but that's actually a good idea,' Holly said.

Anne laughed, as did Edmund. The sound of only the two of them made Anne immediately uncomfortable, and she stopped.

'I hate spreadsheets,' Holly said.

'You should ask Ovidia to do it for you,' Edmund said, looking up as Ovidia joined them again. 'Implementation plans are her thing. She can make spreadsheets with her eyes closed.'

'Well, Ovidia will be there, too,' Holly said. Anne wondered if this was a question or an order.

Ovidia returned to the stool beside Edmund. Her face seemed drawn, as if she'd aged in the half hour since she'd left the room.

'The wedding?' Ovidia joined in the conversation. 'It depends on when it is – do you know yet? I'm going to take a few months off. I have this big plan to travel this year – like a late gap year. I've ordered pizza. I hope you don't mind. We don't entertain much, so we're not really equipped with, um, food and things.'

Anne watched as Ovidia shook her head as if to clear it. Her speech was rapid and indecisive, and Anne was left wondering if Ovidia had, in fact, ordered any pizza.

'They might like pot noodles,' Edmund suggested, taking Ovidia's hand as she sat down.

'Really? You don't entertain? This is a lovely place for it – built for it,' Anne said. It reminded her of the kitchen extension she'd desperately wanted, sleek and contemporary, yet retaining some of the '70s charm that had appealed to them when they bought it. The extension they had built, that they'd endured weeks of inconvenience for, eating microwaved meals and washing their dishes in the bathroom for, had turned out no more than a dull conservatory. John had complained that the furnishing she'd selected was not his style, and they had rowed about everything until, apart from the extra space it gave them, the final effect had been nothing like what she'd envisioned. When the girls had drawn on the freshly painted walls and every nook was filled with toys, she'd said nothing. 'Clean, sleek,' she finished.

'A bit child unfriendly,' John said. 'Don't get me wrong. To every man his style, but I can just imagine the girls breaking their necks on that flooring.' He was speaking to Anne when he said this.

'John, don't be rude,' Anne replied under her breath.

'Look, I'm sorry about the extension, all right,' he whispered back. 'We should have agreed everything before.'

'John, stop,' Anne said, louder.

Edmund stroked the back of his head and shifted his weight in his seat. Anne watched as Ovidia glanced at the floor and then away, and then looked back to Edmund.

'I know,' Jasper said. 'We could hold the engagement party here, since it's so perfect for entertaining.' He hadn't spoken for a while, and the sound of his voice jarred, as if he'd leapt in from a far-off room. He leaned forward, glaring at Edmund.

Holly's eyes lit up. Anne made eye contact and shook her head. It seemed to her an awful idea. Though the house seemed like the perfect location – its address, its size, its owner's status, were all perfect – Anne could tell Jasper's suggestion was a challenge of some kind, a test. Though she knew she didn't have enough information about whatever it was that Edmund and Ovidia were involved in, what issue they were facing, she could see that this was the wrong time for a challenge. She looked at the two of them for validation, noticing how Ovidia's seat was lower than Edmund's, enhancing the difference in their height and making Ovidia seem small and submissive.

She was right, it was a challenge, Anne thought, when Edmund hesitated, seeming distinctly uncertain.

'We've never...' Edmund began, looking at Ovidia for support, but she was gazing into the distance, her expression that of someone whose thoughts were miles away. 'I suppose we could get an event planner?'

'Ovidia?' Jasper asked.

After Edmund tapped her hand lightly, she said, 'I probably won't be here.'

'Leaving for your gap year so quickly?' Jasper said, and Holly started. Anne was also surprised at his rudeness, but Jasper had just learned that his brother had kept a relationship from him for four years – she was surprised that Jasper hadn't marched out of the house in anger.

'Yes, I was thinking of leaving on Thursday,' Ovidia replied, her gaze directed above their heads, as if she wasn't really conversing with them.

Anne saw Edmund flinch. Jasper leaned back into his seat with a smug look on his face. As if something pleased him about Ovidia leaving so abruptly.

Anne was trying to analyse whatever it was in Jasper's demeanour that was wrong. His performance was imperfect – the Jasper she knew, when under stress, cracked or exploded. He disappeared, he ranted, he cried, he imbibed wine until incomprehensible and unsteady. He didn't lean back and try to act as if everything was all right. Everyone else was too preoccupied to recognise it. Ovidia talking about going on gap years, Edmund lost in pyjamas, Holly focused on her impending marriage, and John. John should have been able to see it, but he too was distracted. Anne could see the way he tapped his fingers along the side of his leg, ran his fingers up and down the trouser seams along his thighs, and the way he held her gaze for too long and too intensely – like he did when he lied to her, or when he was trying to seduce her when she'd already said no.

'Wonderful, where to?' John asked, his fingers abruptly ending their journey.

'But you could wait just a couple of weeks, couldn't you?' Holly directed her question at Edmund as if she expected him to tell Ovidia to change her plans.

'I could, but I don't want to,' Ovidia replied firmly. Then she crossed her legs and looked at her audience. 'I'm planning to go to Ghana – where my dad's from.' This time the words stumbled out. 'I've only visited it once with my parents when I was a child. We sat outdoors with my aunts and uncles, went down to the beach, played with my cousins, and talked and talked and talked late into the evening. And I've had this idea' – she leaned forward – 'about designing an engineering boot camp for girls. Then again, I might just hang out in the sun.'

'Ghana,' John said. 'Sounds perfect – but it won't be the same though.'

'I know,' Ovidia replied.

'I grew up in Singapore,' John went on. 'Went back after nearly twenty years and couldn't stand the place. Even the heat was nothing like I remembered. It was oppressive, and it rained all the time. I'd romanticised it, made it perfect in my memory. All my friends had moved on, places I loved had been bulldozed over.' He shrugged.

Anne had gone with him. They'd left London excited at the prospect of visiting such an exotic place. But almost as soon as they got there, he'd begun to complain.

'Well, that wasn't here when I lived here,' he'd said at every turn and, 'But now it's all so touristy.'

She remembered how his constant griping had begun to grate. It had been so unlike him. He'd seemed angry at the city for changing. Since then, she'd come to understand that he'd gone looking for something, or someone, specific, that he expected it to be there waiting for him.

Halfway through their trip, Anne had turned to him and barked, 'What is wrong with you?'

'Nothing.' His voice had been too loud, his tone too aggressive. He'd softened his stance. 'Nothing,' he'd repeated quietly and then paused. 'It's just as if everyone, every friend I had, has vanished.'

Anne had massaged his shoulder, having guessed but never discussed how a childhood spent with nomadic parents moving from country to country and even cities within a state had left him with few people with whom he shared memories of his youth. They'd never talked about the many transient friendships made and lost in his lifetime. Sometimes she'd sense his disbelief when she talked about people she'd known since her first day at school, or when she'd introduce him to someone she'd known for twenty-five years.

Nonetheless, he'd kept moaning about the city, and Anne's patience had become strained, exacerbated by the extremes of the humid heat and the powerfully cold air conditioning. She'd been pregnant, and their firstborn – they'd not yet known it would be a girl – had started kicking while she was alone in their hotel room and John was out. She'd immediately sent him a text, excited, and he'd replied, 'Wonderful. Don't forget we're roaming.'

He'd returned to their hotel room that night, late, traces of another woman on his clothes and in the way he turned away from her in bed, feigning drunkenness. She'd lain in bed, staring at the sterile, glossy furniture that filled the bland space. They'd spent a week more in Singapore – both hating everything about it.

Then they'd returned to London. As soon as the door closed behind them, she'd turned and slapped him as hard as she could, surprised at her own strength when he fell back against the door, briefly stunned. Anne had walked away, restraining the boiling hatred that was frothing within her, holding down the simmering need to scream and hit him again and again and harder. She'd never before imagined hitting someone, certainly not a man, and definitely not her partner. Sometimes she looked at her hand and wondered how she'd stopped herself from carrying on.

'Daydreaming?' John asked, elbowing her gently. He topped up her wine, not offering anyone else a refill, and caught her eye.

'Something about her gives me the creeps,' he whispered.

'John!' Anne hissed, but no one else seemed to have heard.

'Jasper,' she whispered back to John, 'is in pain.'

'I know,' John said, before saying much louder, 'By the way, we probably should take the girls somewhere special tomorrow, so don't have too much to drink.'

19

'What's the urgency?' Holly demanded, her forehead furrowed in annoyance. 'Does it have to be right away – if it's not a family anniversary, can't it wait?'

Ovidia didn't answer, squinting thoughtfully out of the glass ceiling at some birds as they passed. Holly was annoyed for a moment. She felt Ovidia was shrugging her off. But Ovidia was Edmund's partner, she had to be at his brother's wedding, she thought. *What was wrong with these two?*

'It doesn't matter, Holly,' Jasper said, placing his hand on her shoulder. 'There are a thousand places we can have an engagement party.' The warmth of his hand reassured her, and she clutched it. He was right, they could have it anywhere. What was important was that they were to be married. She exhaled, still tense. It was uncomfortable having found out that Edmund was in a relationship by walking in on him. But Jasper seemed to be dealing with it, though he was a little on edge, she could tell. He couldn't sit still. She could sense the rise and fall of his mood through his posture; one minute he'd be as stiff as a board, the next his limbs would be loose, his arms heavy at his side. He was still here, though. If he was really upset, he'd have left, wouldn't he?

Edmund and Ovidia seemed like such nice people, though maybe a little off. It would have been nice to leave and come back when Edmund was better – who wants to have a bunch of people parked in your house when you're quite clearly ill? But the wine had made her even more joyous than when she'd arrived this morning. She wasn't going to ruin her own day by wandering into the city and looking for some other means of celebrating her engagement.

'So, Edmund, how's work?' Holly heard John cut in like a reluctant onlooker breaking up a fight. 'Still in the city?'

'Still,' Edmund replied. Holly got the impression he was amused. 'And it's still as dull as it's ever been.'

Her tension relieved, Holly giggled. Anne chuckled. John appeared confused, as though he hadn't expected that response. Jasper had described Edmund's work as seeming to consist primarily of flying to exotic locations to talk to people about money, but he said that Edmund loved his job – that he'd found what he was destined to do.

'Your job's dull? Weren't you in Seoul only just after Christmas, and New York just before? If I get to go down the road for my work, it's excitement redefined,' John complained.

'Seoul – really?' Holly said.

'That was Tokyo. Two weeks of talking through a translator, being repeatedly assailed by something called a Pikachu, and sleeping in a room the size of a large wardrobe. I don't think it stopped raining even for a second – oh yes, really exciting,' Edmund replied. 'I'd much rather have been at home.'

'If you don't like it, then why don't you quit and do something that excites you?' Anne suggested. 'Run a charity or something?'

'What could possibly be exciting about running a charity? They don't make any money.'

Holly found it difficult to tell if Edmund was joking. 'I do what I do because I make a lot of money. I haven't done dishes or laundry in years. I haven't had to worry about my car breaking down or if my kids will...' He broke off. 'And, I can afford to make sure my brother and his wife have their dream wedding,' he continued.

Holly was taken aback, interpreting it as an offer. Even with Jasper, she'd never considered realising her dream wedding, one in which everything she wanted – her dress, the venue, the menu – was exactly like the pictures she stored on Pinterest. Perhaps because she was, to a certain extent, realistic. She knew that dreams – winning the lottery, being a D-cup, or having a job that involved flying to various parts of the world to meet designers and models – tended to remain dreams. Instead, she moved within the realm of what was possible: meeting local celebrities and mid-level writers in trendy but reasonably priced cafés that had been featured in local magazines. She went to book launches and to Paris or Reykjavik for long weekends, and she owned a one-thousand-pound painting that hung in her and Jasper's living room and was dramatic enough to be commented on by everyone who entered their flat. She'd always dreamed affordable dreams; she wouldn't know what to do with someone else's money.

'Speaking of jobs – what do you do Ovidia?' John asked. Everyone had fallen silent again. It seemed the job of filling in silences had fallen on him and Anne. Jasper spoke only occasionally, and Holly was finding it hard to find anything to say. She was beginning to feel as if this gathering had lost its focus: her and Jasper getting married. She didn't want to come across as over eager, she knew sometimes she did.

'Hey, Ovidia,' Edmund said softly as he touched her, rubbing his forefinger gently on the skin of her knee. 'Listening?'

'Sorry, what?'

Edmund's touch seemed to bring Ovidia back from wherever her attention had wandered.

'John asked what you do?' he said quietly.

'I'm in financial management. I...' Ovidia trailed off as if an explanation was beyond her. 'Or...' she started.

'Edmund said you were the queen of spreadsheets?' John said.

Holly nodded. 'It would really help with the wedding planning if we could have someone organised like that.' She wanted to lead the conversation back to the wedding.

Still Ovidia didn't reply, appearing more disorientated.

After a pause, John leaned forward and said quietly to Edmund, 'Again, if this is a bad time for you guys, we can...'

Holly thought his suggestion made sense. There was clearly something wrong with Edmund and now Ovidia. The difference between the woman who had so suavely introduced herself that morning and the fidgeting, distracted person before them now was noticeable. She saw Jasper had gripped a cushion and gone pale.

Edmund could just take her inside, Holly thought. Ovidia looked as if she needed to lie down. Edmund leaned over to Ovidia and whispered. Holly, despite herself, strained to listen but couldn't make out what Edmund said to her. She saw Ovidia shake her head and then, after Edmund spoke again, she heard Ovidia whisper 'Okay' and nod.

'Make you a cup of tea?' Edmund asked, loud enough for the rest to hear.

'I'm all right.' Ovidia put her hand on his shoulder as if to steady herself.

It was strange how, now that Jasper knew about the two of them, they were now completely blatant about their relationship, whispering and touching each other, she thought. It was as if there was no real reason he hadn't told Jasper, or whatever the reason had been just didn't matter anymore.

They all lapsed into silence again. Holly hoped they would nurture the quiet for a little while and allow Ovidia to recover, but the silence once again felt oppressive. When John cleared his throat, a sense of relief flooded through Holly as if he'd given them all permission to relax.

'I wouldn't mind a cup myself,' John said, slapping his hands against his thighs and leaning forward as if he meant to make it himself.

'You know, I could do with some tea, too,' Anne said, a hand on John's shoulder. 'If you just point me the right way, I can make it.'

'I'll have some,' Holly chimed in, wanting to leave the extension. 'Need any help?'

'No thanks, I'll manage,' Anne replied. 'Ovidia?'

Ovidia nodded this time, looking up at Anne, her eyes refocused, perhaps thankful.

'John, Edmund, Jasper?' Her voice was brisk, and she was already on her way towards the French doors.

'I'll have a cup, thanks,' Edmund said. John nodded and Jasper said nothing. Holly watched as he rubbed his chin and stared at the floor. She tapped his thigh, and, for a moment, she caught his eye, but then he was gone again.

20

Anne was a different shade of blonde when Jasper first met her. Her hair was darker, richer, and cut and styled with a military precision that gave her the quiet elegance of a 1950s housewife.

'We tidied,' John had said by way of greeting. Anne had stood behind him, a fraction of an inch taller than him in a belted cardigan and flowing midi skirt.

Jasper had arrived at their house on time. He'd taken a taxi when he could have easily taken public transport and had waited at a café near the tube station for nearly an hour beforehand. He'd had a milkshake, a sickly sweet concoction that, in the absence of solid food, gave him the energy he needed for the evening.

'It's lovely to finally meet you,' Anne had said, stepping forward, though Jasper had only met John a fortnight earlier. She didn't say *'I've heard so much about you'* or give away any clues if she knew about the circumstances in which he and John had met. He'd felt a warmth radiate from her as he shook her hand.

He'd held out the brown paper bag he was carrying. It had been covered in cheerful red and orange apple prints from an eco-toy shop across the road from his house. Jasper would never have thought of it before, but Edmund had reminded him to take a gift, as if he knew that his brother now felt socially inept, incapable of recalling the conventions of a simple dinner party. Without reminding, he'd ironed his clothes after work but had been aware that his blue shirt sagged around him and his jeans were too big and held up by an extra notch he'd punched in his belt using a corkscrew.

He'd seen the relief in Edmund's face when he'd told him he'd been invited to dinner. Edmund had long since stopped urging him to socialise or to participate in activities that would take his mind off things. In fact, especially since Jasper had quit work, citing medical reasons, Edmund and his parents had become the only people he spoke to on a regular basis, until he met John.

'A puzzle, how lovely.' Anne had pulled the box out, looked it over, and closed it back into the bag. 'We farmed them out for the evening, but the girls will love it.'

'With my mum and dad,' John had interjected with a smile. 'Thought we'd get them out of the way.'

Anne had jabbed him with her elbow. 'Come on in.'

They'd entered a large combined living and dining room with light wood floors and creased linen lamp shades. A large grey cashmere throw covered a good part of a dark brown sofa. The room had been arranged in a way that suggested conversations with friends. A series of small black and white pictures of their daughters ran along the wall opposite the deep brown armchair in which he was invited to sit.

'This is lovely,' Jasper had said, trying to recall what one said at a dinner party. 'It's very Nordic.'

'You see,' Anne had poked John. 'I told you it was a style. Thanks so much. I'd have gone for something bolder and more minimalist – this was sort of a compromise.'

'It's cosy yet stylish,' Jasper had added, shifting his weight and realising that the armchair was rather comfortable.

'Anne's dream is to end up in a magazine.' John had sat down on the sofa at the side nearest Jasper. 'I'm more of a home-is-for-living-in type.'

'In that case, well done. You've got both,' Jasper had said, and Anne looked even more bashful.

He'd liked Anne immediately. He'd liked them, John and Anne together, their banter, the way they seemed so comfortable with each other. But Anne was not Louisa. He was sure then, he hadn't mixed up her name. The afternoon he'd met John, Jasper had been confused when John said, *'My wife.'* It explained the way John had kissed Louisa – an erotic, passionate act in front of a man they'd only just met and, at the time, never expected to see again.

Here in her castle, Anne was most certainly his wife. Small framed photos showed pictures of the two of them and their daughters in various poses, on a beach, in a garden. Each picture was carefully arranged yet was deeply personal.

Anne had offered him something to drink. He'd hesitated, wondering if his lack of food would suit beer or wine better and had been about to opt for beer, when John said, 'Maybe we could have it with dinner, if it's ready. I'm starving.'

Anne had been taken aback. 'It's almost ready, but is Jasper?' She'd looked towards him.

'I can wait until dinner.' He'd felt relieved.

They'd talked to Anne as she served the meal she'd taken from *Vegetarian Living*. 'I hope you like chickpeas. I'm trying to eat healthily.'

'Diet,' John had mouthed and was rewarded by a glare from Anne. 'You're the one who wants to lose weight. I have no complaints.'

'It's all right until I'm faced with – sit please.' She'd waved them to the table. 'With the likes of Louisa Trent. Three kids under six and not a spare bit of fat on her body.'

Jasper's eyes had flicked towards John, who had given no visible response to what his wife had just said.

'I'd wanted to invite her over tonight,' she'd said, and Jasper saw that she was watching as he spooned the food on his plate. 'Physiotherapist at my hospital, single –' she'd begun but let her words drift as she looked at Jasper poking at his food. 'It won't bite, you know,' she'd said abruptly.

'Anne,' John had intervened sternly.

'Whatever it is, starving yourself won't cure it,' she'd continued. 'Trust me.' She'd stood and fetched condiments from the kitchen island.

Jasper had lifted his fork, discomfited that Anne had noticed, and ate a few mouthfuls. He'd guessed from what she'd said, John must have mentioned something, though how much detail he'd given his wife, Jasper couldn't have known.

Anne had said something about a new exhibition at a gallery near where she worked, and the conversation evolved from there. John had brought out the wine, and they went back to the living room. Jasper discovered a strange sense of normality in their home and banter, and he had found he could sit near Anne without a sense of dread or confusion.

'John would never bring a client home,' she'd said when John had excused himself. 'So, if you're not one of them, I can ask what's bothering you.'

He'd smiled at her direct manner. 'The usual. Broken dreams, a bit too much drink, etcetera.'

'No one can help, if you don't say.'

Jasper had shuffled in his seat.

Resting her chin on her hand, Anne had continued. 'When I met John, I was bulimic and in a pretty desperate state.'

'A patient?'

'No, never.' She'd quickly glanced at the door, as if checking if John was in hearing range. 'I've never even told him. I'd had a lot of practice hiding it.'

'And now you're cured?'

'I don't know about cured, but I do know that I can eat now and keep it all down and raise two kids.' She'd glanced again towards the door at the sound of John's footsteps. 'Try looking after yourself, even if that's the only thing you do.'

Jasper had nodded involuntarily.

John had returned to his seat. He'd held out a new bottle of wine and asked, 'Chilean?'

It had been nearing midnight, and John had put Anne – who'd had too much to drink – to bed, and they'd remained talking in low tones until Jasper said he really should go home. He'd ordered a taxi despite John's protests that there was still more wine.

They had been standing by the door when John said, 'I left certain things out when I told Anne how we met.'

Jasper had nodded.

'If she ever does bring the subject up, I'd appreciate it if you kept Louisa out of things,' John had said.

Jasper had nodded again, choosing to stay silent.

'It wasn't anything...' John had cocked his head, as if to say illicit, unsavoury – extramarital.

This time Jasper had raised his chin, a small act of defiance.

'Louisa is a friend...' John had begun.

'I'm not stupid,' Jasper had said. 'A bit confused, maybe, but not stupid.'

The taxi had stopped at the kerb.

'Are you still on for drinks on Friday?' John had asked as they stared at the vehicle in silence.

'Yes.' Jasper had breathed in relief, glad John hadn't changed his mind about being friends.

21

In the kitchen on her own, Anne exhaled, realising that Holly had offered to come with her because she too wanted to escape the others. She felt the tension accumulating in her gut. The kettle stood on the counter, and Anne noticed that the debris of an earlier breakfast had been emptied into the sink.

The kitchen gave the impression of being immaculate because it was expensive. The surfaces would remain forever unmarked, every drop and every spill could be easily wiped off the durable, technologically devised material. Not a corner, counter, or stool was scuffed or marked. If it was, it would be replaced. The cutlery drawer slid out silently, revealing a selection of perfectly matched tableware. Still, when she looked into nooks and corners, she saw more of the shoddy cleaning, crumbs that accumulated and aged in corners and beside the toaster.

This house was hiding its owners from those they loved most, she thought, as she filled the kettle, plugged it in, and pushed the button. Their lives pivoted around this house. From here they went out to work, to socialise, to exercise, and then returned, most likely, each night; yet they didn't care about or for it. She could tell Ovidia cared about her clothes; they were clean and in excellent condition. She was wearing make-up, and her hair was perfect – had she imagined that she'd receive guests, she'd have had someone clean up at least the bathroom. It meant she hadn't used the bathroom nearest the kitchen long enough for the smell of disuse to creep in.

Why didn't Jasper know about this house? He hadn't even known its address. She'd always thought it strange that Jasper and Edmund usually met in cafés and restaurants or went out somewhere. It made sense now – he didn't want Jasper to know about his secret life for reasons the brothers were keeping to themselves. Not knowing this reason was maddening, and Anne hoped the house would give her clues.

Since Holly had moved in with Jasper, she knew Edmund only dropped by Jasper's flat sporadically, though he'd helped his brother select and pay for the flat. But such habits were easy to fall into, like the way she never met John at his office. Also, John knew Edmund to a degree, yet he had believed Edmund to live in a penthouse. If this had changed, he'd have told her. What possible reason could he have not to?

Edmund had been hiding this life from his brother. It could be something just as simple as Edmund not wanting Jasper judging his tastes – but that, Anne thought, sounded much too petty.

She couldn't ask Edmund and Ovidia, but not knowing was chafing at her. She didn't know the couple enough to interrogate them or demand an explanation. She was like a bystander at a sudden public altercation, the history and the event and what came after might never be known. She wasn't sure she could accept that.

She looked around. If she was to get any answers, she'd have to find them herself.

A kitchen like this, Anne thought, *will have a mess drawer.* A place where little scraps of things go: cast-off shopping lists, reminders, old hair bands, loose change. She assured herself that she could claim to be looking for accoutrements for the tea, if she was found. She opened every drawer, relieved that they were so silent, until she found it. The picture was in the drawer near the wine cooler. Everything around it neatly arranged – bills, envelopes, pieces of paper, deformed paperclips, and other photographs.

Anne gently tugged out the picture, trying not to upset the drawer's order. It showed a photo of a baby in hospital, tubes and cables attached to his fingers and leading from his nostrils. As a nurse, she immediately recognised the equipment as life support. It wasn't a newborn – she guessed it had to be about six months old. Its eyes were closed.

She put the picture back carefully and found others.

Only then did she understand whose pictures she held in her hand.

She leaned forward and rested her hand on her chin. Since they'd arrived, there had been no mention of a child, or life support, and nothing in what she'd seen of the house so far bore any evidence that a child had ever lived here. She thought she remembered Edmund saying, the first time they'd met, that he didn't have any children – or had he just shrugged? Having children of her own, it was a question she'd have asked anyone his age. Maybe he'd given her a vague response that she simply interpreted as being a no – when in fact he'd told her nothing.

She set the pictures down and exhaled, trying to free the knot that had formed in her throat.

There were six photos. She looked at each one. Then stopped and caressed the image of a baby asleep in an expensive cot, its new clothes all in pale blue. The other photos showed it had brown eyes and brown afro curls. It was unmistakably both Edmund and Ovidia – a perfect blend of the best of each parent.

If Edmund had a child – surely Jasper would have known?

Another photo showed the baby with its eyes wide open, staring. It was a boy, she guessed, since everything around him was blue and his blankets appliquéd with images of little cars. These were parents who were not interested in bucking convention, in pursuing new or radical ways of raising their child. Perhaps because they were older, maybe because they'd waited, maybe Edmund, or even Ovidia, had never planned on having children. One of the pictures showed half of Edmund; she guessed it was him from his clothes. He held the baby with ease, its large head peeking over his shoulder, still too young to see as far as the camera that was taking its image.

Though taken at different stages in the child's life, they all looked as if they were printed at the same time and then put away – none of the images were crinkled, marked, or smudged. Anne did that herself sometimes. She'd empty her camera phone and pick out four or five of her favourite shots of the girls and have them printed. There was still something reassuring about photos on paper. Somehow, as long as everything was stored in a digital memory, there was the danger that it might disappear, a hard drive might fail, a camera may be stolen – but pictures on paper would remain.

Anne tucked the photos back where she'd found them. With them was a webpage printed out that had been folded and refolded repeatedly, its creases dirty.

How long does it take to die after removing a breathing machine or life support?

Being a nurse, these websites were familiar. Written by well-meaning charities, they were supposed to be reassuring, to guide people through the prospect of losing someone they loved.

'Oh, Jasper,' she sighed. Faced with the enormity of Edmund's secret life, she felt a fathomless pity for her friend. All the phone calls, the lunches in the city, meeting at their parents' home, all those things that Jasper read as a sign of the strength of their filial affection, were meaningless if Edmund hadn't told Jasper he had this other life.

She rooted around more, less aware of the people outside, and found a private-hospital flyer, folded in two, names of doctors, notes on medication, and a date – vague, almost illegible, perhaps today.

Edmund and Ovidia had a baby, and it was in hospital. There could be no other conclusion, though she wanted one.

She felt certain sadness for Edmund and Ovidia. Being a nurse, she'd seen people waiting for someone to die. She'd seen families sitting in corridors and hoping for miracles until the end and even after. She'd seen some people in a daze, unable to speak or comprehend what was said to them and others who tried to continue as if everything was normal. She'd seen those who tried to be strong and those who crumpled to the floor in tears.

Finally, Anne poured the hot water into the teapot. She arranged a tray with a milk jug, sugar bowl, and four cups and saucers, which was the most she could manage, and returned to the extension.

22

Jasper's phone buzzed repeatedly, and he looked at the incoming messages, a smiling emoji from Saskia congratulating him. He didn't respond. On instinct, he scrolled down through the most recent messages, past this morning to the previous night.

Jasper had never saved Edmund's number as a profile. Edmund had been using the same number for years, perhaps even a decade. Jasper had committed it to memory along the way. Before asking Holly to marry him the previous night, he'd tried to call Edmund. *'He's not feeling well,'* his mother had chirped between glasses of champagne. He'd called Edmund once but hadn't been bothered enough to follow up with a message. But in the taxi back home, he'd sent a text on the spur of the moment.

He must have been distracted, happy. He'd typed in the first few digits of Edmund's number and sent the message. He hadn't noticed the response from the mobile provider saying his message had not been sent.

Edmund had received no warning that Jasper would be coming.

Jasper let his head fall forward, and he swore silently. The house and its contents were not part of a conspiracy.

Edmund and Ovidia hadn't planned an elaborate charade. He had unwittingly intruded into their real life.

Holly elbowed him gently. She was laughing about something. Holly was the future. Tomorrow, they'd carry on as if today hadn't happened, he and Holly. Last week, they'd been looking at changing paint colours in their living room – such a safe, mundane activity. They'd begin planning their wedding; she'd take him through pages and pages of magazines and catalogues. Her sister and mother would whisk her off for fittings and make-up and whatever else her big day required.

Holly had been part of a renewed sense of normality. She hadn't saved him – he'd found her as he was swimming upwards from the depths into which he'd plunged when Ovidia had left him. For a long time, he hadn't been able to pretend. Then he'd been finally able to keep a job, to socialise – to put on a performance to the outside world that he was an ordinary man, even if at times his head felt it would explode with the effort of maintaining the façade. At first, he'd been cautious, almost fearful. But a certain folly propelled him forward. He dared himself to trust Holly, but was vigilant, replaying events and conversations in his mind and analysing them for warning signs of impending aggression.

On workdays, they kissed passionately before she left; when apart, they sent each other texts reminding the other of the need for milk and cheese and asked if they really wanted to see the show if Moe was able to get tickets. The show would still be irrelevant. He'd watch and clap at the right times, but he was with Holly, which was what was important.

If he left this house right now, he could go back to that life.

But he couldn't leave. He was rooted to the chair watching Edmund and Ovidia, taking in every movement, the way they vacillated between comfortable and confident to uncertain and jumpy. Perhaps his presence was affecting them – guilt, regret maybe.

Holly had updated her status to 'Engaged' at some point in the morning, and felicitations were saturating her Facebook page. The likes and comments had entered the hundreds. Jasper had been fighting the urge to check Facebook all morning, though usually he could go for weeks without even glancing at it. He'd tap his phone and get as far as typing in her name, 'Ovidia', then his nerve would give way. He wanted to go to the bathroom now, but he didn't relish the thought of learning more about Edmund and Ovidia's home.

Holly had tagged him, and he was now receiving a constant assault of notifications cheering on his engagement – the reason he was here.

'What a beautiful couple.'

That morning Holly had put up a picture of her and Jasper that his father had taken the previous night.

'Show us the ring then!!'

'What! You got there before me!'

'Luv u both. Mwah Mwah!'

Happy faces, hearts, emojis, memes, and gifs were pouring in, and Jasper knew that later Holly would go through every single one adding a like and occasionally a thoughtful response.

Jasper's account was usually all but inactive. It had become a virtual viewing platform from where he watched the rest of the world go about their online lives. Holly kept encouraging him, never understanding his aversion towards it. She never desisted from posting pictures of herself, tagging him, sharing articles on his page. He responded once every two or three months. It all seemed silly, though he didn't tell Holly what he thought. He'd accepted almost every friend request he'd received, regardless of who sent it, and his profile looked healthy, with references to new restaurants, trips, and events that made them seem like sophisticates living in London, with jobs with impressive titles.

Now, he finally typed in *Ovidia Attigah*. Her name came up right away, as it always did.

'There is only one me!' Ovidia used to sing. She'd told Jasper she'd never come across anyone with the same name as she had. As he'd searched for her over the years, he'd found it was true, and wherever her name appeared online it referred to his Ovidia.

Jasper's heart fluttered when he saw her profile. He hadn't looked at it for years. He'd googled Ovidia constantly, once upon a time. He'd tried to keep up with her, to know where she was, and find out what she was doing. At some point, she'd removed him from her list of friends – he'd cried that night.

After all that, here he was looking at her profile and realising how little it told him about her.

Ovidia's profile belonged to someone who didn't bother with security settings, because she posted nothing that required privacy. It was generally impersonal with sporadic bursts of conversation and the very occasional picture.

Of the few posts on it, most were about running: articles, profiles, advice, ultramarathon pages. Ovidia had also shared a few articles on engineering and finance, perhaps two over the past year. She'd taken a trip to Iceland and posted a picture of Icelandic horses. Someone tagged her in 'Gloria's Wedding!' – where she posed beside her sister and a group of smiling black women. In that picture, Ovidia looked as he'd once known her, her hair longer, straightened to her shoulders, parted in the middle and curled into a bob. Her face was fuller, and Jasper could see her legs, slender yet soft, demurely crossed. He stopped at it for a moment, taking in her face.

Jasper scrolled through her history, occasionally looking up to assess the conversation that continued around him. He found a link for an accolade in a newspaper – 'Forty Black Britons Under Forty Making Waves in Science' – explaining that she had taken up marathon running and had been on a team that engineered some new construction technology that would cut the cost of constructing public housing.

Jasper scrolled back even further.

There, posted on her page, by an Edmund Edward, just over four years previously, a video – 'Yoshimi Battles the Pink Robots'. Twenty likes.

'From the vaults,' Gloria commented. One like.

'Didn't take you for a Flaming Lips fan?' Ovidia commented. One like.

'Not quite your type of music,' Josh said, whose profile picture was of Noel Gallagher in profile. Two likes.

'What kind of nonsense is this?' her sister Doris commented. Five likes.

'I'm not,' Edmund Edward replied to Ovidia's question.

'I used to think this was soooo cool! <3,' Leandra said. Four likes.

'Am I the only person who thinks this is crap?' Jeanette said. Eight likes.

'I didn't say you were pink, did I?' Ovidia said.

'You don't remember?' Edmund Edward replied.

'My best friend at uni had a tattoo of a pink robot. She's been trying to get rid of it for years,' Jade said.

'Friends?' Edmund Edward said. One like from Ovidia.

'There's this group 'The Banging' sounds just like Flaming L. Wanna go this weekend?' Josh asked.

'No,' Ovidia said. Eleven likes.

'Have I missed the punchline?' Gloria said. Eight likes.

The conversation ended. Perhaps the other participants realised they too had missed the punchline.

It was the only conversation between them.

Looking up briefly, Jasper smiled at Holly. 'You've got 139 likes,' he said, trying to be discreet as he tapped Edmund Edward's profile picture and was directed to his profile.

Had it not been for the conversation with Ovidia, there would have been no reason to think it was his Edmund's page. Not one of the hundreds of photos gave a clue as to their taker. Not one of the names was familiar; his friends, the books he read, the personalities he quoted.

Some of the posts referred to another person. *'SHE's taking photos of bricks again,'* he said in Hong Kong, and *'Left carrying the bags at yet another race.'* Nowhere was Ovidia tagged or anything shared with her. Abuja, Shanghai, New York. There were photographs of a village in the South of France – a place Edmund may have mentioned – and other destinations such as Cape Town and Moscow.

The pages Edmund liked belonged to tailors and designers – showing male models impeccably dressed. Jasper recognised some of the brands Edmund wore, exclusive, bespoke tailors that were listed in top magazines.

None of these were strange for a financier, Jasper thought – pausing and muttering a few sentences in reply to a question from John – but for a man who'd never considered himself cool or trendy or had shown any aspiration to be so, this was unlike Edmund. However, if this Edmund Edward was Edmund, then Edmund had been lying to him not just about Ovidia, but about his life.

The last woman he'd met his brother with had been at least a decade ago. She'd been slender, with brown hair that cascaded past her shoulders, and wore pale linen pants and a sleeveless white top and delicate, discreet jewellery. Edmund had said that she always dressed like that. That was the kind of woman he associated with Edmund.

Jasper looked up. But this too was Edmund, talking to his guests in a dirty dressing gown and slippers beside a woman with a partly shaven head, bouffant slippers, and a top with a shade of orange that could be used as a safety beacon.

The dressing gown Edmund wore, when Jasper looked carefully, bore a quality-brand name discreetly etched into the lapel. Scrutinising his brother harder, he realised that there was nothing innately outmoded about the gown, and the pyjamas, if worn by a chiselled featured model in a magazine, would appeal to many young and fashionable men.

Jasper stuffed his phone back in his pocket and looked at the woman beside Edmund, the one who kept him here, rooted to this garden sofa unable to leave. He wanted to seize Holly by the hand, stand, and declare that the charade was over, that Edmund's joke had gone too far, and leave. But he couldn't.

The doorbell rang.

'Is that the time? That must be the pizza,' Ovidia said. Jasper watched her leave, going to answer the door, the sound of her slippers padding along still seemed ridiculous.

He'd had enough.

Jasper gave her a moment, then making sure to pre-empt anyone else, he said, 'I'll go help.'

He sped after her, looking back only briefly at Holly who remained sitting in the middle of the sofa, a space on either side. Holly looked perplexed but then slid to her left to fill the space nearest Edmund, the space that been empty since they arrived.

Jasper arrived in the kitchen as a stocky, acne-riddled delivery man unloaded six boxes of pizza onto the kitchen peninsula. Jasper waited silently as the man hitched up his trousers and left. He hesitated a little longer as Ovidia attended to the boxes, opening them and checking against their labels and frowning at their contents as if displeased.

Ovidia seemed unsteady, repeating her actions, rubbing her hands together, dropping things. Jasper had never seen her that uncertain or confused.

She was spending too long reading the labels and staring at the food. Jasper was sure she knew he was behind her, but she did not turn to him. Watching her, he finally allowed the memory of the last time he saw her replay itself in his head.

He shut his eyes as he saw that evening in brief and violent eruptions of memories. He heard a raised voice – hers. He recalled a jolt of fire striking his face again and again. His legs had crumpled beneath him and he'd dropped to the floor. He could see her face from where he had fallen, cowering on the carpet of the flat they'd shared, her fists landing on his face, her knee in his stomach. She'd hurled words at him, hissed and poisonous, their syllables stabbing like a knife. The beige carpet had softened his fall, but his head smacked against the oak shelves that held their books, music, TV, little trinkets collected on weekend trips, and pictures of them in each other's arms. His head throbbed with the impact.

Daring to open his eyes and watch her five years later, he thought of the time when it felt as if he lived on the floor, dodging blows that seemed never-ending. Ovidia's voice, when she was angry, was harsh – like a long-time drinker. At times, she'd raised her voice – but rarely, mostly her words came out in a cruel whisper, or in an abrupt change of tone.

That evening had been different – volatile. Then finally, Ovidia had screamed at Jasper, standing above him, before launching herself at him, hitting and slapping his face, something she'd never done before. How many mornings had he examined his belly, small round blue and black bruises formed on his skin, tiny lacerations formed where one of her rings slashed his skin?

She'd called him stupid. Whatever had upset her, he couldn't recall. In fact, he was sure he'd never really known. He'd apologised repeatedly, though he couldn't imagine what he'd done wrong – again. He was always so careful, so certain that he couldn't have done anything to hurt her.

'Ovidia, please, you're hurting me.' Crying, Jasper had raised his hands to protect his face, leaving the rest of him defenceless.

The blows had stopped, there and then. She'd sprung back and stood for a moment, looking down at him, the insanity in her eyes extinguished. She turned in a frenzy, bumping into their blue sofa as she escaped, seizing her bag from the table and running out into the night. The door slammed, and its locks clanged behind her.

'Ovidia!' he'd called, stumbling to the window when he realised that she was fleeing. Those moments he took to find his feet were enough for her to get away. He watched from the window of their flat as she ran and ran until his view of her was blocked by trees and lampposts.

Jasper didn't chase her. He couldn't. It wasn't that his lip was cut and his face burned in pain. It wasn't because someone would notice. Something stopped him. An unseen force. Perhaps an epiphany, a guardian angel that finally held him back just long enough to let her go.

Just long enough.

But once he realised she was gone, Jasper spiralled into a panic, terrified. She was going, leaving. He grabbed the door handle but had no idea what route she'd have taken. He couldn't imagine where she'd go.

He rang her mobile number over and over. Hour after hour, he paced the little flat, her phone ringing unanswered. Finally, after midnight, a groggy female voice answered. It wasn't her.

'Hi, Jasper. Ovidia says not to call her.'

He couldn't recognise the voice. 'Where is she? I need to talk to her,' he asked, restraining himself, wanting to scream at this stranger.

'Look, she says she needs to get away from you, and that she's getting a new number in the morning,' the sleepy voice replied.

'Please, I…'

'Hey, you arsehole, God knows what you've been doing to her, but no more!' She fired the accusation at him.

He choked back a response and ended the call. He looked at Ovidia's number and the profile picture that lingered with a mounting sense of fear.

When he tried again in the morning, after a night spent tossing and turning, the number had gone offline. None of her friends would tell him where she was, and even their mutual friends seemed unwilling to help – most of them were as surprised at her disappearance as he.

Finally, he'd trudged to her family's house, a head sock pulled low on his head and his collar raised high to hide his bruises. He'd stood outside their terraced house where, only a few weeks earlier, he'd met her family at Ovidia's suggestion. He'd felt proud to finally be introduced.

Standing outside their house, where her mother had fed him a selection of cake and her father plied him with wine, he'd realised he could find Ovidia if he really tried. He could wait outside her office, hire a private detective, harangue her and her friends on social media. He could find her, and he'd beg at her feet, he'd make any and every promise he needed to convince her to return to him. But what if she did take him back?

Her parents' front door opened, and he fled. He turned away and ran down the street.

'Ovidia.' He returned to the present.

She turned to him, still preoccupied.

'What's going on here?' Jasper asked, quietly. 'What is all this, you and Edmund, this place?' He gestured at the house, the kitchen, looking up at the ceiling.

'Do you want me to tell you that you're dreaming?' Ovidia shrugged and turned back to the peninsula and looked about, as if she'd been in the middle of something but was unable to remember what it had been. He watched her examine her hands for a moment, turning them over once and then tucking them in her pockets.

'Well, I must be. Because there is no logical explanation for you being here,' he replied.

'What am I supposed to say?' She leaned forward – away from him – and gripped the counter, emphasising her shoulders, hard and muscular, so unlike what he remembered.

'You're not scared I'll say something to Edmund?' he asked. It was his only leverage, though he wouldn't use it, of course.

What could he say to Edmund? Sometimes, Jasper's time with her seemed as if it had been a nightmare from which he'd long ago woken, the details seeming nebulous, almost other-worldly. Other times he felt as if their relationship had been only yesterday, everything about it clear and tangible. In the middle of some nights, he'd wake in terror to see her sleeping peacefully beside him, only to realise a moment later that it was Holly.

Even if he told Edmund about the violence, what would he say? Would Edmund believe him? What proof could he offer Edmund of the nature of his and Ovidia's relationship? What Ovidia had done to him? The scars had faded and bruises healed, he'd moved house and jobs, he'd repaired himself and found a new love and was about to marry.

'About?' Ovidia asked.

'About?' he repeated. About their love, he thought. About the two years of his life that he spent devoted to her.

She couldn't tell him it had all been his imagination. When he let himself, he remembered everything beginning with the first night they met.

He'd been invited out by friends. Ovidia had arrived late, appearing first to be dressed entirely in black. After waving to their party, she'd sat down and unbuttoned her sweater to reveal a vintage 1970s polyester blouson in lurid pink and orange. Jasper had hiccoughed with laughter at the sight of it. In that single act – the sweater unbuttoned – he was hers. He'd become giddy; he'd felt himself grow warm as he stared at her. He'd watched her kiss their mutual friends on the cheek.

'You're late,' Heath had said, tugging at her top. 'Now this is bright, even for you.'

'It's crease proof. Pure polyester,' she had replied, as if that was enough justification for her choice of colour.

Now a party of six, they had sat around a table made for four. It had been the only way they could get a table in the tiny but immensely popular new restaurant.

'Could you move over a little,' Ovidia had said to Jasper, glancing at him.

Jasper's date was named Claire. And he hadn't seen her since. She'd had a dark pixie cut, but he remembered very little else about her. He'd pressed a bit closer to Ovidia, unintentionally – but she seemed oblivious to him – while Claire asked about his work. Jasper could hear snatches of Ovidia's conversation but not all. Ovidia had said something about a man trying to grab her as she'd left her office, which elicited gasps from her audience.

'Last week?' Gemma had said. 'Oh, I haven't seen you since. You could have called.'

Pressed against Ovidia, Jasper couldn't study her without seeming overfamiliar. From the corner of his eye, he could see that she talked with her hands in her lap, that traces of make-up emphasised her eyes and lips.

'Oh God! But what's that got to do with today?' Heath had asked.

'So the police came around to my office this afternoon saying they were following up on my report. From what I could wrestle out of them, the same guy raped and nearly killed a woman in the next building,' Ovidia had explained.

Jasper and Claire had joined the chorus of horror, and Jasper took the opportunity to join the others in conversation.

Ovidia had shrugged. Then she had looked, but only for a moment, as if she was about to cry.

'Where's the bloody waiter?' Gemma had demanded, swivelling in her seat as best as she could.

Heath had taken Ovidia's hand. 'But you're okay, hun? He didn't... do anything to you?'

'No.' Ovidia had taken deep breaths. 'A couple of bruises, but nothing serious. I'm just so mad. If the police had listened to me...'

'The bastards,' Gemma had breathed.

'But, of course, black woman makes a complaint about an assault – minor assault – of course no one's interested.'

'Oh Ovidia, that's not true...' Claire had said, indignant. 'The police don't take any woman seriously. It's not race that's the issue.'

The others had glared at her.

'I just really want to hit someone.' Ovidia had been agitated but didn't cry. 'The police, the idiot himself. I've lived in this city all my life. I've worked at that office for years. How do I just go about my business? How do I return to normal life? I'm scared all the time now.'

Heath had hugged her, being the only person, apart from Jasper, who could reach her. 'Sorry, I've nothing constructive to say, so I'll just cuddle and pay for drinks.'

'Free drinks!' Ovidia had tried to joke. 'I should get nearly murdered more often.'

'Good girl,' Gemma had said. 'It's over now.'

The physical sensation of being seated against her had been surprisingly unnerving. He'd felt her every move, and when she'd extricated herself from their confined seating arrangement to go to the ladies, she'd momentarily lost her balance and seized his shoulder to stop herself from falling.

The extra space had afforded them a chance to relax, but he'd felt exposed, wanting her back against him.

'Try to be a little less obvious.' Gemma had leaned towards him. 'Your date looks as if she's about to storm out, and' – she'd looked around – 'you look like you wouldn't give chase.'

Jasper had realised he'd been keeping turned away from Claire as his attention had been focused on Ovidia since she'd described the attack. He'd grimaced. 'I have no defence,' he'd whispered back. 'I feel like a bit of an arse. Claire must be having an awful evening.' He'd given a last furtive whisper as Ovidia returned. 'I can't help it.' And the two of them had moved apart.

When they'd finished their meal and were standing outside the restaurant talking about what to do next, Jasper had immediately gone to her. Bold, as he was those days, unafraid.

'It must have been absolutely terrifying,' he had said. 'I might sound patronising, but you did pretty well coming out tonight. Much braver than I would be.'

She'd squinted at him, as if trying to place him, considering his finer details. 'Really? What would you do in my situation?'

He'd thought for a moment, pushing his hands into his pocket. 'Hide. Go round to my mum and dad's? Anywhere but to meet a bunch of people in a restaurant down a dark alley.'

He'd seen a flicker of a smile. Standing, she'd still had to look up at him even in her heels.

'There are far more dangerous places than London, and people don't lock themselves up in their homes.'

Her eyes had been bright. He'd thought with excitement rather than alcohol. He'd opened his mouth to invite her out.

'Guys, pub!' Gemma had called. 'There's a brilliant one down here, was in a mag last week.'

'Do we have to hang out the windows like last time?' Ovidia had turned to follow her.

Heath had elbowed him. 'You haven't even got rid of Claire and you're lining up the next one? I wish I had your confidence.'

'Where on earth did you find her? She's amazing.' The two of them had started after the others.

'That vintage shop my sister runs. She had a friends and family sale. Believe it or not, Ovidia's a regular.'

'She's electric,' Jasper had said. 'Is she with anyone?'

'Not that I know of. She's been single for a while.'

'Give me her number.'

'Ask her yourself,' Heath had replied.

'She's just found out that she could have been raped and murdered – I'll give her a day or two.'

This was a night out in London. This is why they lived here, enduring maddening delays on the trains, endless waits for buses, flipping through pages reading the latest horrible knife crime. This summer night full of people out enjoying themselves, friends guffawing in laughter, lovers in embrace.

In the pub, Gemma had waved her glass dangerously close to his white T-shirt, a nonsensical logo splashed across it designed by a London graphic designer. 'Has he told you that his brother's loaded and buys absolutely everything for him?' She had been addressing Claire, but Ovidia was right next to her.

For the first time, Jasper was embarrassed about Edmund's generosity. He hadn't wanted Ovidia to think him a wastrel living off others. 'He doesn't. He's just offered to cover my deposit.' He'd glared at Gemma, who made a playful face.

'Great brother,' Ovidia had replied. 'Can I have him? My sister's moved back in with our parents while she's saving. I'd rather die than move back in with my parents.'

'I'd move in with your parents in an instant – I adore them.' Gemma had squeezed her.

Ovidia had smiled. He had been pleased she approved.

Jasper had waited until the next morning, and then, unable to contain himself any longer, he'd called her.

He rarely allowed himself to think of the bliss of those first few months. When he tried, a sense of foreboding, a terror, dread, would rise in him, because he knew the future. He knew how her girlish whispers upon crawling in between their newly purchased sheets had become the whispered cursing, the accusations and rants that she unleashed as they stood apart, facing the bed that he dreaded getting into each night. He knew the playful slap on his bare arm as she swatted at a mosquito in Mersing as they overlooked the ocean had become a punch, the first time in his life that he'd been hit outside of a school playground.

Even when he did allow himself to think about it, clenching his fists in anticipation of the blows, he could never really remember when it first started.

But he supposed it began with words.

'You've got no idea, have you?' she'd said one Friday evening as the clock ticked towards midnight. She had spent hours calculating and recalculating what, to him, appeared to be gibberish. She'd said there was an error in her proposal and her deadline was that Monday.

He'd asked about a bank-holiday trip they had planned.

'It's not as if I just play about with pictures,' she'd said, of his work.

She'd said previously how cool it would be to be artistically inclined like he was, how exciting his office and the people that he got to work with were. He'd blushed at her praise – but later, when she'd left him, he imagined she'd been grooming him for disaster, lifting him on to a pedestal so that the fall was farther, harder, and would hurt much more.

He'd shaken his head at her comment, saying to himself that she was under pressure. A lot of money had been invested in her proposal. Her future as a civil engineer would be elevated and she would move up the professional ladder.

He recalled another time. The two of them were returning from his parents' house. Ovidia was driving.

'They're racist,' she'd said, speeding up as a light turned green and a row of new builds dissolved into bland, outdated apartments on one side and old terraces on the other.

'Who are?' Jasper had said

'Your parents, who else?'

She'd said it as if it were a matter of fact, something that was not up for discussion.

He'd jerked up, suddenly alert, annoyed on her behalf. 'What? Did they do something? What did they say?' Incredulous. His parents.

'Don't pretend you didn't see it. The way they looked at me. The silly questions they asked. Your dad had the balls to ask me where I got my degree.'

'He asks anyone I date that.' Jasper had settled back down into the seat. 'He's sizing you up, picking up the best bits to show off about at his book club: *"My daughter-in-law is prettier and smarter than yours."*'

She'd shaken her head. 'You're determined to believe I'm stupid.'

They'd slowed for roadworks and had come to a halt, waiting for the light to change. In the near darkness, he'd watched her hands resting on the steering wheel. He remembered she'd had her nails and hair done in anticipation of that evening. Her fingers had flexed and straightened, flexed and straightened. The lights had changed and she'd sworn quietly as she sped up. They'd sat in silence as they completed their journey home.

When she'd hit him that night, there had been no apologies, no promises. In bed, he'd contemplated what had happened and told himself it would never happen again.

'About... us,' Jasper hesitated, the smell of pizza making his stomach lurch.

'Please let's not talk about this. I don't think I can.' She wrapped her arms around herself. 'Not today.' She looked back at the pizza boxes.

'What about Edmund?' Jasper insisted. 'He has the right to know about us.'

'Edmund?' she asked, breathing in, still not looking at him. 'He knows all about us.'

'What do you mean "he knows"?'

'He found out while I was still with you. That's how we really met.' Ovidia stroked the counter. 'Edmund turned up on my doorstep and told me I had to leave you alone, or he'd make sure I left you alone,' she explained, her eyes nearly closed as she outlined the story of how she met Edmund. 'I don't think I believed him. But something in me clicked. I think.'

Jasper balled and unfurled his fists.

'He'd figured out what I was doing to you. I guess he saw the state you were in and put two and two together. I threatened to call the police. He just turned away and repeated that I should leave you alone.'

'He knew all that time!' Jasper repeated. His disbelief began to turn to anger.

'I'm glad he did. I might not have left you if he hadn't done something. He saved you from me.'

They were both silent.

'I wanted to find you, call you or something, but...' She shook her head. 'I had no idea where to start. I'm not being callous... sorry.'

There was a silence.

Jasper turned to leave, to return to the annex, to return to Holly.

'That night, later, I saw that I'd become a monster,' Ovidia continued.

The distant, nervous stranger reappeared in front of him. 'So many times, I've been dressed, ready to come and find you, but what was I going to say? I've never understood what happened. I've always been normal – I don't even know people like that... like me. When I left you, I tried all sorts of things, therapy, books. There was just nothing for women like I was.' She stopped for air. 'Then I found running and... I bought a flat. It was hard, but I had to remember the person I had been. I thought, *when I find the words, I'll go and explain it to him – apologise.* But I've never found them. Then I met – again – Edmund. And I started to believe that I could be a decent human being again.'

'And you've had an affair with him for four years?' Jasper asked.

Ovidia paused for a moment. 'It's not an affair. We, well, I just couldn't find a way to tell you. I know you don't want to hear it, but I've been happy.'

He snorted. 'What about me?'

'Knowing that you had to find out was the one thing that kept me from being completely happy.' She sighed. He saw her clutch the counter. 'Maybe we could talk another time, I can't...' she stopped.

For a moment, something about her distress made him glad, but the feeling didn't last. Her remorse was insufficient, but there was nothing else he could hope or ask for. He waited, but she stood with her eyes closed once again, this time tightly shut, as if she was blocking tears from running.

'You never came back, not even to even find out what I did with your stuff?' he asked quietly. Jasper had broken a lot of it and shredded her clothes with a sharp pair of scissors. He'd swept her books off the shelves onto the floor and pulled up her rugs. Anything that survived the first month of his rage and unhappiness, he'd carted off to a recycling centre in a rented van.

'There was nothing there I wanted, even if it was everything I owned. I needed a clean break from you and, well, Edmund did threaten me if...' she stopped.

23

What if I'm wrong? Edmund had questioned himself over and over before making his decision.

What if he was right, and did nothing?

The previous night Edmund had finally confirmed what he'd suspected for months. There, just beneath Jasper's collar, the browns and blues of new and old bruising.

Edmund had long ago stopped asking about Ovidia, but Jasper had kept on telling him about her. What he said about her had changed though. Now he stated facts: 'Ovidia got a promotion,' 'Ovidia bought a new rug,' 'Ovidia says I should try a different line of work.'

Ovidia was no longer 'perfect', 'amazing', or 'the one I want to be with for the rest of my life'. The spark in Jasper's eye when he talked about her had died. It was obvious he was not happy, though he insisted he was.

Now there was an emptiness, a lack of expression in his tired gaze. Edmund had asked him time and again what was wrong.

'Nothing.' Jasper had brushed him off the evening before, as the two of them had an early dinner. Jasper had been eating a grilled steak that he said he didn't think much of, especially not at that price. Yet when the waiter had arrived, Jasper said nothing, being almost apologetic when Edmund prompted him to complain.

Edmund had sat wondering what he was supposed to say or do about the situation. His brother had changed – unable to protest to a waiter about overcooked meat, his eyes flitting across the room from person to person as he chewed. Jasper had given up his flat and was living with Ovidia. From what Jasper had told, all his own belongings were in storage. He'd taken only his clothes and the things he needed at hand with him. His explanation had been that it was until they could get a place that was truly shared, which was taking time. He'd rejected Edmund's offer of financial assistance, saying that Ovidia was an engineer; they didn't need Edmund's money.

'He's a bit nervous about things,' their mother had said in some sort of agreement. 'And he didn't come for my birthday – he said Ovidia had something important on at work.'

But she'd brushed off her concerns. 'He's in love. He just wants to keep her happy. Boys change when they find love.' She'd sighed and Edmund could see that she wasn't satisfied with her own explanation. 'I thought I liked Ovidia when she came around to see us the first time. Now I'm not so sure. We've seen her twice since then, and one of those times was just for a few minutes.' His mother had paused. 'Jasper thinks the world of her, and I'm not sure that's a good thing.' Then she'd gone to refill the kettle, the conversation seemingly over. 'He as much as accused me of being racist.' She'd slammed the kettle onto the counter.

'What was so important that you couldn't come for Mummy's birthday?' Edmund had asked Jasper at dinner.

'Ovidia had something on with work,' Jasper had said. 'You didn't go either.'

'I was in Japan.'

'You can go to Japan any old time.'

'It was for work.'

'So your work is more important than Ovidia's?'

'I didn't say that.'

'You didn't have to.'

Edmund had backed down, not wanting to get into an argument. It had seemed any disagreement with Jasper quickly became volatile. He could go from a calm discussion to leaping to his feet and marching away, sometimes only as far as the men's room before he returned. It had been clear that Edmund wouldn't be able to convince his brother to leave Ovidia. What reason would he give him? *I think she's physically violent towards you.*

He'd spent some time reading about violence in relationships. It was a subject he had no experience with, at least not with men being the victims. He'd corroborated what he saw in Jasper with what had been documented – which surprisingly wasn't much. Most of the information available had been about men hitting women – not the other way around. One point that kept arising was that men and women usually had to decide for themselves to leave with phrases like 'hit rock bottom' and 'I was sure he was going to kill me'.

But Edmund wasn't going to let that happen. Now that he was, almost, sure of what was happening, he was going to help his brother.

A woman had slapped him once. Edmund had recalled the weak, ineffectual blow. He'd felt no pain, but he had been surprised. Even at the schools he'd gone to, fighting and violence had been reserved for a certain group of boys, brawling types whose playground punch-ups were immediately reported to a teacher by fleet-footed onlookers.

That had signalled the end of their relationship.

But, standing in front of the address he'd been given, Edmund had hesitated. Maybe the fault had been his own. Had he been too busy with his own life? Perhaps if he'd paid more attention to Jasper's relationship, visited, and made an effort to meet and get to know Ovidia, he would have seen it sooner?

His plan had been to meet her and talk to her. He would either verify his suspicion or know that he had to look for another cause for the bruising around Jasper's neck. Unlike at work, where he knew what to say and do, that day he'd felt completely unequipped for his mission.

He'd knocked on the door, hoping she was there so it could all be cleared up right away.

The door had opened and Ovidia emerged. He'd guessed it was Ovidia. She had been smaller than he'd expected. He'd only had his parents' and Jasper's descriptions of her and some professionally taken photographs on the internet that gave him little idea of the scale of her.

He'd expected someone bigger, someone capable of frightening a fully grown man.

In one hand she'd held a mobile, and he'd got the impression he'd disturbed her.

'Hi,' she'd said politely. 'Are you looking for someone?'

'Yes. I'm looking for Ovidia,' he'd replied, pulling himself up to his full stature, though he was already towering over her.

'That's me,' she'd said, her tone still friendly.

'I'm…'

'Jasper's brother, right – Edmund?' She'd held out her hand and smiled. 'You look just like him.'

'Or the other way around, perhaps.' He'd shaken her outstretched hand and smiled back. Her friendliness had been an unexpected setback.

'He's not here, but…'

'Leave him alone.' The words had flung from his mouth with more force than intended. As he'd let go of her hand, he'd seen that her right hand was bruised along her knuckles and the flat of her fingers. He knew little of violence, but he'd dated a woman for a while who'd taken martial arts classes and was constantly unable to form a proper fist, walking around week after week with bruised knuckles until she gave it up.

Ovidia had backed away. She'd tried to close the door between them, but he'd easily stopped her.

'Leave him,' he'd repeated, this time less violently. 'Or I'm going to get the police involved.'

'What the hell are you talking about?' She'd pushed the door harder against him, but he'd forced it back open. She could have screamed for help – it was a ground floor flat with neighbours on every side – but she hadn't.

Once inside, he'd marched through the small flat. Though the phone had been in her hands, she didn't call the police.

He was right, he'd concluded. He'd walked through the room from the front door, taking in the pictures on the wall, the blue sofa and its scattering of colourful cushions. He couldn't recognise a single item as Jasper's, except for the laptop on the kitchen table and clothes in a pile in a corner. Pictures of her family had sat in frames, books on engineering and math and popular women's literature and the standard classics had stood on shelves. Jasper had owned a larger and newer TV and an expansive leather sofa that was of some value. Both items were far superior to the ones in this room. His framed posters had been nowhere to be seen, nor was the family photo that Jasper had had professionally framed. His books about art and design that were normally in piles in corners had been missing. Jasper wasn't living in this flat, Edmund had thought. He was imprisoned here, being let out occasionally to play a charade at lunch and dinner with his brother and family.

'What have you been doing to him?' How long had he been complicit in his brother's misery by brushing away the signs and not paying enough attention? How long had Jasper needed him to intervene? 'You hit him, didn't you?'

'Right. I'm calling the police.' Though she'd sounded decisive, Ovidia still hadn't dialled, the mobile forgotten in her hand. She'd been in front of the door, facing him with a defiant stance, her feet slightly apart and arms crossed.

He'd got to the end of the room and turned back to her.

'Jasper's my only brother.'

She had begun to speak, but he'd cut her off.

'I'll do anything to keep him safe...' He'd nodded a goodbye.

He'd never in his life made a threat of physical harm to anyone. But his words had been spontaneous, barely disguising the rage inside him. The idea of his brother living in terror for all that time without being able to come to him for help had incensed him. Without regret, he'd strode back through the front door and slammed it shut as he left.

24

'Edmund threatened you?' Holly shrieked, a few feet ahead of Anne.

Ovidia was startled, not having heard them enter. How much had they heard? Holly looked cheerful, buoyed by the wine that, though being drunk slowly, was having an effect. Anne looked pensive. Ovidia guessed she must have heard something significant enough to have to think over.

Edmund had never apologised for threatening her. He'd never, even as they had settled into their lives, retracted what he said or told her that he never really meant it. She'd never asked him if he would have gone through with it, neither did she worry that he ever would. It was one of those obstacles that they seemed to agree to let lie – history that cannot be changed.

'Returning to the theme of invading aliens,' Ovidia said with a sudden and bright smile that she hoped concealed the conversation that had just transpired. She'd stopped drinking earlier, holding on to the same half-full glass. She wished she'd had more: enough to get drunk, enough to forget. She glanced at the clock on the microwave and hoped for a moment it had stopped. The numbers moved forward by a minute. It hadn't. It was only past one.

Holly laughed, tinkling like a bell, honestly, happily. 'I'll believe that. Right now – Edmund says – he's not saying it's women's work, but he did open the champagne, so can we get dishes and things. We're having lunch out in the extension – your cubey thing is just *made* for spring days.'

Holly's laughter helped. Or it could have been that Ovidia had finally spoken to Jasper? She'd been dreading that encounter since he'd tapped her shoulder that morning. She'd imagined what they'd say to each other if alone, how much longer they could continue the charade outdoors. She'd tried to explain, but her words seemed inadequate. She wanted to tell him how much she'd gone through, but she didn't want it to be about her. She'd hurt Jasper, over and over, again and again. And she knew it hadn't stopped when she had run away.

She'd never forgotten what she'd done. Over the years, Jasper had become something she accepted would never leave her. Edmund told her about him on rare occasions and always briefly. He had only told her about Jasper's new relationship when Holly had moved in with Jasper. Occasionally, a friend would mention that they'd spotted him at an event or walking down the street. But, despite being in the same city, she hadn't seen him even once. London was an enormous place filled with millions of people; their professions and families were unconnected. Had it not been for Edmund, they might never have seen each other again.

She heard Jasper breathing heavily, his chest rising and falling beneath his shirt. It seemed unfair that on the first day of his engagement he should find himself faced with her. It wasn't a situation she'd imagined – Jasper walking into her kitchen. She was sure he hated her, that was, if he felt anything for her at all.

She'd often wondered if he was safe now. Did this new woman, with her tresses and girlish laughter, ever hurt him like she had?

Some days, thoughts of Jasper were as brief as a flash of light, other days it was a weight that she carried for hours. She carried the guilt for what she'd done with her not as a word or a single thought. It was integral to who she was now, so thoroughly enmeshed in her life that she knew it was something of which she could never divest herself. She couldn't say at any moment, *I feel guilty for what I did*. Instead, her constant regret was formless, intangible. The feeling lurked within her; it did not announce itself and then berate her for what she did, but it drifted in as a cloud in a sunny sky, a smudge on her laptop screen, a kiss from Edmund that was briefer than she wanted it to be. Then she'd be reminded of how she'd tortured a man who had done nothing to deserve it.

She wondered if her remorse had anything to do with her feelings for Edmund. She'd weighed the question, analysed it, watched the man she loved with an intense gaze, but how would she know even if there was a connection? She could never be the person she was before Jasper, and, no matter how much she wished, she could not erase time.

She wanted to run out to Edmund and bury herself against him. There she would feel safe from herself.

'Not to pry' – Holly came to a stop in front of the cutlery drawers – 'but what's the pile of woody stuff in the corner of the garden?'

'It was one of these garden rooms,' Ovidia said without hesitating. She was battling to appear normal. She reminded herself that Holly and Anne didn't know. If they did, they would not be here. 'That corner looked so, erm, disused, and we didn't want to add any more greenery, so we thought of a garden retreat.'

'And it lost its life due to…?' Anne asked.

'We never used it. We'd made all sorts of plans for it, but we won't need it now.' Her eyes held Jasper's briefly and then she turned away. He was still standing where he'd been when their conversation ended. 'We should have sold it, but we couldn't get ourselves organised.'

'Couldn't get yourselves organised?' Holly hooted. 'I think you two were born organised – look at this cutlery drawer.' She marvelled at the perfectly arranged contents of the drawers.

'You said you're an engineer, didn't you?' Anne asked.

'Civil,' Jasper said, inadvertently alluding to their shared past, always adding 'civil' whenever anyone asked if she was an engineer.

'I *was*,' Ovidia corrected Anne. 'I did a few finance courses a couple of years ago and basically forgot about them. Then one day I saw an ad that needed engineering and finance, and shadowing and mentoring were provided, and suddenly – bang – I was a financial engineer. Really lovely office, and I never had to work outdoors again.'

She didn't say that she'd being trying to create a new life, fleeing the world she'd lived in with Jasper.

'You didn't need to start from scratch or do a new degree?' Anne asked.

'No,' she said, omitting that she'd had the job for less than a year.

'You make it sound so easy,' Anne said. 'Nobody said you're a woman or too old or too…?'

'Black?' Ovidia suggested. 'There is always someone telling you that you're too something. You have to choose who you listen to. I even got people telling me that I was too successful, that I made too much money…'

'Made too much money?' Holly screeched. 'Is that even possible?'

'You'd be surprised,' Ovidia said. 'People said things like, as a black woman I should be less selfish and more community orientated, or that I should be less assertive because it shows a bad example to young black girls…'

'No,' Holly gasped and clasped her hand over her mouth.

'I wasn't making that much money anyway.' Ovidia was glad that the women had joined them. She was sure Edmund had sent them in to intervene. He'd have been worried about her and Jasper alone together.

'You gave it up?' Anne must have noticed her use of the past tense.

Ovidia didn't answer. Instead, she pulled a large knife from a wooden knife block kept in one of the cabinets.

Anne continued. 'A couple of years ago, I started a design course. John put me off it – he says nursing is far more reliable. It is, but wouldn't it be nice to do something a bit more glamorous? I feel I'm creative, but I never have the opportunity to express it. Well, I have a design blog, but it's not very popular, and John doesn't know.'

'You have a blog? You didn't tell me about it.' Holly turned swiftly to Anne. 'You could make it into a side business. Just like John has his books and public speaking and stuff – that's not strictly related to his job.'

'Yes, but he says…'

'Screw what he says,' Ovidia replied, 'and if he doesn't like it, chuck him and get yourself a flashier model.' She felt a spark of excitement at talking with the two women, perhaps a momentary freedom from the choking feeling she'd had for most of the day.

Anne chuckled, but Holly winced, saying, 'Don't think like that. He'd be upset, but once he gets used to the idea, he'll come round. Luckily, Jasper and I have similar interests, and there's plenty of space to express our creativity in our lines of business.'

Ovidia glanced at Jasper again. He'd remained quiet, though he was watching the women. They were talking as if he wasn't there anymore, like women speak without their men. The three women passed cutlery and crockery and organised the meal as if they were living a generation ago when it would have been expected of them. It felt oddly natural. When she was a teenager at family get togethers, especially on her father's side of her family who still retained many of their Ghanaian norms, the girls always found themselves stuck doing the cooking, cleaning, and serving. As she'd grown older, she'd railed against the expectation that the women of the family would continue to act as the previous generations had done, but time had made her objection nearly irrelevant. As the children of her peers entered their early teens, boys found themselves stuck alongside their sisters serving their elders at parties.

'You know, this is really weird.' Holly was the first to articulate it. 'We could be sisters-in-law soon – common-law sisters-in-law, if there's such a thing. And Anne's always around at ours and Jasper's mum's. Imagine we could end up doing this quite a bit – if only you and Edmund come out of the closet.'

Anne chuckled. 'Out of the closet? They're not gay.'

'I mean leading a double life, hiding. It must be pretty lonely and scary even – wondering if someone will find out,' Holly elaborated.

'It's not like there're any real repercussions. Some people would be pretty upset, but I'm sure they'd get over it,' Anne said.

Ovidia wanted to tell them that the repercussions would not matter, because the relationship would be over before the end of the day. She wanted to say she and Edmund wouldn't be together to face the furore and confusion, that each of them would deal with the disapproval or questioning without the other to lean on.

Instead, she clung to Anne's and Holly's cheerfulness, knowing it would help her get through the afternoon.

'It's not like we're the only ones who do it,' Ovidia said. 'Anne has her secret life in design. But what about you Holly? You must have a secret, too?'

'Well, Jasper's sneaked out now, you may as well tell us,' Anne egged her on. Ovidia turned and realised Anne was right – Jasper was gone.

Holly looked around, hesitating. Then she blurted out, 'I have about thirty years' worth of *Archie* and *Sabrina* at my parents' house.'

Anne stared at her and then erupted in laughter. 'The comics?'

Holly looked embarrassed. 'My mother got me a subscription when I was about eight, and I just can't let it go. I read every one and keep them in storage boxes in the garage. I'm not quite sure how to tell Jasper. They're still delivered to my parents' address.'

'Why?' Anne asked.

'I don't know. I love Archie comics, I really do. When I was about eighteen, my mum tried to throw them away. I cried so hard, she had to fish them out of the bins and wipe them down.'

Ovidia wasn't laughing. The secret was silly, flippant, but she had hoped Holly would say no, that she could never think of keeping something from her husband-to-be. She'd hoped that Holly, unlike herself, would be beyond reproach, that Holly would be a woman she could trust with Jasper. She crossed her arms and, suppressing her emotion, said, 'I don't get it – you seem so normal.'

'Maybe I'm too normal,' Holly replied. 'I know it sounds old-fashioned, but I'm one of those women who has wanted to fall in love and get married almost all her life. But I haven't been willing to compromise about it. I've had relationships before, but, apart from Immanuel, Jasper is the first guy that I can say unequivocally that I want to spend the rest of my life with, and I've known that since pretty much the third time we met – we're inseparable.'

Ovidia bit her finger, her nerves taut. Had she ever been able to talk about Jasper like that, to say she wanted to spend the rest of her life with him? She must have, at least at first. They'd introduced the other to family and friends. Surely that was a sign that they had been in love? At some point, her love must have died, because people don't torment those they love.

'That's lovely to hear,' Anne said, taking her friend's hand, and Ovidia nodded.

25

Jasper was on the ground floor, having left without saying anything as the women talked among themselves. He stopped briefly and looked out over the cube, where he could see John and Edmund in a slow conversation. He looked around the room they'd entered the house through. A few books were neatly piled on a side table. Even they looked as if a designer had laid them there. The room was as if it had been organised for a public viewing. He couldn't imagine Ovidia living here – at least not as she once had been, with her floral prints, engineering texts, and boots muddied from visiting a construction site.

He climbed up another floor and exhaled in preparation, visualising opening one of the doors and finding Ovidia and Edmund's bedroom, the place where they'd make love and afterwards sleep with their arms wrapped around each other.

He steeled himself and pushed open the first door. He found what appeared to be a TV room. He could see that this was where their lives really took place. It was large, and in its centre was a long velveteen sofa in deep grey, with a scattering of cushions in bold bird and floral prints. To one side of the sofa were several women's magazines neatly arranged, unread, unopened in their plastic wrapping. On them were two wine glasses, dredges of red wine dried within them. In a magazine rack were copies of *The Economist* and *National Geographic*. Edmund had had subscriptions to both magazines since he was a teenager. On the wall was a large flat-screen TV. A single shelf extended along the width of the wall at his eye level, and on it were books that had really been read – their spines were bent and folded, and here and there a ripped piece of paper marked a place where its reader had abandoned the book. *Two Hundred Classic Cryptic Crosswords* had a pencil jammed within, its covers dog eared from Edmund's efforts.

Jasper could imagine Ovidia here, though someone had come in after and straightened her notebooks and tidied her cache of pencils into matching pale wood cups. Three giant photo prints of Icelandic ponies in motion, their manes flowing in the breeze, were mounted on the wall, each in tones of grey framed in the same pale wood. On the sofa was a throw, a simple hand-knitted pattern, amateur but neatly done. He remembered Ovidia saying that if she ever had more time she'd knit – but she'd always been too busy when they were together.

It seemed she'd found the time since she'd left him. Jasper stroked the throw with his fingers and visualised her bent over it, knitting, the needles clack-clacking, stopping every so often to see how much she'd done. He realised that in his mind, she still had shoulder-length hair, but it was gone – as were the reasons why she could not find enough time to knit.

Jasper sat down on the coffee table with his head in his hands and imagined Edmund beside her, holding the knitting magazine, pointing out where she'd gone wrong and helping her untangle the wool. He imagined them giggling like lovers so often do.

He and Ovidia had had wonderful times, too, especially in the beginning. They'd spent whole mornings in bed, escaping only to make a cup of tea and toast.

'I've met someone special,' he'd told Edmund when they'd met soon after at their parents' house. 'No, I'm not going into details now. I don't want to jinx it.'

'Jinx it! What are you twelve? Tell me or don't tell me.'

'She's beautiful, smart – a civil engineer. I know that doesn't make her sound particularly special, but I can't put how I feel into words. She does talk quite a bit, though.'

They'd both shrugged in good humour. 'You're used to it,' Edmund had said, referring to their mother.

'She's not like Mummy. She can talk about absolutely anything on earth, no matter how trivial or ridiculous, and make it sound intelligent.'

'I'm sure that's what Dad says about Mummy, too,' his brother had replied. 'Well, I can't wait to meet this woman. I'll bring my earplugs.' He'd patted Jasper affectionately on the shoulder and handed him another beer.

'You'd really like her. I know you would,' Jasper had replied, and Edmund had nodded.

Obviously, Edmund did like Ovidia. Edmund had also recognised that Ovidia was in fact beautiful and amazing and smart, and this house was theirs. Jasper slammed his fist against his thigh.

The last time Edmund had bought a flat, Jasper had been his first guest. They'd arrived at the building and, as they entered the lift, Edmund had thrown his jacket over his arm, while Jasper remained in his, drops of rain clinging to its fabric.

'Well, what do you think?' Edmund had asked, gesturing ahead of them as the lift doors opened.

Its front door had been open. A man had been polishing already immaculate wood floors with a large machine. He'd nodded at their entrance, not stopping to take the earbuds from his ears.

'Oh my god.' Jasper's line of sight had been immediately drawn to the view of the city and the river. 'This is really nice.'

Jasper had greeted the cleaner over the sound of the machine, though he'd barely looked at the man as he was already distracted by his opulent surroundings. Edmund had headed directly to the large glass windows that stretched across the expanse of the wall and stepped through onto a terrace.

'What was wrong with the last one?' Jasper had asked as he followed his brother, turning around twice to see as much of the sitting room as he could on his way. The finishing in the flat had been in dark greys and black, almost in contrast to the late-autumn blue sky that the flat had looked out upon. Penthouse, Jasper had corrected himself. 'Except that it was tiny by comparison.'

'Sold it,' Edmund had said, running his hands along the railing that encompassed the enormous balcony. Jasper had joined him outside, pulling his jacket around him.

'Really?' Jasper had replied 'I kind of liked it. This one's great, but I don't know, a little trendy maybe.'

'What's wrong with it being trendy?'

'Well, if you like it – nothing,' Jasper had replied off-handedly, turning back to the view and realising he could see a restaurant that he and Ovidia had recently been to and liked. 'It's not something I'd thought you'd choose.'

'Really?' Edmund had replied. Then he'd nodded. 'Good. I just wanted a second opinion. This one's a financial stretch. It'll be a good investment.'

'Another investment,' Jasper had said, childishly skipping a few steps across the balcony to test his nerve – they had been on the twelfth floor. He'd skipped back to Edmund and asked, 'When are you going to buy somewhere to live? You know, where you're not going to think about how much it'll be worth next year, and, I don't know, paint it yellow and install floor-to-ceiling pine panelling.'

They'd both laughed, recalling their childhood home, which had been built in the sixties and never substantially redecorated until both sons had moved out.

'God, it must have taken years to convince them to get rid of that panelling.' Jasper had leaned against the railing beside his brother. 'Dad seriously thought it would ruin the house price.'

'Probably doubled in value over night,' Edmund had said. 'Do you remember Mummy's face when she first saw the sitting room without the panelling? She looked devastated.'

'I would have put it back up, if I could.' Jasper had thought about how miserable she'd looked as they'd shown her the newly plastered and painted walls in a duck-egg blue, the pale yellow gone forever.

'I guess they'd been so proud of what was then a fashionable house that they didn't realise it had just become ridiculous,' Edmund had said. 'Well, not ridiculous…'

Jasper had thought he knew what Edmund had been trying to say, that they had underestimated how much the house's outdated décor had meant to the two who'd worked hard to buy and care for it.

'I asked them if they'd consider moving, but they seemed content with a new conservatory,' Edmund had said. 'Insisted that the house held too many memories to leave it to strangers.'

'Memories,' Jasper had scoffed. 'Of what? Projectile vomiting and loose teeth? It's not as if we had the most exciting family life.'

'I remember the first night you ever got drunk,' Edmund had said. 'I took you out, remember? Mummy had sat up waiting for us the whole night and, when we came home, she served you dinner at two in the morning.'

'I can't believe she sanctioned a night of illegal drinking. She'd never have let me out without you. Absolutely everyone else was going to that party.'

'And I had to spend a Saturday night with a bunch of fifteen-year-olds. At least if the party had been near a pub, I could have gone for a drink around the corner. But I knew she'd kill me if anything happened. I spent the party staring at the ceiling and avoiding the attentions of underage girls from your school.'

'Yeah, but you were quite discreet, I remember. No one knew I'd been chaperoned by my big brother.' They'd both laughed. 'Strange to think half of those teens now have kids and responsible jobs, houses and things.'

'Well, you could have all that soon,' Edmund had said, he'd winked and crossed the balcony and stood at the large windows. 'One-way glass,' he'd said. 'No one can see in. I can have my privacy while watching the rest of the world.'

'And that's your plan?' Jasper had asked. He'd known he was repeating the question, but his brother had been, as usual, making plans that never seemed to involve, or leave room for, another person.

His own relationship with Ovidia had been solid. Their evenings had been spent together, or if they were apart it would only be for a short while. Something about Edmund sitting watching the world from his penthouse had struck him as incredibly lonely.

'Well, I need furniture first.' Edmund had tapped the glass. Jasper could see he was dismissing the question.

'It sounds as if you're not even looking.'

'I'm not,' Edmund had shrugged.

'You don't see yourself with a pine-panelled yellow living room of your own? Kids...'

'Kids...' Edmund had given a comic imitation of shock.

'You and Ovidia are at the thinking-about-kids stage?'

'Not yet. But we are moving in together properly soon. And yeah, we talk about things like that. It's not on the cards immediately, but' – he'd nodded, his heart swelling in happiness at the idea – 'I see kids in our future.'

The cleaner had leaned in and waved once, indicating that he was going. They'd both nodded in response, and Edmund had thanked him.

'Remember, my offer's still open for your deposit.'

'We talked about it, but Ovidia's keen to do it on her own. She moved a few times when she was young. I think her family had a few financial hiccoughs. I guess that's why she's pretty much obsessed with buying a flat. But then, you're obsessed with property, but you're just making money.'

Jasper had darted from the room, realising that he hadn't seen the whole flat. While it was majestic, it didn't mean anything, he'd thought. It was just an investment. That realisation had dampened his enthusiasm for it. The polished wood floors had continued into two large bedrooms, each large and empty, the fixtures gleaming, unused and unspoilt. Each bedroom had pale, contemporary marble tiling and windows that were operated with a switch. The master bedroom had been enormous. In the middle of its floor had been a large bed, also new. A kilim rug at the foot of the bed had lent some colour. Several suitcases had lain neatly on their sides, and a few large, unopened boxes were labelled 'books'.

'What do you think of that view?' Edmund had asked, appearing behind him.

Jasper hadn't even looked out of the window. He'd glanced out.

'It this all of your stuff?' Jasper had demanded, and Edmund nodded nonchalantly. 'Where're the things from your old place?'

'Nothing worth keeping.' Edmund had shrugged.

'But,' Jasper had stuttered, 'you're over forty, and this is all you've accumulated? What about souvenirs and, I don't know, junk?'

Edmund had snorted. 'You mean my equivalent of pine panelling. You know I don't like to hold onto things.'

'Still, this is a bit extreme. It's so cold, so impersonal. There're no memories.'

'And I'll fill it with new memories.'

'But you're selling it.'

'It's just stuff, Jasper, and this is just a house. There's nothing special about it. Someone lived in it before me and someone will come after. Someone out there's lying on my old sofa thinking what a deal he got from Oxfam.'

Jasper had shaken his head. 'That was a perfectly good sofa. If I didn't have such a cool one myself, I'd have nabbed it.'

'Then next time I move, you'll be first to go through my rubbish.' Edmund had sat down on the bed and crossed his legs in satisfaction.

26

It was the afternoon after a race. Ovidia and Edmund had been in a family-owned café in a small seaside town. It had been raining since morning, and Ovidia was sitting with Edmund in a small glass conservatory from which they could see the sea in the distance. A scattering of dogwalkers and determined tourists clad in waterproofs tramped across the sand. Occasionally, a small huddle of a family or a lone passer rushed by trying to get somewhere without being soaked.

'Are we boring?' Ovidia had asked. After hours of exertion, her feet plodding on the gravel country roads, her legs had ached pleasantly, her feet throbbed gently, and a magazine lay on her lap unread. At times like this, she felt a peace and happiness and, glancing at Edmund, the feeling intensified.

Sunlight had been filtering in between the light rainclouds, which drifted away only to be replaced. In the background, on a radio show, a panel of experts discussed a book, lauding its merits.

'We're in a village in Somerset eating cake?' Edmund had flipped the magazine he was reading closed. Slices of apple cake lay half eaten, empty cups of tea and a pot beside them. 'We were in Cape Town a few months ago.'

'Eating cake and drinking tea.'

'We had a fair amount of wine, too.' He'd chuckled.

Ovidia had laughed. She'd hoped he knew what she meant. They'd settled into a way of life that she wasn't sure how to define. He had his flat and she had hers. They ate out, they travelled, they did almost everything together, even very occasionally socialising, tentatively meeting other people together. But that wasn't what she meant.

'The term you're looking for is "old married couple",' Edmund had offered.

'That's not it.'

He'd leaned towards her, moving his cake away of the way. 'It's the question of what happens now, I think,' he'd suggested. He'd inhaled deeply before he began. 'Jasper has made enough progress. This girlfriend seems to actually be a positive influence. He's putting on a little weight. I think it's time for us to consider telling him.'

'Why?' Ovidia had said after a pause. And how, she'd thought. And when?

'We're back here again, aren't we?' Edmund had said. 'We have to.'

'So we've said, I don't know how many times.' She'd shaken her head. 'But it's not as if it's hurting our relationship. Or is it, and I just can't see it?' Ovidia had scratched the back of her head. 'It's not as if we're sneaking around. The whole world can see us. I still haven't heard the hammer of angry fists on our front door.'

'I imagine that, when I tell him, he'll completely break down... or worse,' Edmund had said. 'What if it gets so bad that it ruins what we have?'

She saw him ponder it. She'd known part of him hated keeping their relationship from Jasper. The other part she hadn't been so sure of.

'Let's go for a walk,' he'd said. She could tell he was putting off the conversation he'd started.

'It's raining,' she'd replied.

'Not that hard.'

They'd paid and bade the teller goodbye, despite her offer to refill their pot for free if they'd wanted to wait for a while.

'Old married couples,' Ovidia had said as she tucked her arm in his, 'make plans for the future. They acknowledge each other's place in their lives. I feel as if we live in the now, as if we were twenty-five-year-olds who don't really believe that they'll last together.'

'I would marry you in an instant,' he'd said. 'But that for me would be pushing our secrecy too far. To have a wedding, no matter how small, and not invite my family would be too much. I think you feel the same way about yours.'

He'd been right. Even though they had what she'd felt was an idyllic relationship, the secret was a wall around utopia, making it something that couldn't be shared.

'The way I see it,' Edmund had said, 'when we tell him, or I tell him – it's my responsibility. No, it is.' He'd stopped her as she opened her mouth. 'I know you still carry a lot of pain and guilt, but Jasper is my brother.'

She'd forced herself not to argue.

'We'll pretend it's just happened. That our relationship is new.'

'What?' She'd stopped.

'Think about it. It's much longer since you two broke up, if we say we met last week or even last month and that it's all new…'

She could see he was excited about his idea.

'We could say we wanted to tell him before we took it any further,' she'd suggested. 'It would be nowhere near as painful as the truth.'

There had been a lightness in her step as they'd continued their walk. They'd looked like everyone around them, she thought, an innocuous couple. She'd felt a thrill. Soon Jasper would know, and the two of them together, even if Edmund had insisted it was his responsibility, would help him heal. They'd have to pretend for just a little while. Edmund would be faultless in front of his brother and family – he deserved that.

'What would we do if Jasper told your family about what I did, in this new scenario?'

'He won't.'

'But what if he…'

'Ovidia… this is the best idea we have. We'd be free.'

They'd climbed over a low beach wall onto the beach of damp grey sand and gravel. Their hoods pulled over their heads. The rain had been forgivingly light. Still, Ovidia had felt a drop or two running down her back.

'Then we'll tell Jasper as soon as we can,' she'd said. 'So you can marry me.'

'Well, no – I haven't actually asked you yet.' He'd squeezed her tighter.

'I could ask you,' she'd said.

'No way. And it's not about being hopelessly old-fashioned, it's because –' His phone had rung. 'Sorry,' he'd said, and answered it.

She'd stepped away to give him his privacy.

'Something happened?' she'd asked as he looked at his phone, suddenly seeming tired, and put it in his pocket.

'Work,' he'd said.

Ovidia had known he was lying. It was a subtle exchange; he kept her from Jasper and Jasper from her. She knew not every call he received or emergency meeting was from work. She knew that it was work if he was specific: *Stocks are down* or *my director's in hospital*. She knew if Jasper's calls or visits were planned, Edmund would say: *I'm meeting Jasper for lunch or I'm going down to my parents' for the weekend.*

However, other times he was vague. Or other times he lied – like this one. When he hadn't made eye contact with her, when his jaw had become tense, and he'd glared at the sky as if it were somehow at fault. She didn't know how he decided it was something he shouldn't tell her. Maybe when he'd felt that Jasper's needs had been intruding too often, or when it had clashed directly with something they had planned. A few times, she'd happened upon his phone, showing Jasper's or Lucinda's numbers coinciding with a call that he'd received previously that had made him leave in a hurry.

'Do you have to go?' She could have asked, *Is he okay?* But that would have been unfair. She could see he was flustered; work never made him flustered – it excited him.

'Yes. I have to go right away. Can you hire a car for the day or something?'

'I'll manage,' she'd said. 'I might spend the night and come back tomorrow. I'm still a little sore.'

'You will,' he'd looked relieved. She'd offered him more time to be with his brother, whose unhappiness she was responsible for.

'I love you,' he'd said, and turned, hurrying up the beach towards the car park.

27

It had been Holly.

The crisis.

Edmund had driven back as fast as the speed limits would let him, terrified that this time would be *that* time. The time that he'd be too late, too far away.

Edmund had vacillated between excitement at the prospect of Jasper finally finding someone and the fear that she might be awful to him.

Perhaps, he'd thought, cruising towards his brother's flat, he should have put his reservations aside and made an effort to meet her. From a nearer vantage point, he'd be able to keep a better watch on the two of them. While Jasper had been with Ovidia, the distance that she created between the brothers helped mask the situation he was in for much longer. That his brother's state was Ovidia's fault was something he couldn't run away from, but he tried. Still, at times like this, he found himself on the verge of resenting her.

Edmund had let himself in the flat. He'd jingled the keys in his hands, delaying his mission for just a moment. Then, as had become a habit, he'd checked himself for any traces of Ovidia, though there never was. He'd imagined sometimes that Jasper might recognise a stray hair, an image on his phone, or a receipt for a dinner for two.

Jasper had called, saying in a monotone that she was gone and life wasn't worth living. No crying, no hysterics.

All the lights had been on.

'Jas,' he'd called as he shut the door behind him

He'd heard a moan in response and felt a wave of relief.

The smell of vomit had hit him as he moved towards the living room. He'd found Jasper lying on the sofa, a soft blue blanket over him. The television had been on, showing American reality TV.

'What's going on?' Edmund had asked.

'Nothing, let me sleep.' Jasper's breathing had been laboured, as if exhausted.

'Holly?'

'Gone.' Jasper had wiped his nose and turned over.

Carefully examining the sofa before sitting down beside his brother, Edmund had tried to think of what to say or ask.

Edmund had never told Ovidia of the state Jasper had ended up in. He'd never told her the extent of the wreck she'd left behind. She'd believed that Jasper, as Edmund had said, had a tendency for depressive episodes, describing them as him feeling low and just needing to withdraw and find someone to talk to. Edmund had told her that Jasper needed propping up every now and then, wanting her to believe that Jasper was an attention seeker, demanding to be centre of Edmund's and their parents' attention, though he was sure she didn't believe him.

Edmund hadn't told her how low those lows were, the whispered contemplations of *ending it all*, the internet browsing history that terrified him with its graphic instructions in order to leave as little to clean up as possible.

He'd been honest when he said Holly had made it better. Now when they spoke, it was quite often normal, about the trivialities of life, the mundane as well as the exciting. Jasper's face showed life.

'How did we get here, Jasper?'

He'd received a groan in answer.

'How long are we supposed to continue like this? What happened with Holly?' His voice had rung louder than he wanted.

Nothing.

'Did she get fed up and walk out?' he'd demanded. Jasper had lain deadly still.

'Did she say she just couldn't take it anymore? That she'd had enough, and she needed to get her own life?'

Jasper had shifted his weight, pulling the blanket off his face.

Edmund calmed down, reminding himself that Jasper wasn't just being difficult, as his mother had gently suggested.

'What do you expect from her? Do you expect her to just put up with whatever you throw at her? She has nothing to do with what brought you here. You can't expect her undying patience.'

'I know,' Jasper had whispered, turning on to his back.

'I've run out of things to say.' His and Jasper's eyes had met. 'I'm out of possible solutions.'

'If she doesn't come back,' Jasper had said, 'I don't know what I'll do.'

'Neither do I.'

Edmund had picked up the remote and turned down the sound on the TV. Keeping it on had almost been an extra presence in the room, so that he wasn't alone with his brother.

'I should clean myself up. What if she's forgotten something and comes back?' Jasper had shifted his weight but remained as he was.

He spoke minutes later, raising himself into a seated position. 'I' – his voice had hovered – 'don't want her to ever know how weak and stupid I've been.'

Edmund had risen, his mouth opening to protest. Jasper had never told him what had happened between him and Ovidia, but at times he referred to it without putting it in words.

'And I don't want her to ever see me like this. With Holly and the new places we go and the new people I meet, I feel as if I am something like a normal man.'

Edmund had dropped his face into his hands.

'When I think about it' – a manic look had crept onto Jasper's face – 'it's good that no one knew, right?'

Jasper's speech had descended into a babble that Edmund stopped following. It had happened before, the resolutions, the declarations, the looking on the bright side of things and having a meaningful, lifelong relationship with Holly. It would wear off, and he'd be back on the sofa begging his body to sleep.

Edmund had successfully put off any opportunity to meet Holly – sometimes by forces outside his control, work commitments, Ovidia's races disguised as obligations – but other times he'd simply lied. He had no idea what he'd say to this woman, what he was *supposed* to say to her. *'You know me – work, work, and crossword puzzles.'* He'd always tried to find out if Holly would be there when his parents would invite him and Jasper for the weekend. A few times he'd found himself in the company of Anne and John, to whom he felt a certain gratitude for maintaining a friendship with Jasper – though he hadn't the time or energy to spare to get to know them.

But Edmund had been to see Holly several times, though she didn't know it.

He'd been to her office. He'd gone up to the door. The office took up two floors of a concrete and dark glass building that had been built at the height of the sixties' modernism; its heritage appreciated only by a few aficionados. He'd found a large room styled as an open-plan office. Whoever was designated to receive guests had been absent, and only two of three heads were visible, bent over their work. He had glanced around the room, careful, knowing that his resemblance to his brother would have given him away if she saw him.

'Can I help you?' An older woman had peeped over her partition.

'I'm looking for Holly?'

'They've all gone out for coffee, I think,' she'd said.

'Right, thanks,' he'd said and turned to leave, knowing she'd ask if he wanted to wait or leave a message.

His plan had been to speak to her, try to learn something about her. Instead, he'd emerged from the building and quickly turned left as he saw a clutch of people, a blonde at their centre, returning. He'd had a good idea of what she looked like, as he'd frequently scanned her Facebook page. He'd gone through her LinkedIn profile and various other sites. He'd read her work; it was all in entertainment and art. She knew her subject matter and wrote well, but nothing she wrote was memorable. Her professional profile photo did her looks a disservice – she'd appeared a bland blonde woman in a staid, high-necked top. She was far more attractive in person.

He'd sat on a bench and watched her, as the little group had come to a halt outside the building. They'd seemed to be waiting for one of their number to finish a cigarette, each of them with a reusable mug. The conversation was animated, though he couldn't make out their words. He'd wanted to assign certain characteristics to the way she moved, the way she giggled with her hand hovering over her mouth. His first impression of her was honest and innocent. She'd seemed, in a single word, nice. But that to him sounded as if he was saying Ovidia wasn't those things. Ovidia was honest, boldly honest, the kind of woman who left an imprint in conversations about politics and morality. He'd realised he was searching for the reason Jasper would love Holly. Had Jasper chosen a woman who was the antithesis of Ovidia?

Edmund had been shocked at how much of an impact Jasper's relationship with Ovidia had had on his brother's life. He'd never imagined that an individual could rend a life apart. No matter how much he loved her – Edmund was realistic – Ovidia would always be that speck less than perfect, ever so slightly tarnished by her relationship with his brother.

Holly was offering his brother a new life, but Edmund couldn't bring himself to invest in their relationship. He was afraid, yes. Afraid that Holly would prove as destructive a force in Jasper's life as Ovidia had been, and, if that happened, he wasn't sure Jasper would survive.

Holly had seemed benign. On Facebook, she'd announced the places she went to and what she did casually; long weekend trips to popular spots on the continent, a weekend at home hillwalking with her parents, an art exhibition, and media training at a local charity. Her tastes were in no way exceptional, neither were they mediocre.

He'd turned back to Holly. She had been standing full height. She was taller than Ovidia, and her clothes in pale summery colours.

As he'd watched Holly, he'd pondered his own relationship with Ovidia. They were settled, considering the future, hinting *'when we are old'* or *'it's the kind of place we should retire to'*. They'd spoken of themselves as single unit.

He wanted that for Jasper. But what would happen when Jasper saw Ovidia again, when he recalled how vivacious she was, or how when he made love to her, the rest of the world, the history and the future, became irrelevant? What happened when he remembered when she sang songs from musicals badly?

Would Holly hold up to the comparison?

It was okay. His thoughts were his own, he'd reminded himself. Ovidia was his, perfect for him. She had been completely wrong for Jasper. If Jasper was serious about Holly, he must have felt that there was something different about her, that she was good.

His gaze having shifted to the street, his attention had been drawn back to the group. Holly had burst into laughter, a sudden violent eruption, during which she gently shoved her colleague's shoulder. Edmund had steeled himself at that move. The colleague had laughed along.

In his brother's flat, as Jasper – emboldened by some trick of serotonin or dopamine or whatever brain chemical the latest theory assigned his raging to – had paced the room, Edmund had made himself a cup of tea and settled on the sofa, listening and then not listening to his brother, imagining what Ovidia was doing in a village outside Weston-Super-Mare on a rainy evening.

Jasper had sat down, eyeing Edmund's feet.

'Don't ever tell Holly, please?' he'd asked, his eyes imploring.

Sitting in his extension, neat and friendly, Holly seemed everything Edmund wanted for his brother. He wondered what she would do next. Jasper wouldn't be the same after today. Holly had never met the Jasper of before. She didn't know what Edmund had lost.

28

Anne smiled at Jasper as he came downstairs to the kitchen and joined Holly and her. She saw him stroke Holly's shoulder, and Holly whispered something to him, smiling. Holly handed him a plate, and Anne saw his reluctance. He picked up a slice of pizza with a fork and let it lie there untouched. She recalled the Jasper she'd first met, emaciated and miserable, who took half an hour to finish a bowl of soup, and wondered what it would take for him to descend to those depths again. She looked at the time on her watch and realised that, though it was early afternoon, for a group of friends celebrating an engagement, it felt ages since they'd arrived.

As Holly kissed Jasper, Anne escaped, saying, 'second helping,' though it was her third as she scooted past them to pick up another slice of pizza before returning to the annex.

'Come on,' Holly said, and she and Jasper followed Anne through the door.

There, John was explaining what it took to write a book. 'It's difficult to say. It was harder and easier than I thought it would be.'

Ovidia was twisting about in her seat, looking for something. She seized Edmund's lapel, her other hand aimed at his pocket.

'I said I don't have it,' Edmund whispered loudly to Ovidia, interrupting John. He brushed her away. 'It's not in my pocket. You called for pizza, remember?'

'Lucky, there was a bit of developmental support, too,' John continued. 'The editor helped to really flesh out the concept.'

Ovidia went to the kitchen and called to Edmund from the door. 'It's not here.'

Edmund looked annoyed briefly, stood and followed her inside. 'You've just left it on the table somewhere.'

'That editor, who kept calling me "darling",' Anne said. She was pretending now that Ovidia and Edmund weren't acting odder than before. 'I can't see how she could have been any help.'

'He's taken it – the delivery guy.' Ovidia's raised, tense voice came through the open doors.

Edmund's voice was raised too, but he was further away, and Anne couldn't hear what he said in response.

'My pictures,' Ovidia said. 'It has my pictures – I need them. Call the restaurant.'

'Well, let's make sure it's really gone. We don't want to embarrass ourselves.' He must have moved closer to the doors, as they heard him clearly.

Edmund returned to the annex. Now they were all watching. Without speaking, he started rifling through the cushions in his chair and examined the space in which Ovidia had been sitting.

'I want it back, my pictures,' Ovidia's voice rang.

'Phone gone?' John asked, as everyone watched.

'She thinks it's the delivery guy. Do people still do that? I thought mobiles had no resale value.' Edmund looked annoyed and inconvenienced. He sat down again, looking as tired and dejected as when they'd found him that morning.

'Are you okay?' Anne said as the colour drained from Edmund's face. 'Guys, could we all look around? It's probably just lying around somewhere.'

Jasper appeared to hesitate, but he left when Holly gently tugged his hand.

'Are you okay?' Anne repeated, sitting on the stool at Edmund's side where Ovidia had been.

'Fine,' Edmund replied after a moment, taking several deep breaths and rising.

'No, sit,' Anne ordered, and Edmund acquiesced. The tone of her voice came from being accustomed to dealing with reluctant patients, people who wanted their own way, or to escape their hospital beds. 'The others will find it.'

'It's just a bloody phone,' Edmund said, his teeth gritted.

'It isn't just a phone, is it?' Anne asked, and Edmund realised that she knew it wasn't.

'I kept telling her to back up her things, download her pictures of...' he paused '... her photos. But she never gets round to anything. She was an engineer, for heaven's sake, now she can't find a bloody cable for her hard drive.'

He stopped abruptly, his eyes unfocused. Anne knew how it felt the first time you spoke negatively about your spouse aloud – that jolt of pain when you first admitted to the rest of the world that he or she was less than perfect.

'I don't know her, but she looks capable of getting herself together. She probably just needs time,' said Anne. 'When we were in the kitchen, she referred to herself as assertive, and I could see what she meant.'

'She's fallen apart,' Edmund said.

'And why not? So what if Ovidia's clever, witty, beautiful – it doesn't mean losing a child would be any easier for her than anyone else,' said Anne.

Edmund stiffened, his eyes narrowing.

Anne's hand went to her breast. 'I'm so sorry... I found something in the kitchen... I didn't mean...' she said, fumbling her words. 'I haven't said anything to the others. Really I haven't.'

He leaned back silently and she said, 'Can I ask...'

'No,' he snapped, loud and fierce enough to frighten her.

In the brief silence that followed, Anne thought for a moment that she should leave but remembered she was with a man who'd spent most of a day with his brother unable or unwilling to tell him that he had a child who was dying. She couldn't conceive of a reason Edmund should choose to suffer in silence, except maybe that he was trying to protect his brother from the enormity of his lie.

'When Jasper finds out...' she began, but she couldn't continue. Edmund didn't respond. She was aware he knew far better than she what might happen.

She changed direction, her words stumbling out. 'If we leave, you two can have some time to yourselves.'

'Then who'll tell Jasper?' Edmund asked, his voice flat.

'Well, maybe Jasper shouldn't be your priority right now. Maybe think of yourself and Ovidia.'

Edmund looked at the ceiling, and they were both silent.

Edmund stood purposefully. 'Thank you,' he said to Anne as she also rose.

She followed him back into the kitchen.

'Found it!' Holly chirped cheerfully. The four of them stood in the kitchen, Jasper stone faced, John chewing his lip as if trying not to smile. Ovidia, apart from them, held her phone in her hand, looking at it.

'Can we get back to lunch?' John looked amused as he marched back to Anne. He stopped beside her and whispered to her, 'This woman's lost the plot.'

Anne nodded.

'Jasper's not far behind,' he continued.

'Yeah,' she said vaguely.

'I think we should go,' John said.

'How?' she replied, her eyes locking with his. 'We can't leave Jasper.'

29

Edmund waited for the others to file back into the annex, leaving him with Ovidia.

'That was embarrassing,' she said. 'It was right there. I don't know how I didn't see it.' She leaned back against the counter and looked to the floor.

He took a few steps towards her but didn't touch her. She looked tired or, rather, defeated.

'They must think I've lost it.'

Edmund thought back to what Anne had just said. 'Maybe you have.'

She started, looking up at him, annoyed.

'Which isn't what I meant to say,' he said. He let himself touch her. 'We don't have to pretend anymore. There's nothing left to hide, not even our madness.'

'You, mad?' She put her arm around his waist and sighed.

'You've no idea how desperately hard it's been to take care of you and to keep going to work, to keep functioning and pretending that nothing has happened when all I want to do is crawl into bed and never get up again.' He said this quietly, refusing to look at her, gazing instead at the wall where pictures were once affixed.

He felt her arm tighten around him.

'I have been so lonely,' he said. 'You don't stop to see how I am, to see if I need help. There's no one to –' he stopped. 'Anyway, I'm not leaving you because I blame you,' Edmund said. It came out bluntly. It wasn't something they'd put into words, but he knew it was inevitable. 'No, that's a lie. I do blame you. I wish we could continue, but I just don't see how we can.'

'If we want to badly enough...' she began, but Edmund interrupted.

'It's not about wanting to anymore. It's about no longer deluding ourselves. It's about waking up from a fantasy.'

'This is not a fantasy, it's my life.'

'It's my life, too.' His voice rose. He felt agitated, but he paused, took a deep breath, and continued. 'This mess we're in is my fault. I should never have texted you, never have come to your flat. I have been lying to Jasper and the world every day for the last four years, because I love you, and now I'm going to lose you, too.'

Ovidia let go, pulling away from him.

'And you know what? It's perfectly fair,' Edmund said, wishing he could stop. 'If you could have seen what Jasper became because of what you did to him –'

'Stop,' Ovidia barked. 'Not today. Tell me this any day but today. I know it's all my fault, but today's not about Jasper.'

He stopped. He heard Holly's laugh from outside. Though the others were so close, the kitchen felt like a marble mausoleum, devoid of life yet created beautifully. He couldn't go outside to face Anne now she'd seen behind his mask. He glanced at the clock – it was almost time.

'But Jasper and I did talk, by the way,' Ovidia said, clearing her throat.

Edmund lifted his head in response.

'It wasn't very constructive,' Ovidia continued. 'But it's done. We've finally met that first time.'

Edmund nodded.

'Could you tell him I'm sorry?' she said. 'I don't think I actually told him I was sorry.'

'It would be more meaningful if you told him yourself,' Edmund replied after a moment. 'And took responsibility for your actions.'

'I've got so much to apologise for,' she replied. 'I've had five years to do it. I shouldn't have waited until now.'

Edmund put his arm around her waist. 'We did what worked. If I'd any idea he'd show up at my house with his fiancée one morning, maybe I'd have done some things differently. I've had the most wonderful years of my life with you. I won't apologise for that.'

Ovidia smiled at him, whispering thank you.

They stood still – time arrested. Edmund felt as if something had changed. The heaviness in the air had dissipated, if only a little. He let her go reluctantly, knowing they could not stand there forever.

He hesitated at the door to the extension.

'Why don't you go upstairs, take a long shower or something?' Ovidia said after a moment. She must have sensed his reluctance.

'You want to go out there on your own?'

'Yes,' she said, raising herself to full height. 'I do.' She stepped in front of him and exited.

He almost followed her, but then turned away, slowly making his way to their bedroom. There, he sat and waited.

I'm ready, he said to himself after what felt like an eternity, and he rose to get changed.

Ovidia had used the bathroom since he'd last been in it. Her white towel, now dry, hung on the towel rack. The one he'd abandoned on the floor earlier that morning had been thrown on the back of a chair. Her shower gel tube was open, and her sponge placed precariously on the edge of the shower rack. He showered, dried his hair, and returned to his usual uniform.

He sat on their bed as he pulled his socks on, wondering when he'd last read the books that lay beside it. He tried to recall when he and Ovidia last sat in bed talking, books abandoned, bedside lamps on, the rest of the world seeming so far away. Now either he or she would already be in bed with their back turned, and the other would be unable or unwilling to instigate a conversation. They'd made love the previous night, and he'd held her tightly. It had been months since the last time – four months at least.

He was lying in this bed a year and half ago when she'd prodded him awake one morning, waving a home pregnancy test inches from his face.

'You're joking?' he'd demanded, wiping the sleep from his eyes and prying the stick from her hand, wanting to see the evidence for himself. She'd let him have it, her eyes wet with tears.

Now, he looked in the mirror, relieved that he at least looked like himself again. He entered the kitchen, forcing his shoulders back as if going to war. Then he looked at them all through the window, back in the annex, their postures and expressions revealing various degrees of tension or confusion. He knew it would be impolite, he knew it was unfair to Jasper and to Holly, but he decided to give himself a little longer alone. He turned into a corridor and found a wall to lean against and waited.

30

John hung up his mobile again. His daughters were demanding to know when they could go home, bickering with their grandparents. He'd reassured them that he would take them somewhere amazing the next day, though he couldn't imagine at that point where that would be.

He stayed on the line longer than he should, revelling in their voices yet knowing he had to get back to Jasper. He peered back into the annex, realising he was reluctant to return. It was warm outside and he'd ambled to and fro across the clipped garden lawn as he spoke, hoping the others would think he simply wanted a quiet place to speak. He'd made it as far as the pile of wooden debris, poked at it with his foot and was certain it was not a garden room as they'd been told.

His friendship with Jasper rode crests and falls, but it had never been as tested as today. He didn't know the details, but he knew Jasper well enough to know he was suffering.

When he'd met Jasper, he could easily have handed him a business card and the two of them would have become client and therapist, but he didn't – not that Jasper would have been ready to accept it. Instead, Jasper became the first person in John's adult life that he would have considered a best friend. It wasn't about him 'helping' Jasper; it was a mutual relationship. Jasper was someone with whom time spent felt fulfilling, full of camaraderie and trust.

Watching the group, John could see Jasper pretending to listen to Holly, his lack of attention given away by his furtive glances at the annex door and constant kneading of his knee with his fingers. Holly looked resigned to his inattention. John could tell that Edmund's revelation had struck Jasper in the heart – why, then, wouldn't he just leave? He focused on the others in the annex. From where he stood, they seemed at ease, even happy – a stranger looking through the glass would have no reason to think they were anything but friends. The last few hours had been spent discussing anything between the mundane and the exciting, emotions had risen and fallen but never too high or too low – the undercurrent of Jasper's unhappiness and Edmund's deceit masked by conversation. Ovidia had given them glimpses into her intelligence and wit – only glimpses, he felt – yet she no longer seemed like such an unlikely partner for Edmund.

'I still feel as if we should leave, but I don't want to be the one to suggest it,' he whispered to Anne as she came out into the garden and asked if he was all right. He glanced at the time on his phone and it was almost half past three. He thought how he felt as if so much more time had passed, but it hadn't. 'By the way, Lucy wants ice cream, and your mum won't give her any. I suggest we have a tub of it by the time she gets home.'

'There's a reason Mum won't give her any; it's not healthy,' Anne replied. 'We should stop indulging her. I keep telling you.'

'You know how much she hates being away from us...' John changed the subject. 'Do you think they'll survive this?'

Anne looked startled. 'Who? Edmund and Ovidia?'

John looked at her. 'No, Jasper and Holly.'

'Oh, no. This is between Jasper and Edmund – Holly will just have to put up with some sulking for a few days, and they'll be fine,' Anne said.

'But what about if she won't put up with it? This is the first day of her engagement – what if she realises that this is it, that Jasper is always going to be hard work, even if he does love her?'

'He's just found out his brother's been lying to him for four years – I'd be pissed off, too.'

'Yes, but look at him, he's completely miserable. He's the only one who can let us out of here. He knows I can't leave him here, and neither can Holly.' John paused. 'Edmund must know how vulnerable Jasper is. How could he lie like that?'

'Don't you judge – you of all people.'

John recoiled at the ferocity of Anne's words. 'What do you mean?' He knew how to make himself appear confused and offended, as if she had accused him of the unthinkable. Nonetheless, she'd never spoken with such vehemence before.

Anne waved him away with a quick sweep of her hand and turned, leaving him to face the back of her head. She marched towards the splintered building and looked down at it, her back straight and forbidding. For a moment he felt lost, an unfamiliar feeling when with Anne.

John followed and stood quietly beside her for a while and then took her hand. For the first time since Singapore, she shook it away.

'Listen,' he said calmly, leaning towards her. 'The world is full of crazy stories. Jasper's never going to be the same again and probably neither is Holly. But we can't let today affect us. These are our friends, but we are not them. We were together before we ever knew them.'

He gently sought her hand again. This time she let him take it. He relaxed knowing she couldn't hold anything against him for long.

'I can't imagine how Edmund's done this to his own brother, I really can't,' he said again as they returned to the annex. In his work, his clients described far worse acts that brother wreaked upon brother – violence, manipulation, stupidity – however, it was all relayed to him sometimes years after the event. In his own experience, his family life, his friends – until now – brothers didn't keep such secrets from each other.

They smiled at the others as they sat down, but Holly's tale continued despite the distraction.

They watched Jasper and Holly for a moment. The urge to leave was growing, but all he could think of was to say, 'I really need to pee.' He slapped her thigh playfully and she nodded, touching his hand in return. *Yes, another breather*, he thought. He'd take as long about this as Anne had taken about the tea.

He followed the same directions Anne had been given, unfazed by the house. To him, it was a show house from an era when houses were meant to impress and even intimidate guests and neighbours, an exhibition of wealth. He sneered at the clawfoot tub – did they expect guests to take a quick bath when they came to visit?

He washed his hands and rubbed them on his jeans, not wanting to have to neatly fold the hand towels again. The house probably wasn't as ostentatious as he wanted to believe it was. Maybe for now he wanted to resent everything about Edmund. Perhaps, in other circumstances, he'd have appreciated the house and its décor. When he'd arrived this morning, John had felt a hint of the attraction he'd had to Edmund, but, after witnessing Edmund's manipulative and even cruel behaviour to his own brother, the attraction had soured.

John was coming back from the bathroom, taking his time examining the details of the house, when Edmund passed, returning to his guests.

'Just having a sniff around,' he smiled, still trying to compensate for the gaffe two years ago that Edmund, without a word, would not let him forget. He had never felt entirely comfortable in Edmund's presence since.

'I see,' Edmund said, disinterested, moving on.

'Edmund.' John stopped him. 'This *is* my business, so don't tell me it's not. Jasper's my friend. Are you going to apologise to him? Somehow iron this out?'

He was surprised when Edmund responded.

'I can't imagine how I can iron it out, but yes, I am going to apologise to him. I've hurt him, and I'm not proud of what I've done.'

'But why, for god's sake, didn't you just tell him all this time?'

'Because, John.' Edmund looked down at him, his expression one John had seen on him many times before – calm and reassured. 'No matter how clever I am, successful or wealthy – I can't tell the future. If I'd had any idea that one morning you lot would show up on my doorstop, I may have done things differently. But, I didn't. And now I have to deal with the consequences.'

Edmund continued his interrupted journey, leaving John in the corridor.

An explanation so simple that it had to be true. John watched him walk away, wishing Edmund had brushed him off or lied.

31

Ovidia left when Edmund returned. He sat down in his armchair as she stood. He squeezed her hand and immediately let go. Jasper looked as if he'd decided once again to indulge Holly, contorting his face into some semblance of cheerfulness while his eyes remained flat and distant.

He'd whispered to Holly inches from her face and wiggled his eyebrows. Holly had punched his arm happily, perhaps hoping that the day was getting better. Ovidia had felt a stab of regret, recalling that he used to do the same to her.

Ovidia glanced back at him as she left. He was trying too hard to be funny yet sitting much too rigidly in his seat and every now and then attacking his nails with his teeth. She wondered why he didn't leave. She guessed he was still looking for an explanation – that he still didn't believe what he was seeing.

It was her turn to change her clothes. She rifled through the walk-in wardrobe for something suitable. It was difficult. The clothes she was happiest in were bright and colourful. She was forced to root through the clothes she'd worn when she used to work. When she finally settled on a charcoal-black suit, she decided she looked much too sombre. She tried on an orange scarf, but looking at herself in the mirror the colour screamed back at her, garish and inappropriate.

The scarf was a favourite, and she'd once worn it often to brighten up outfits in black or blue. Today, it refused to sit in harmony with the rest of her clothes.

Ovidia returned to the group in the new outfit, having settled for a grey dress that ended just above her knees. The conversation had continued without her: Holly's mother's love of Christmas decorating, Anne and John's daughters who didn't believe in Santa Claus, and how hard it was to find the perfect gift.

Ovidia had stopped at the French doors with one foot in the kitchen. When Edmund turned and saw her, he checked his watch.

'I'm sorry. We have to go,' Edmund said to his guests, rising to his feet. 'Please lock the door behind you, if we're not back by the time you leave.'

They all started in their seats.

'What?' Holly said, springing up. 'Right now?'

'Something better to do?' Jasper asked in a loud, accusing voice.

Edmund joined Ovidia at the door without answering either question. He was beside Ovidia when she found herself rooted where she stood, incapable of movement.

'No,' she said, her voice strangled, barely audible.

Edmund said nothing. He put an arm around her and gently tried to steer her away into the kitchen.

'Edmund, where you going?' Jasper demanded, standing up and following his brother to the door, stopping inches from Ovidia. 'Or is that also a big secret?'

'Jasper – not now,' Anne hissed.

'You can't just go,' Jasper barked. Ovidia's stomach coiled at the force of his voice. 'No wait, you can. You can keep your whole life a secret from me. I'm just your brother.'

Edmund still didn't answer. For a moment she was afraid of him, the look in his eyes was unlike any emotion she'd ever seen him in.

Ovidia gripped the door. She shut her eyes tightly, trying to shut out reality. She was not going to move, she declared silently.

Edmund whispered gently, 'Let's go, let's go now.' She felt him prying her fingers loose from the door frame, still unable to open her eyes. He gripped her wrist much too hard; she winced.

'Hey, you're hurting her,' Holly said, and Ovidia opened her eyes to Holly springing from her chair towards her. When Holly got to her, Ovidia brushed her hand away and looked at the others for help.

John stood, but Ovidia saw Anne grab his hand and pull him down, shaking her head when he looked at her.

'No, Edmund, don't make me go. Please,' Ovidia said, her eyes still shut. 'You go, I'll stay here. I need to lie down.'

'Ovidia, you promised.' Edmund gently yet firmly guided her into the kitchen.

'I can't do this!' Ovidia insisted, the sound of rising hysteria in her voice. She could hear her heart pounding, and she felt faint.

'We agreed.' Tense and determined, Edmund tightened his grip on her wrists seemingly oblivious to the pain he was causing.

'No. You just want him out of the way so you can get rid of me.' Looking Edmund in the eye, she resorted to that desperate accusation.

'You know that's a lie,' Edmund replied, looking hurt, his grip tightening on her arms.

Ovidia yelped at the pain. Edmund had never hurt her before.

'Leave her alone!' John barked. Pushing past Anne, he darted forward and pulled Ovidia away. Edmund relinquished his grip without contest. Holly stood behind them, her hand over her mouth.

Ovidia's heart sank as she watched Edmund stare down at his hands. Ovidia saw then that they were bruised and scabbed from having demolished the playhouse early that morning. For the first time, she understood how unhappy he must have been.

'I'm sorry, Ovidia.' His voice came in a whisper. 'But we have to go now.'

'Is this what he does to you? Is this why it's a big secret?' Jasper, who hadn't moved when John had intervened, said.

'It's not at all what you think,' Ovidia replied. She could see the assumption on his face and was offended that anyone could imagine that of Edmund. Taking Edmund's hand, she nodded, and the two of them began what seemed to her an interminable trek to the front door and to the taxi waiting outside.

EVENING

32

'Are we just going to let them leave? He might hurt her again,' John asked as Ovidia and Edmund walked slowly up the stairs to the front door.

Holly was shocked by her own inaction and that of those around her. The way Edmund had tried to drag Ovidia out had frightened her. She felt ashamed that she had not done anything. At least John had tried. It was only when John had pursued Edmund and Ovidia into the kitchen, followed by Jasper, that she followed, too.

'Ovidia,' Jasper had said, as Edmund and Ovidia started out towards the taxi. 'Didn't I mean anything to you at all?'

Holly's heart had immediately begun to race, pulsating, sending blood much too fast to her head. In an instant, she was dazed and nauseated, tension building in her gut about to explode – she was confused.

Neither Ovidia nor Edmund had reacted, continuing their journey with Edmund steering them away, perhaps a little faster, disappearing, and a door closing behind them.

Holly could feel herself breathing heavily, quickly. She'd been unable to speak as they left, myriad explanations hurtled around her head, each more ridiculous than the last.

But now she had found her words. 'What did you mean – "mean anything to you"?' She put a hand on her chest, but the feel of her heart racing frightened her, and she let her hand drop.

Jasper didn't reply. His gaze was fixed on the now empty corridor that Edmund and Ovidia had travelled down.

'What did you mean?' Holly repeated louder, in case he hadn't heard her the first time, though she was sure he had.

'You and Ovidia?' John asked.

Holly didn't want her suspicions confirmed by John. She wanted Jasper to say it aloud, so she could hear it from him.

Jasper remained frozen, looking down an empty corridor. 'You and Ovidia?' Holly echoed, her face contorting with emotion. 'The woman with Edmund?' She pointed in the direction that Edmund and Ovidia had walked, as if it could have been any other Ovidia.

Jasper exhaled, a loud puff of air. To Holly, in lieu of words, it told her that he and Ovidia knew each other. That morning and afternoon, she realised, had been spent in the company of the woman who was responsible for the condition Jasper had been in when she first met him. Ovidia was the woman for whom he'd pined until he had nearly wasted away – physically and emotionally.

Everyone was silent and waiting for an explanation. Anne's mouth was open, her hands clenched. John's hand was at his chin, rubbing it.

'It was long before we met,' Jasper said, his voice tremulous. 'I haven't seen her since then.'

'For how long?' Holly demanded, her chest heaving. 'How long were you together?'

'A while.'

'It wasn't a one-night stand, not a fling? You were properly together?' Holly had to know, her overriding emotion was now that of utter humiliation. Her face reddened; she closed her eyes, feeling her skin burning. Holly stood clenching her jaw, her hands gripping the kitchen peninsula, yet still feeling as if she would fall. She breathed in through her nose, filling her lungs, trying to tame the relentless lurching in her stomach.

'Let's go home,' Holly said abruptly. No one replied. 'I can't stay here. It's not like our being here was so important to them that couldn't postpone wherever they were going.'

Jasper and John looked at each other for approval.

John shrugged. 'I agree, absolutely.'

Holly could see that Jasper was relieved. Had he expected her to scream or to make a scene?

'Yes, let's forget about Edmund. His little brother tells him he's getting married and he runs off.' He pulled her towards to him and, with his arm around her waist, kissed her on her ear.

Holly flinched. 'My bag's in the cube thing.' She pulled away from him. Jasper with Ovidia explained everything: the strained atmosphere, Jasper's relentless fidgeting, his brother's defiant attitude – Edmund hadn't been ill or preoccupied; he'd been, what, ashamed?

Jasper kept a hold of her hand. 'I'm sorry. I should have had the courage to leave earlier.'

His words sounded flat to Holly, as if he was just saying it to pacify her. She shook her hand free of his.

She walked briskly into the annex. Once outside, she picked up her bag and clutched it, squeezing it to her chest, fighting back tears. Her worst suspicions were confirmed. He wasn't over her, the woman that broke his heart. It was a subject they never discussed. Not even once had they talked about the cause of the pain that even now occasionally made him sink into bouts of unhappiness that lasted hours and sometimes days. In the worst of times, a whole day would pass in which they didn't speak to each other, and she'd scrape uneaten food into the bins, and, in the bathroom, she'd catch the lingering odour of vomit.

She'd wanted so many times to confront him about how he wasn't doing anything to deal with the fugue he often fell into. But she told herself that John was a therapist and Jasper's friend, so surely John was helping him resolve it.

Holly told herself that 'this' (she still wasn't sure what it was) was such a small part of their feelings for each other that they could afford to overlook it. She repeated over and over again that time would take care of them, that the past would get further and further away until it was insignificant.

'You and I have a lot to talk about,' John was saying, as she walked back into the kitchen. 'Of course, now's not the time – but, shit, why didn't you say something? Your brother's with your…' He stopped.

Jasper was silent.

'You've been lying all day,' John said, as if reluctant to end the conversation. He scratched his head and went to where Anne stood and took hold of a corner of her blouse.

'Shall we go?' Holly asked. That was all she wanted to do now, escape, to leave Edmund and Ovidia and their silly, tasteless mansion. She glanced around – strange how the house now looked absolutely soulless.

'Yes.' John nodded and then shook his head. 'I want to get out of here, too, but I still don't feel right about just leaving. Edmund was being pretty rough with her. I'm worried he might do something.'

'She doesn't need us to worry about her,' Jasper said, his teeth gritted.

'Really? I see women in trouble every week, women whose husbands are unstable, on edge,' John insisted. 'All it takes is the right provocation, and he could really hurt her. Jasper, can't you call them or something?'

'I don't want to call my ex-girlfriend,' Jasper insisted loudly, his voice raspy. 'Look, I don't know what all this is about. I don't understand this suburban mansion business, the kitchen extension, the Nordic garden set. Edmund never told me that he and my ex were playing house.'

Holly felt a little better. Jasper just hadn't known what to do. He hadn't deliberately tried to deceive her.

He took a few slow steps to one of the barstools, where he sat heavily as if defeated, weighted down. 'I don't know where he is or what he's going to do to Ovidia. And I don't think she's my responsibility. So, Holly's right, let's get out of here.' He slid off the seat and quickly backed away from the others, towards the front door, but stopped. Holly took a few steps towards him, following.

'I mean look at this... all this. You know Edmund' – his eyes appealed to John – 'does any of this look like him to you? This guy goes to coffee competitions for Christ's sake. What are our parents going to say when they find out? Am I supposed to join in, keep it all secret for him?' Jasper stopped and planted his hands in his pockets. 'Coming here was such a stupid idea. Let's find a fucking pub and celebrate my engagement.'

Holly nodded, she reached for him. He looked on the point of tears; she didn't want him to cry, not the day after their engagement. Today was meant to be one of the happiest days of their lives. She scolded herself, but only briefly, at how quickly her anger at him had receded.

Anne spoke so quietly that Holly could barely hear her. 'You really should stay and wait for Edmund. He needs you.'

'Needs me for *what*?' Jasper sneered, moving before Holly could touch him. 'What on earth does he need me for? He has his own enormous slice of the suburban dream.'

'They have a little boy,' Anne said. 'And he's not well.'

There was silence.

'He's dying.' She finished and looked at Jasper.

33

'It's not a situation I ever imagined finding myself in.' Jasper was explaining the truth about Ovidia to John. They sat in the extension, the door closed between them and Anne and Holly, who were in the kitchen. He could hear snatches of the sounds of their cleaning and putting things away.

'And now' – he leaned back into the armchair Edmund had been sitting in – 'I'm trapped in her house.'

John hadn't asked, but Jasper felt compelled to tell him. Jasper had decided to stay, felt he had to be there for his brother. He'd thought a little about his relationship with Holly, sure it would be over, but Ovidia dominated his thoughts. He didn't want to call Edmund. The truth, if he heard it now, might be too brutal for him to stand. Yet his gut churned with a desire to find out about the child.

Anne couldn't tell him what he needed to know. It was a baby boy, she repeated; she didn't know what was wrong with him. Her eyes met Jasper's. No, she didn't know why they had to leave just then. Her gaze averted, flickered towards the back wall, where there was nothing to be seen.

The easiest thing, Jasper decided, was to be here when Ovidia and Edmund returned. He went out into the cube and sat down, feeling entombed.

Holly had refused to leave without Jasper when he'd suggested she, John, and Anne leave, so she stayed, her face telling him she was unhappy. It was John who'd suggested they divide in two to clean up. Everyone agreed, and Jasper was, in a way, glad that he hadn't been left alone with his thoughts in his brother's house.

'You could have hinted, given some kind of sign or just said "let's get out of here",' John said gently.

'I couldn't. I had to...' Jasper paused, not being able to put in words the conflicting emotions he'd been experiencing since that morning. 'I had to know. It was as if I was dreaming or hallucinating. If I left, I'd never have known if today really happened.'

'Okay, so you couldn't really think it through, I understand that,' John said, his words came out clipped and taut. 'But why have you never told me about Ovidia?'

'Why are you so offended? It was before we met.' Jasper's first instinct was to circumvent the question.

'This relationship was important to you. I can see that, and so can Holly. That's two years – a gap – in your life that I know nothing about, that you have deliberately kept from me. You have never, ever, made any reference to her,' John answered. 'Why?'

Jasper sat back in his chair and the fingers of one hand gripped the armrest.

'Jas?' John's eyes met Jasper's, his voice reassuring yet firm, a gentle demand. 'Why?'

'She used to hit me.' He articulated his words slowly. It was the first time he'd ever told anyone outright. He'd never even told Edmund, though he now knew his brother had guessed.

John shuddered, a brief, involuntary movement. 'She physically abused you?' he asked, leaning further forward, disbelief visible in his wide eyes.

'I saw that,' Jasper said, referring to that momentary expression of revulsion. 'You responded like that – and you're a professional.'

'I'm sorry,' John apologised, looking contrite. 'That was the very last thing I expected you to say.' John massaged his forehead with his knuckles. 'And yes, for a second there I didn't believe you. Shit, I'm sorry.' He apologised again and paused, the ball of his thumb between his teeth. 'You're my friend, and I didn't believe you. So, you're right to not have told me. I did exactly what you were afraid I'd do.'

'I sat in a room once, nine guys in some church hall, and that's what they all said – no one ever believes you. I don't get it, though. It was so obvious. I wondered how the whole world hadn't noticed. I couldn't go to the gym, go swimming, take my shirt off on a hot day. I couldn't look people in the eye when they asked how I was,' Jasper explained. 'I've asked myself so many times, what it was about me that she saw as a target. I still don't know. I'm from a happy home, I have loving parents, a job and an education – but somehow, she saw a huge sign over my head saying "please, kick me".'

Jasper continued, after pausing to catch his breath. 'It was as if, somewhere along the way, Ovidia decided she was going to kill me. And, apparently, she would have, if Edmund hadn't stopped her,' he added bitterly. 'I found that out today, too.' He paused again. 'Then you meet a great guy and his wife – they become your best friends, so when and how do you tell them? *"Hi John, hi Anne, lovely summer we're having – by the way, I was a victim of repeated and sustained intimate partner violence for two years. Do you still like me? Have you lost all respect for me? Have I become an anecdote you tell your friends?"* When is the right time to say that?'

'Two years?' John asked quietly, in a firm but reassuring voice to which his clients were drawn, comforted and inspired.

'More like two lifetimes. It didn't start right away, of course. At first, our relationship was a dream – well, I thought it was. Later, I was sure the only way to leave was to kill myself. I couldn't see any other way to get away.'

'And then she left you?'

'Literally. Ran down the road. Never saw her again until today.' Jasper slumped back in the seat, fighting back tears, looking up at the sky through the glass roof. With Edmund, he'd only talked about what came after the abuse – depression, loneliness, sadness. He'd never really spoken about his abusive relationship with Ovidia to anyone so openly. He'd sat in that room, a support group for male victims of domestic violence and not said a word. He'd taken a place in a circle of fabric-upholstered metal conference chairs in a brightly lit, century-old room. There'd been a draught that had relentlessly assaulted his ankles, giving him something to divert his attention to when he felt the need to cry. Some men had. As he'd watched them sobbing, shoulders shuddering, their words choked back or abandoned, he realised that, even in that room that was meant to be safe, in a group created for them to speak, every single man was fighting to hide the expression of their pain. The men battled against their tears, they battened down their words, they hoisted shame onto their own shoulders and carried it until they cracked. Breaking down in elevators, in locked bathrooms, garages, and emergency rooms.

As he left, Jasper had picked up a brochure. He'd learned the terminology and why he shouldn't suffer in silence. He'd nodded to the other men as they left, watching them pat each other on the back and make plans to meet for a drink. He'd never returned.

'It's nothing to be ashamed of,' John said.

'Of course it's something to be ashamed of. I'm weak. I'm stupid. I allowed myself to be sucked into hell thinking I was in love. I let her reduce me to absolutely nothing. It's been five years and still I fly into a panic at the sound of a book slamming shut.' Jasper's eyes were wet. He closed them and cleared his throat, and then opened his eyes again.

'Jasper. You are none of those things.'

'I've told myself that. It doesn't help. Look at me, I'm sitting here thinking about Ovidia when I should be thinking of my brother, or at least about Holly.'

'Absolutely, everything you're feeling is valid and justified,' John said. 'I know that sounds like a therapist talking, because it is. I'm not just your friend right now, talk to me.'

Jasper looked at him for a moment, weighing up what he just said. 'I met her mother and father once. They were wonderful. Her sister was wonderful – religious, but wonderful. I wanted monsters. I wanted to see people that would explain what their daughter was. But everything they said about their daughter that night was exactly what I love about her.'

He saw John raise his eyebrows and realised he'd used the present tense.

'What are you going to do now?' John asked after a silence.

Jasper cleared his throat. 'I can't just leave Edmund on his own. He's been there for me when I needed him. He's slept on my sofa, sat with me while I ate – and then he's gone to work in the morning. Remember,' he digressed, 'the day we met, and he came when you called him?' His voice trailed off. He calculated how long Ovidia and Edmund had been together and tried to recall exactly when that day had been and then wondered if, the next morning, Edmund had come here to Ovidia. He silently cursed them both.

Jasper slapped his hands against his thighs, slumped forward, and continued. 'I may be a wreck, but if he hadn't stepped in when he had, I could've been much worse, dead even. I can't leave a woman who might beat him senseless to take care of him. Oh, and our parents, they'll be devastated if they find out – and his son, well I should be there for him, too.'

'You're forgetting someone,' John prompted him.

'Holly? I can't expect her to stick around. She puts up with so much nonsense from me already. I can't ask any more of her. Maybe this is it for us.' Jasper paused.

John shook his head. 'I meant – what about you?'

'Me?' Jasper asked. 'What do you mean me?'

34

Holly and Anne had long since filled the dishwasher, cleared the counters, and emptied the detritus of food and drinks into the recycling and rubbish bins. They avoided subjects of any importance. Anne felt ill-equipped to discuss Jasper's relationship with Ovidia. Instead, they talked about Anne's daughters, about how Anne and John were doing an excellent job. The conversation faded, being harder to stoke until, eventually, they sat perched on the barstools in silence with wine glasses half full.

'Are you okay, Holly?' Anne finally asked. She didn't know how else to get Holly to talk.

'I'm...' Holly started. 'Ask me tomorrow. I need to think, but I don't want to. Is there a way to turn the sound off in my head?' She smiled unsteadily.

Anne thought about a night about a month ago. John had arrived home, earphones on, and kissed her on the mouth. 'The girls?' he'd asked and whistled off in search of them.

He had been perhaps twenty minutes later than usual. There had been nothing about his clothes, his coat, his smell, or even the way he whistled cheerfully that had said that he'd been with another woman. Nothing. But she had been certain of it.

'If you don't talk about it, it will gnaw at you until you think you're going mad,' Anne said, knowing immediately she shouldn't have. Holly studied her for a moment, looked perplexed, but said nothing.

John's infidelity wasn't something Anne thought of constantly. Instead, thoughts of him with another woman, or women, stabbed her when she was least equipped to fight back – after seeing a particularly difficult patient or in the midst of excruciating period pain. She sometimes wondered if she should hire a private detective to find out for certain. But she couldn't, because some mornings she woke bathed in dread, afraid of what knowing the truth would bring.

They'd have to split. There would be no excuse to stay, especially after what had happened in Singapore. After that trip, she and John had painfully stitched their life back together again. He'd declared he'd never leave her and that he would do whatever it took to stay. He came home straight from work, he'd scoured the shops with Anne for what they needed for the baby, he cooked and cleaned – as he still did. They'd talked seemingly endlessly about love, their future, their baby. They'd discussed everything, except, she'd realised long after, what he'd done and why he'd done it. Anne had been left without an explanation.

'Come on. I'm going to have a look around,' Anne said, sliding off her seat, deferring thinking about her own life for later.

'What, go snooping? Anne, we can't,' Holly said.

'You can stay if you like,' Anne suggested. 'But I don't want to just sit here. It's too depressing.' She didn't want to think about deceit – Edmund's or John's.

'Wait for me,' Holly called. Anne was already at the foot of the stairs.

Holly caught up with her, glancing behind her as they went.

'Can you imagine what it feels like – to lose a baby? You're a nurse, you must have seen it a lot,' Holly asked as they arrived on the ground floor and glanced around the large, soulless room before continuing up the stairs.

'No, actually, I haven't. It's not TV, it doesn't happen that often – not in this country anyway,' Anne replied.

'I had a miscarriage at three months,' Holly said as they arrived on the first floor and out of earshot.

Anne froze.

'I'd been planning to get rid of it, and then suddenly it was beyond my control,' Holly explained, stopping and straightening a picture on the wall absentmindedly. 'That's what really hurt. I'd been so certain I wasn't going to keep it, and then it wasn't my choice anymore.'

'With Jasper?' Anne asked.

Holly nodded. 'We'd been dating for just over three months. Two adults, above thirty, tertiary-level education, and not using birth control – would you believe that? It's not like we were silly teenagers. I felt so stupid.' She emphasised stupid. 'What was I doing sleeping with a guy I'd just met without protection? How was I so sure he was the one?'

'Did you tell him?' Anne asked. They stopped at the top of the staircase.

'No. I said I was having an unusually bad period. It took me weeks to get over it. I'd never been so miserable in my life.'

She'd found herself weeks later wrapped in a blanket on her sofa awakening from the fugue she'd descended into after her miscarriage. In that state, she'd realised what it must be like to be Jasper, the man with whom she was in love. She'd felt her unhappiness surging through her body like currents too powerful to control. She'd known what it was like to stand in front of her colleagues at work, fighting back tears as she spoke, to watch her mobile ringing and yet be unable to face the idea of speaking to her own mother. But, for her, it had ended swiftly in comparison to Jasper. She felt spurred to continue with him, putting in the additional work, that extra patience that he needed.

Holly shook her head. 'I've kept it from him. It never occurred to me that he might have secrets too.' She leaned against the wall. 'I'm such an idiot, Anne. I should have demanded more from him, made him deal with whatever it was that was bothering him.'

'What's the problem? Is it that he never told you about her, or that she's with Edmund?' Anne asked.

'Both,' Holly replied. 'Jasper sat there the whole day without saying who she was. I thought she was nice – I talked about us becoming sisters-in-law. And he has never, never said a word about her – why not?' She stopped. 'No. I'm not going to talk or think about it until I've talked to Jasper.'

'Good idea,' Anne said as she pondered which door to open first.

They saw a master bedroom, a room with a TV and pictures of Icelandic ponies that Holly had called stunning, and a guest room. Finally, they opened the door to the last room. Anne found what she was looking for. The nursery.

OLIVER was emblazoned above the cot in metal letters painted in cobalt blue. Someone cleaned the room often and well – unlike the rest of the house. Neither dust nor dirt were visible anywhere. Anne could see that the nursery belonged to a baby whose parents had lavished their child with every conceivable luxury. Anne recognised the furniture from décor shops that she visited and magazines that she bought, designs she couldn't even dream of being able to afford. The books on the shelves were traditional titles, books that Anne knew would be abandoned in favour of new, contemporary titles as parents searched for something that would hold their baby's attention.

Anne picked up a framed picture of Oliver. 'Look, he's so gorgeous – what beautiful brown eyes. You know, I never realised that Edmund had really nice eyes until now. Maybe because they looked so sad today.'

'Aww cute,' Holly said, glancing only briefly and then too swiftly turning to something else, perhaps avoiding Oliver's picture.

Anne opened a few drawers, careful not to disturb anything. 'I hope we get to see Ovidia again, one day, when they're over this.'

'If she stays with Edmund, it will be inevitable. I still can't imagine what she sees in him, though,' Holly said. 'But she did seem nice, until… well. I just don't get how she can go out with two brothers – even if it there was a good amount of time between them. Oh, look at this!'

Holly quietly pulled open another drawer. She mouthed an 'Oh' and held up an ultrasound picture. 'Wow,' she said quietly, squinting as she examined the image. 'My baby would have been almost like this. Look, you can see his outline. He's so human.' Without showing it to Anne, she hurriedly put the scan back in its place, slamming the drawer with surprising force. 'I'm sure the last thing they want to find when they get home is us picking through their son's bedroom,' Holly said. 'Or in their house, for that matter. I'd leave, but I don't want Jasper here with her. Did you see the look on his face when she didn't turn back? He was devastated. He's obviously not over her, and he won't be over her tomorrow or the day after...' She paused, lost in thought. 'I want to have this, too: a baby and a man who looks at me with adoration,' Holly continued. 'I want to be like you and John, ten years together, a family – grandparents falling over each other to get to look after their grandkids.' She sat down in the nursing chair and raised her feet from the floor, pointing her toes. 'He says he loves me, but he's never looked at me the way Edmund looked at Ovidia today.'

Anne thought how John looked at her like that all the time, yet it meant little and guaranteed even less. 'That's just what you see. If there's anything I've learned today, it's how deep secrets can run,' Anne replied. 'Come on, let's go.'

'You know what just occurred to me,' Holly said as they opened the door to leave. 'When Oliver is okay, and if Jasper and I are still together, our kids would probably use some of this stuff – you know, hand me downs from their older cousin.'

Anne thought Holly suddenly looked more cheerful. Even when the smile left her face, Holly's eyes still appeared brighter. Holly was fooling herself, Anne decided. Holly believed her life with Jasper would return to the path it was on before today. Holly hadn't seen Jasper at his worst, or in the state Anne had met him in. She wasn't sure Holly would be able to cope.

Was she supposed to encourage Holly to stick by Jasper, or was she supposed to support Holly if she decided to leave Jasper? Jasper's mental health was precarious. He could have a complete breakdown – was Holly supposed to commit to him for better or worse when the near future looked highly likely to be worse?

They returned to the kitchen to John pouring wine into two glasses. Jasper's eyes were red and the skin around them agitated, but neither of the women asked why. Anne saw Holly look at the floor, averting her eyes from her fiancé. She thought of their Facebook announcement and wondered what would happen if Holly deleted her status – what would her friends think, and what would they say or not say?

Holly and Anne said nothing about their exploration, either. Anne brought out a jumbo packet of crisps she found when she'd been cleaning up. The others thanked her, and they sat, waiting again, crunching in silence.

35

Oliver's brief life was over.

Ovidia and Edmund had taken a taxi home. Occasionally, she'd glanced at Edmund. His expression was not one she'd ever seen before. It was one of complete defeat, she'd decided.

She'd delayed their mission as long as she could. That morning, when Edmund had asked – or had he accused? – her of going on her run on such a day, she'd been afraid that she wouldn't have an excuse not to go to the hospital as early as it was permissible. She'd been that afraid that the staff would have greeted them cheerfully and then said, *'since you are here early'*, and Oliver would have lost half a day of his life.

Ovidia stroked her phone's interface. She observed her short, jagged nails and the dry, grey and flaking skin of her knuckles. A notification message was emblazoned across her mobile's screen. Doris had sent her a message. Ovidia didn't open it. She knew it was a prayer or a quote from the bible, but she knew it had nothing to do with Oliver. Her family didn't know she was here, in a taxi, being driven across the city with Edmund beside her.

Without Jasper, Anne, Holly, and John, neither she nor Edmund had seemed able to speak. She watched Edmund's hands, gently restless in his lap, his fingers moving in a slow wave-like motion as if following a piece of silent music. She had wanted to take his hands and feel the music too, to be transported away from the faux-leather seats, talk radio, and incessant beeping of the driver's mobile phone.

Ovidia sat in the back of the taxi thinking about divine retribution and about punishment for one's sins. Of course, at times, she'd thought that she'd deserved the death of her child, and maybe Edmund had to some extent, as well, but she'd told herself that was all nonsense. She knew the universe didn't work that way – she believed in the laws of science, that existence was composed of atoms, molecules, energy, and everything else that lay only in the physical realm. Yet, despite not having been to church since she was a teenager, she recalled the supplications. She clenched her hands in her lap, disguising their pose with her phone – not wanting Edmund to see her pray.

She thought back to last year in spring, at this time of the evening when she was still expecting Oliver. She'd been sitting in the annex with her feet on a stool, and she'd thought Edmund was working on his laptop in the kitchen, staying close to her. He'd suddenly flown out of the kitchen, laptop in hand.

'Look at this. Isn't it just fabulous!' His eyes had been ablaze with childish delight.

He'd shown her the webpage of a décor magazine; it showed a children's playhouse set within a wild, English garden. Three children, their backs to the camera, dressed as pirates, raced around and on the playhouse, their hair streaming behind them and toys strewn on the ground.

'You do realise it'll be years before he can get on that thing?' she'd asked, though she'd been immediately captured by the image herself, already considering simple safety measures that could be added and perhaps a slight change in colour.

'I know,' Edmund had said, resting his chin on her shoulder. 'A bit of forward planning won't hurt.' He'd nestled his face against her neck.

By this point, their baby had already been named Adam, Noah, Lucian, and even Evelyn. They'd been sure of his name and then they weren't, once again editing the list. Would they need a middle name, and, if they did, should he use a hyphenated last name? They'd discussed which second language would be most useful and if the two of them should learn it as well.

Like the playhouse, they'd imagined what his interests would be. Would he be inclined to sport or music, and when would he be the right age to take up art and piano lessons? They'd paused in sports shops to ask about the best bicycles for a beginner, not admitting the future cyclist was yet to be born.

Last year, the future had been something they anticipated. It was so certain that it was almost tangible – they were having a child, it would be loved, it would grow into an adult, with every day of its life bringing them joy.

But now he was gone. No one else who mattered in their lives knew. It was still light outside, just after eight. Ovidia watched the city's denizens walking home from parks and playgrounds, towels slung over their shoulders, skin pink and tender from too long spent in the weak sun. Outside restaurants, she saw small groups congregating for dinner, seeking missing members of their complements, tapping furiously on their screens or leaning away from their friends, heads cocked against their phones. Some had already had too much to drink and were making their way home, their pace uneven and path meandering, tempers simmering like kindling waiting to ignite. At home their partners would be waiting, some angry, some ambivalent.

She was pretty certain that, for most people, this night was a lot like the previous one or at least like their previous Saturday. Her sister Doris would be on her way to an evening prayer session at her church, as she'd done almost every Saturday night for years. Her parents would be settling down for Saturday evening TV; they'd have a packet of crisps and beer. The sound on the TV would be a little too loud, her mother refusing to acknowledge the slight loss of hearing that had come with her age.

She tried to think about the city, former colleagues, friends and former friends, acquaintances – anything that was neither immediate nor important. Her thoughts kept returning to Edmund and to Oliver.

Right now, Edmund's mother would still be exhilarated from the previous night's news of Jasper's impending marriage. She'd be talking nothing but weddings, mentally compiling guest lists, weighing up her options for a venue, adding to her wish list those regrets that she still carried from her own wedding – as mothers often did. Ovidia wondered if Edmund would phone them to tell them his news, to ruin their happiness. *'The grandchild that you never knew is now dead.'* They'd be confused, perhaps outraged. *'How did you have a baby and not tell us?'* Ovidia could imagine Edmund's mother saying.

Ovidia closed her eyes and leaned back in the seat. How would Edmund tell her to leave? Or would he just expect her to go without having to say so. There was nothing to keep them together now. When the cab stopped outside their house, his house, would she go inside or cross the road and go back to her flat?

When they'd arrived at the hospital, the doctors had explained everything to them – what was going to happen, that they'd turn off the machines, that it might take days for their baby to die, or just a few minutes.

Beside Oliver's hospital bed, Ovidia had made a few remarks about when he was born, about how dark his hair had been and about the roundness of his cheeks. Edmund had nodded. He'd sighed and glanced out of the window – a window that faced the wall of the adjacent building. Edmund had asked her if she would like them to take turns waiting or if they should wait together until he was gone – they'd had no idea how long he'd live once the life support was turned off.

When the doctor and nurse had begun, Ovidia had closed her eyes. She could sense their shadowy forms moving through her eyelids. She'd reopened her eyes when the sound of the machines had stopped. The sound that she'd become accustomed to, the noises that told her Oliver was still alive. She'd allowed herself to believe that, once he was free of the beeping, tubes, and lights, he'd open his eyes. She'd imagined that one day she'd play with him again, that one day these months in hospital would all be a distant memory.

This, Ovidia had reminded herself, was the last time she'd sit in the intensive care unit. She'd never again have to walk through the corridors bustling with staff whose faces were half-obscured with surgical masks, their shoes soundless as they pushed or skirted around gurneys. Sometimes a child's cry would make Ovidia's heart leap and she'd hurry, thinking, *'Could it be?'* But it never was.

Every day she and Edmund had arrived at Oliver's bedside, and he'd still be lying inert on a bed that was much too big for him, tubes feeding him and machines breathing for him, dressed in blue and white. She'd never given up reading to him, hoping he was listening. She'd imagined him one day when he was older, telling her why the giraffe had a long neck or asking her why he had such vivid memories of a trickster rabbit.

He'd been nearly bald when they'd brought him in – his baby hair, straight and brown, had been shedding, only to have regrown as he slept, this time soft and curly.

When it was over, she'd stroked his hair for the last time and then turned away from him and left the room.

36

Edmund replayed his son's last moments. Oliver's chest, for just a few minutes, had risen and fallen with the air going in and out of his lungs without the help of a machine. Hope had jolted through him – perhaps that miracle he'd been praying for had come. But too soon it was over. Edmund recalled the life creeping out of Oliver's skin, remembering how quickly his baby took on the pallor of the dead.

Edmund was thankful to Jasper for having bought Oliver a few hours of life. Had Jasper and his guests not arrived that morning, there'd have been nothing to stop him and Ovidia from going to the hospital earlier. He knew he could not have made it through the day staring at his son whose death was imminent, scheduled, without begging the staff to end everything immediately.

Ovidia had been beside him, holding his arm at first, letting it fall later. She'd said little as he'd talked to the doctor. His voice had cracked mid-sentence and, when he faltered, she'd asked, 'And how long do we have to make preparations?' She'd stepped in as if to rescue him from the embarrassment of being struck dumb with grief. He'd seen that she hadn't listened for the doctor's response – she'd turned away to watch Oliver dying.

They were allowed to hold their son. His body was lifeless, as it had been for the last four months.

In the taxi, Edmund had inhaled through his nose, hoping to calm down, hoping he could at least get home with some dignity. He could feel his eyes clouding over and blinked rapidly, chasing the tears away each time, the blush of sadness rising and subsiding. Every now and then he'd caught Ovidia's eye. She wasn't crying, she hadn't cried at all. Shock, he decided.

When the taxi had stopped at the last lights before their house, Edmund, unable to hold back his tears, had buried his head in his hands and wept. Ovidia had held him, and, when he finally looked up, he found her watching a group of teens as the taxi passed, half of them laughing and leaping about and the others holding up their mobile phones, texting or making video calls. Her face the picture of misery.

He had opened his mouth and then shut it again. In his mind, where words usually resided, there was nothing but a blackness. He'd wanted to comfort her but couldn't. She'd held him with cold hands as he leaned against her shoulder and cried.

He'd never in his life felt unhappiness like he felt at this moment. When his grandparents had passed away, he'd been sad, but both had aged gently over the years, the crippling effect of their time on earth had been relatively kind to them, both left with dignity, saying sad farewells while their family waited beside them fetching each other cups of tea and sticky buns from the hospital cafeteria.

Oliver had never even said his first word or taken his first steps. He'd never had the chance to become the darling of his grandparents' eyes, the centre of their universe.

Anger at the unfairness of the situation had flared up within Edmund and then it ebbed. Anger was pointless at a time like this, as was blame. It felt out of place; both he and Ovidia were suffering.

The taxi driver had said nothing after he'd picked them up outside the hospital. Edmund had spotted him glancing back at them, he guessed, trying to figure out their story.

Now the driver told them the fare gently as he parked outside their house. Ovidia paid as Edmund straightened his clothes, accepted a piece of tissue from her and wiped his eyes and nose.

'They're still here,' Edmund said. He took Ovidia's hand.

'They really want us to join in their celebration,' Ovidia replied drily.

'Ovidia,' he chided her, gently drawing out her name as if he might never say it again.

'I'm joking.'

'Humour? Now?'

'Doesn't make much difference,' she insisted and chuckled, but he knew the sound of her laughter, and this wasn't it.

'Let's go and hide at my place for a while,' Ovidia suggested. 'They've no idea how long we took.'

Across the road, the curtains in her flat were closed, the two of them could escape there for a little while and not talk to anyone.

'Oh no, I don't have my keys,' she said.

'I have them,' Edmund replied. They were always on his key ring beside his own.

Ovidia turned and Edmund panicked.

'No, come home with me,' he said. 'If you go home, you might stay there.'

Ovidia nodded. They continued standing where they were, just outside the door, neither being first to open it.

Edmund was once again reminded that the door would have to be fixed. It was one more thing he had to do, he thought, in a seemingly endless list of obligations. At first, each time he exited or entered through it he thought, briefly, how it came to be damaged, why the lock refused to stay shut, being prone to slowly swinging open unless they remembered to lock the inner latch, which they often didn't.

He remembered being overcome with fury a few weeks earlier; Ovidia with Oliver at the hospital, his work that he once loved piling up, the growing apprehension that he was going to have to tell someone of his situation or finally break down. The lock had resisted his fumbling as he'd tried to force his key in with shaking hands, and he'd attacked it – slamming his weight against the door, over and over again until he'd felt it give. Only then did he stop, breathe, and examine the destruction he'd wrought and feel that little bit relieved.

With the house alarm going off, the police had arrived within minutes, but a simple explanation that he'd forgotten his keys put them at ease. They'd checked his driver's licence and swept through the house and then bid him goodnight, suggesting that next time he consult a locksmith.

Ovidia had asked about it when she returned. Edmund said the police had told him someone had tried to force their way into the house, but he'd shrugged it off. 'The perks of living in a good neighbourhood and having security response.'

Before opening the door now, Edmund began, his voice a croak, 'I can't believe he's gone. At least before, I could hope.' Ovidia turned away from him towards the street. There was nothing there to see except the same cars that parked there every night, including his.

'Being with you was amazing, it was perfect. I want to be with you for the rest of my life,' Edmund said.' And what's worse, today I got to see the woman I fell in love with again.' He ran his finger along the door's mouldings. 'I should have left yesterday,' he continued, 'before I knew how hard it would be.'

Ovidia stayed quiet.

Edmund stared at the doorknob. 'I'm nearly fifty. I've tried calculating my chances of being in love again, how long it will take to find someone and start a new family. Then I'll be an old man by the time that child's a toddler, maybe senile by the time it gets to university. I'd never get to see my grandchildren. And if I don't find this woman, I'll be alone for the rest of my life.'

Edmund turned the door handle and entered, Ovidia behind him. They heard voices from the kitchen below, and Ovidia froze, stopping in her tracks. Edmund turned to her, and she shook her head.

'I'm going to be sick.' She clutched her stomach and retched on the floor, Edmund catching her before she could fall.

He pulled her away from the puddle of vomit and steered her to the downstairs bathroom. He held her as she leaned over the toilet and spewed the contents of her stomach until she had nothing left to bring up.

Edmund soaked half a hand towel and wiped her face and patches of sick from her dress.

'That towel smells like we nicked it from a tomb,' she said, tears welling up in her eyes but still not crying.

Edmund smiled reluctantly and sat beside her on the floor, and she crumpled against him.

'I can take care of myself,' Ovidia said. 'Don't worry about me.'

'Maybe you can,' he replied. 'I remember thinking, when I saw you that day at the run, that if anything happened to you, I'd hate myself. That still applies.'

They remained on the floor for a while longer, only their breathing audible.

'I'm going to get some stuff together and go back to my place,' she said, and they both got to their feet.

Edmund stifled a protest. That morning he'd wanted this – the end. Now he had it, but he wasn't sure what was supposed to happen now. His heart began to race, and he battened down his rising panic. He swallowed and opened the door, and they exited the bathroom, parting at the stairs.

Edmund arrived in the kitchen to find four people seated with bated breath and expectant faces. He nodded in greeting and paused.

'Ovidia's gone upstairs,' he said. 'She's going to get some sleep.' He waited, hoping they'd excuse themselves. 'I think I'll join her,' he said when they didn't. He didn't want to explain that Ovidia was packing, that his relationship was over.

Edmund turned to go back up the stairs, but Jasper leapt to his feet, his stool wobbling precariously with the momentum.

'Edmund, I have to talk to you,' Jasper said, glancing at Anne as he spoke.

'I'm exhausted. I'm sorry. I'll call you tomorrow,' Edmund replied.

'Just a few minutes. Please,' Jasper said.

Edmund nodded, and Jasper followed him through the French doors to the glass extension and the two of them sat down – Edmund in his armchair and Jasper on the three-seater, leaning in towards his brother.

'I wanted to say I'm sorry about…' Jasper began haltingly. 'You could have told me.'

'I could have told you that I was with the woman who abused you and was happier than I'd ever been in my life?' Edmund asked. 'It didn't seem like a good idea.'

'Well, yes. Why not?' Jasper demanded.

'Really?'

'We'd have rowed a few times. I'd probably have sworn to never speak to you again, but what would I have done about it? I couldn't have stopped you,' Jasper said. 'In time, everything would have been okay.'

Edmund could see Jasper was trying to comfort him, but his brother's eyes said how much pain he was in. Had Jasper known he was with Ovidia, it would certainly have pushed Jasper over that precipice that he had so delicately trodden for the first few years after Ovidia left him.

'Maybe. Or you could have been completely devastated. It was only a year after you broke up. You're my only brother – I'd have lost you,' Edmund replied. 'Jasper, look at yourself. You've never recovered from Ovidia. Do you think it would have been easier knowing she was with me? It would have pushed you over the edge.'

'Most likely,' Jasper confessed, rubbing his eyes. 'That aside, you should have told me when your son was born.'

Edmund didn't reply.

'Or at least, the two of you didn't have to sit here listening to us plan weddings and talk about honeymoons,' Jasper continued in Edmund's silence. 'You didn't have to go through this alone.'

'Yes. I did,' Edmund said finally. 'This is the life I created for myself and these are its consequences. Tomorrow is a new life, filled with new things to go through alone.'

'So, it's over between you and Ovidia?' Jasper asked, sitting up suddenly, his hands falling away from his face.

'It has to be. How can it survive?' Edmund said.

'Relationships do continue after a child's death.'

'If it were just that,' Edmund replied quietly. 'But there's so much more. And besides, you know about it now. Then there's Holly, and John and Anne. Soon it will include Mummy and Dad and Ovidia's family. Everyone will want to know, everyone will demand an explanation, everyone will want to be involved.'

Jasper snorted in suppressed laughter. 'I am not them. I'm the little boy you taught to ride a bike and use chopsticks.'

'And look what you kept from me,' Edmund said quietly.

'I was afraid,' Jasper said, after a moment's indecision. 'I was scared, terrified from morning till night every bloody day. I couldn't see a way out. She was a monster.'

'I know,' Edmund said. 'I asked every expert I could find, I read every article and every thesis I could get a hold of. It took me a long time to understand what I was seeing. Part of the reason it took so long for me to realise was that I'd always thought you'd come to me if you were ever in trouble. And you've always done before – remember? School bullies, getting through your first job? You always told me.'

'And you?' Jasper said quietly. 'You never told me anything. I've realised that today. All that talking we do, it's never about you. I don't think I can even remember your first job.'

Jasper glanced through the glass into the garden. 'This thing with Oliver fills in so many blanks. It explains so many weird little...' He paused and leaned forward. 'That dinner at Mummy and Dad's, when you left?'

'Ovidia called saying she had contractions.' Edmond gripped his arm rest at the memory. 'False alarm in the end. I practically danced my way out the front door.' His voice almost failed him.

'You were that happy and you didn't say.'

Edmund paused, his hand over his mouth.

'Or we didn't notice,' Jasper said, pensive.

They were both silent. Edmund struggled to keep his composure.

'Ovidia told me you threatened her. Did you mean it?' Jasper asked.

'Practically speaking, no,' Edmund replied, his own words reminding him of Ovidia's penchant for ill-timed humour. 'The thought of spending time in prison doesn't appeal to me. But I was going to stop her. Lucky, she took my word for it.' He paused and looked at Jasper. 'But then, when you met Ovidia, it changed you – so who knows?'

'You're saying that when with you she changed completely, that she never said or did anything to you that showed you what she was really like?' Jasper demanded.

Edmund flinched. 'Do you remember the first few months you were with Ovidia? I do. You told me everything about it. I could see the excitement in you when you talked about her,' Edmund said. 'I remember you told me about how funny she was, and intelligent, and she was loving and caring.' He saw Jasper look away from him. 'Well, I had that for four years, four amazing years.'

'You want me to believe that?'

'Yes, I do,' Edmund said.

'And that she became the perfect mother, too?'

Edmund didn't answer, closing his eyes for a moment.

'What happened?' Jasper asked.

Edmund still didn't answer, and his gaze drifted away from his brother onto a puddle, long-dried and now invisible, where the contents of a baby bottle had once spilt and were almost immediately wiped away.

'Fine,' Jasper sighed. 'I'm going to let you go to bed. I've a feeling I'm not going to be this sensible in the next few days. Right now, it's more important that you get through this. Please understand if I don't spend as much time with you as I should.' Jasper stood straightening his trousers. 'And of course there's Holly.'

'And you're not – afraid of Holly?' Edmund asked.

'No. Not of Holly,' Jasper said, a touch of sadness in his voice. With his hand on a door handle he continued. 'Okay, I'm going. You might find that you're short of booze. We helped ourselves while you were out.' Jasper didn't offer an embrace or a firm reassuring handshake; he knew his brother too well.

Jasper paused again. 'Oliver – is he…' He looked for an appropriate euphemism.

'Dead?' Edmund suggested. He nodded, slouching back in the sofa. 'It took less than half an hour in the end.'

37

She was being good, Holly thought to herself. She'd even been to the bathroom to reapply her make-up and straighten her clothes. She reassured herself that the day was almost over, that Jasper would emerge after talking to his brother and feel satisfied that he'd done his fraternal duty. Then they'd all leave, and she'd return to her life as a bride-to-be: wedding planning, thanking her friends for their congratulatory messages, and deciding if she should change her last name to Jasper's or not or perhaps go for the double-barrelled option.

Ovidia, Holly told herself, was just an ex. Jasper and Ovidia's relationship had probably ended in some dramatic scene or perhaps had been embarrassing – like when Immanuel had abandoned her for a wealthy brunette whose family originated from the same part of India as his. Afterward, she had berated herself for not having foreseen that their relationship would not last – his constant references to affluence, her never being introduced to his family, periods of overwhelming attention and affection followed by long disappearances and apathy.

Still in the bathroom, Holly typed Immanuel's name into Facebook but closed it before the search results were listed. The difference between her and Jasper was, if she met Immanuel now, she wouldn't be plunged into an abyss of unhappiness.

But Holly didn't believe herself when, in a whisper, she reassured herself that everything would be all right. Nonetheless, she continued to tell herself that Jasper would explain to her what happened and then everything would be as it had been before. Inside, she could feel her emotions escalating, and all she wanted was to leave the house with Jasper.

Earlier, when Edmund and Ovidia had been out of the house, she and John had coerced Anne into telling them the little more she knew about Oliver and to show them the pictures. Jasper had glanced at them as they handed them to each other, the rest of them lingering on each image. Having seen Edmund's pallor when he arrived, she hadn't needed him to confirm that the baby was dead.

'Do you think I'm being really shallow if all I can think of is my relationship?' she asked, joining Anne and John in the kitchen again. 'What if this wrecks everything? What if Jasper goes back to her?'

'Holly' – John wrapped his hand around hers – 'it's okay to be worried and even scared. This is a pretty bizarre situation.'

'Even if he stays with me, how will I ever socialise with Ovidia? How will I ever like her?' Holly asked, her resolve to be optimistic already disintegrating.

'It's been at least four years, Holly.' Anne leaned in, resting her elbows on the kitchen peninsula. 'He's had time to get over her.'

'Right.' Jasper strolled in with an obviously feigned levity. 'We're through. We can go home now.' He rubbed his hands. 'What a bloody awful day this has been.'

Holly could tell he was pretending to be all right. His eyes refused to meet hers, and he rocked back and forth on his heels. Holly curled her hands into fists.

'What do you mean "a bloody awful day"?' Holly straightened up in her seat, erect and angry. 'We announced our engagement today.'

'You know I didn't mean it that way,' Jasper said, dismissing her reaction with a flick of his head. 'Besides, we can pick up tomorrow where we left off.'

'Really? Burying your nephew is "picking up where we left off"?' Holly said accusingly. 'How are we supposed to have a wedding with your ex sitting at the high table with us. And what about today – are we just expected to never say anything about Edmund's charade or Oliver to anyone?'

'It's no one else's business,' Jasper replied in defence of his brother.

'Well, I don't see why I should have to keep it a secret,' Holly said, feeling her aggression growing. She scratched her fingernails against the top of the kitchen peninsula.

Jasper was becoming agitated. He tapped his fingers against the empty stool and then, resting his weight against it, asked, 'Why would you tell anyone anyway?'

Holly hesitated for a moment. Anne and John were sitting silent, their body language telling of their discomfort. Disregarding their presence, Holly continued. 'That's beside the point.' Again, she paused, jutting out her chin. 'Jasper, why didn't you tell me about her?'

Jasper looked at his shoes.

'Don't tell me it's because it was a long time ago.' Holly forced herself to say it to him. 'You're still in love with her – she left you, and you aren't over her.' Her face reddened and tears came to her eyes.

Jasper didn't respond.

'I'm second best, aren't I?' Holly said, choking back her tears.

'You weren't...' Jasper began and trailed off.

Holly flinched. He'd used the wrong tense. It was tantamount to a confession. She turned to John and Anne looking for help – they must have heard him, too.

Anne and John glanced at each other and then the floor. They looked uncomfortable and desperate to escape.

Anne cleared her throat. 'I think perhaps you guys should wait until tomorrow to talk about this – things will be a bit clearer then,' Anne said. 'Right, Jasper?'

'I have to talk to Ovidia,' Jasper said instead. He turned and hurried up the stairs.

Stunned into silence, Holly slumped on to a barstool and cried.

38

Ovidia wasn't expecting him or anyone else. She was in front of the TV when he found her. It was off. She had been readying herself to leave and instead found herself curled on the sofa, caressing the grey blanket she'd knitted. She'd gone first into Oliver's room, run a hand over his cot and fluffed his pillow. She'd opened and closed his drawers, smoothed down his neatly folded clothes. She stopped in the middle of room and realised every item within it would be removed, that the walls would be repainted, the whole space used for someone else, perhaps not even a baby. She thought of another child wearing his clothes and the other little boy called Oliver who would own the handcrafted metal letters. Somewhere soon, another baby would lie on his back in his cot mesmerised by Oliver's mobile, and another mother would lean over the cot stroking her own baby's face, whispering to him that he was the most wonderful creature who'd ever lived.

Ovidia had said goodbye to the room and its contents, closed its door quietly, and crossed the corridor to the TV room. The first thing she noticed was one of a pair of running shoes that she'd misplaced months earlier. She and Edmund would sit here like polite guests, not touching anything except the TV's remote. Her magazines accumulated unread, and bookmarks remained exactly where they'd been inserted in a previous life when they read and played music.

Ovidia picked up her shoe and recalled the morning four months earlier when its loose insole had been irritating her on her run. She'd come up here afterwards, shoe in hand to examine it. Edmund had been in here, on his mobile, with Oliver asleep in his arms. She'd walked past him, brushing the top of his head in greeting and had sat down on the sofa, completely engrossed in examining the shoe.

A few minutes later, she'd felt Edmund standing above her, still on his phone, holding Oliver out to her.

'Just a minute,' she'd said, trying to extract the insole, turning away from him. He'd left the room, and she'd heard the nursery door close.

She'd been considering her options for a tool to lever out the insole when she'd heard Edmund in the corridor on the phone, asking for something to be repeated when Oliver began wailing, all four months of him. She'd smiled and returned to her shoe. For some reason, the shoe had her attention – Edmund would look after Oliver.

Now, the insole was still as she'd left it, half peeled off, the job incomplete, the shoe neatly placed beneath the chair, the housekeeper knowing that Ovidia didn't like anyone to interfere with her running equipment.

'You were never one for crying,' Jasper said, startling her. She got the impression he'd been watching her for a while. He closed the door behind himself.

He looked frightened. Here, out of earshot of the others, did he still believe she was the woman who'd tortured him all that time ago? How was it, she asked herself, that after five years apart, she could still terrify him?

She watched him take several deep breaths. Jasper sat down at the other end of the sofa, facing her at an angle. What Ovidia saw were the times she and Edmund had sat together on this sofa and watched TV. She'd often put her feet in his lap, or he'd lay his head on her lap, or they'd lean against each other eating popcorn.

'When Edmund mentioned he was watching a show on TV, I should have known a woman was involved,' Jasper said. 'It all feels a bit ridiculous now, all those little hints and giveaways are finally in context.'

Ovidia didn't respond.

'I'm so sorry about Oliver.' Jasper changed track, as if beginning again.

Ovidia nodded.

'Are you going to hold a funeral?' he asked with a tremor in his voice.

'We haven't thought about it,' Ovidia replied, willing him to go away.

'If you did, then I'm sure no one would... confront you about all the secrecy. Everyone would think it was the wrong time,' he suggested.

She thought for a moment that he was about to reach over and touch her. She drew back, repulsed by the memory of his touch. It was a lifetime ago when he'd last held her. She had been a different person, a vile and violent person, someone she didn't want to remember.

'So.' Jasper slapped his thighs and seemed as if he was about to stand up. 'I've seen you again – like I dreamt I would. Still nothing is sorted out, no questions answered.' He scratched his forehead.

'It's not as if I was ready for this either,' Ovidia said.

'It's unfair, Ovidia,' he said. 'Within a year you were in love with someone else, and I was still suffering. Everything you touched turned to gold: great career, you live in a place like this with your partner and child... Where's the justice?'

Ovidia stopped in mid-motion, frozen in the act of stroking the blanket.

'Oh God, no, I didn't mean to insinuate that Oliver's death was anything about justice – I'm sorry,' he blabbered hurriedly.

They were both silent for a moment.

'Anne showed us Oliver's pictures. He was beautiful,' Jasper continued. 'Then I realised that he had my eyes... I'd never really thought about it before, but Edmund and I have the same eyes. It was like seeing what our kids, yours and mine, would have looked like.'

Ovidia resumed stroking the blanket – surprised. It had been such a long time since she'd been in Jasper's presence that the idea that Oliver would have looked like his uncle had never occurred to her. Oliver and Jasper had never existed in the same realm. Jasper and the life she'd lived with him hadn't overlapped with the life of her child.

'Did you ever imagine us with a family?' Jasper asked.

'Never.' Ovidia shook her head. 'I'm glad we didn't make that mistake. I was a frightening, horrible person. No child should have to grow up with a mother like that. We'd have been tied together forever if we had had a child – it'd have always been an excuse. We'd never have been able to escape, to be happy again.'

'And you've been happy with Edmund?' he asked.

'Unbelievably happy,' Ovidia replied. She wanted Jasper to leave so she could be alone with her sadness. 'Jasper, I don't want to be mean, but do we have to talk about this right now?'

'When will you want to talk about it?' he asked. 'When it suits you? When your world is all right and cosy, then you'll want to talk about it – maybe?'

Jasper stood up, straightening his shirt as he rose. 'I can't believe how wrong I was about you. It wasn't enough that you ended up almost killing me, but then you just left. Just like that. Not an "I'm sorry" or a cliché "it's not you, it's me". No. You just went. And now, five years later, living with my brother, you can't spare me an explanation – something. I'm just supposed to be okay?'

She didn't respond.

'I have been on the brink of suicide,' he said, and a jolt shot through her. She'd had no idea. 'I have clutched those pills in my hands. I have held the knife to my wrist. If it weren't for Edmund…'

He took a few steps towards her.

'Did you love me?' he asked her, looking down at her on the sofa.

'I thought I did,' Ovidia replied.

'But when you met Edmund, you realised that you actually hadn't.' Jasper interpreted it for her. 'You never even came back to pick up your books and clothes. You left your photos and stuff from your childhood with me – remember the chipped Take That mug you used every morning?'

'I wrote them off. I thought about calling you and concocting some ludicrous plan where I could get my things and you wouldn't be at home. Then I realised it was all just material, meaningless – I hadn't listened to Take That in years. And their solo careers were…' She stopped herself from rambling. 'It wasn't easy to stay away. And now, again, everything about my life has changed. Over these last few months, I've lost everything. I no longer have a career, or a child, and soon I won't even have my partner. So, there, you have your justice – or something like it.'

Ovidia stood up, holding the grey throw.

Without asking, Jasper put his arms around her. At first, she became rigid, unwilling to concede to his comforting her. Then she let her head fall onto his shoulder and closed her eyes. His familiarity instead became comforting, and she felt the warmth of his breath as he lowered his head until it was just above her. His scent, his heartbeat, everything about him, reminded her of losing Edmund.

'You could have stopped me before this,' Ovidia murmured, her voice muffled in his shirt. 'Why didn't you tell someone, have me locked up?'

Her words became indistinct as they turned into thoughts in her head. She could smell his scent and feel his body through his clothes. Minutes passed, and Ovidia let Jasper hold her, knowing this would be the last time it could ever happen. Then she straightened, being gently woken from a trance.

'You should go,' Ovidia suggested.

Jasper nodded and left the room without turning back.

39

Jasper arrived in the kitchen to find John, whose face was taut with irritation, and Holly, who was resting her face on the kitchen peninsula. Jasper took many deep breaths as he approached, each one feeling more useless than the last.

'Holly was right. It's time to get home,' John said. 'But Anne's making Edmund tea. We're going to be here all night.'

'What did you two talk about?' Holly asked, raising her head, her eyes rimmed red, puffy and bloodshot.

'Oliver,' Jasper replied. His response was too quick to be believable.

'You're lying, Jasper,' Holly accused him, glaring at him.

'Let's call a taxi the minute Anne's finished. We can talk when we get out of here,' Jasper said.

Anne returned, walking briskly back into the kitchen from the extension where she'd been with Edmund.

'Are we ready?' John asked.

Anne went to the furthest door in a row of cabinets and sprung it open revealing an array of dehydrated pot noodles and powdered mashed potato.

'Just a few more minutes.' She peeled off the lid of a noodle cup that proclaimed itself to be authentic Korean flavoured and poured hot water into it.

Holly watched her and then picked up her handbag and said, 'I'm going.'

John went to stand next to Holly. 'Anne, I think these two can take care of themselves.'

'Remember, I didn't even want to come here this morning,' Anne said, holding the hot cardboard pot with a dish towel as she walked back out into the extension.

'Then we just leave her here. She's a big girl, she can find her own way home,' John said.

Taken aback at John's suggestion, Holly and Jasper hesitated before following him up the steps through the ground floor's large lounge and to the front door. Even in his haste, John hesitated.

'Imagine you're a kid with all this to run around in – play hide and seek, break things?' John said. 'Endless fun. What a shame.'

When John put his hand on the front doorknob, Jasper noticed that once again the front door had been unlocked and slightly open. John fiddled with the latch, trying to lock it behind them.

Holly followed him out, breathing in the evening's fresh air as she stopped on the top step, turning to look up at the house. Jasper stopped beside her, taking in its façade, sure that he'd never return. He took Holly's hand, feeling its warmth, and she let him hold it.

'Come on,' he said to her. Holly smiled.

With one foot off the top step, Jasper froze.

'What did she mean?' Jasper asked aloud. He looked at their faces and realised that neither John nor Holly knew the answer.

Looking momentarily at Holly, who again was agape and again on the verge of tears, Jasper spun and raced back into the house, the door sprung against its broken jamb unable to lock them out.

'What now?' John demanded.

Jasper barged into the extension where Anne sat in the three-seater and Edmund, still in his armchair, was eating the pot noodles with a spoon. Edmund was talking in low tones, and Anne was nodding; they stopped, both startled.

'What did she mean when she said I should have stopped her "before this"?' Jasper demanded.

Holly and John caught up with him, remaining just inside the kitchen.

'Edmund?' Jasper's voice rose, nearing hysterical. 'What did she mean?'

Edmund looked up at him.

'Did she –?' Jasper stopped and looked at Edmund's face, which was impassive. He could see his brother deliberately obscuring the answer to his question.

'She hit him?'

'She didn't…' Edmund began without conviction. Unable to meet Jasper's eye, he turned his head away.

'What then? Dropped him? Shook him?' Jasper demanded even louder, looming over his brother.

'Jasper!' Anne shouted.

'She did, didn't she?' Jasper stepped back, horrified.

Edmund rose to stand eye to eye with Jasper. 'Just leave us alone,' Edmund ordered him, his eyes narrowing and his voice calm and deep.

'She killed her own baby,' Jasper said, lowering his voice.

'Get out,' Edmund repeated, menacingly calm.

Anne seized Jasper's arm and pulled him towards the door. He complied, allowing himself to be pulled back into the kitchen. John and Holly moved back to give him room.

'You lied for her,' Jasper yelled to Edmund without turning, knowing his brother was behind him. 'Someone must have asked, social services, the doctors?' He visualised the baby in the picture, visualised the child's eyes – his own eyes. 'I'll report her to the police,' Jasper said to Edmund, who'd followed them into the kitchen, still holding his pot noodles.

'No one would believe you,' Edmund replied flatly. 'And you wouldn't be able to prove it.'

They all fell silent, except for the sound of their fast and frightened breathing.

'What are you saying?' Holly croaked, clearing her throat.

'Let's go,' John whispered to Jasper. 'This is too much.'

Seething, Jasper nodded, knowing he was defeated. He let John pull him towards the exit. He'd never filed a complaint for himself, he'd never told a soul. It would be an accusation by a jealous ex. Everyone, his parents, his friends, would call him a liar.

It was either the noise or fate that brought Ovidia down the stairs, he thought later. He saw her padding towards him in a pair of lion-faced socks.

He felt the blow. He saw the blur of his hand, balled in a fist, hitting her. He felt a burning thud that, in a split second, sent pain racing from his knuckles, up his arm, lighting every sensor in his body.

Jasper saw her fall, ricocheting off the wall and tumbling to the floor, a stream of blood escaping from the side of her mouth.

Anne and Holly screamed, and John's cursing was drowned out as he and Edmund hurled themselves at Jasper.

40

'Why now? Why right now?' John demanded.

They were standing on their upstairs landing, the door to his office open, the fold-up sofa unfurled. They'd opted not have a dedicated spare room – John's career had needed the office space to work on his writing. Anne handed him a set of clean sheets. He snatched them from her and shook them out. His life was coming apart; he knew why, but he refused to accept it.

'Would you rather wait until I slap you again?' Anne replied carelessly.

'Anne, don't joke about violence – not after today,' John said, the echo of Jasper hitting Ovidia still reverberated in his mind, hours after the event.

'I'm not joking,' she replied.

'You can't leave me,' John insisted, his words sounding useless and pathetic to his own ears. He spread the sheet over where he'd be sleeping that night.

'I'm going to give it a go,' she replied.

'Edmund and Ovidia, Jasper and Holly, their relationships are probably going to end tonight, and you want us to do the same?' John tried another tactic.

'I prefer to see it as starting afresh,' Anne said. 'We have to end so I can have a life on my terms.'

'You're being evasive,' John said. 'Please tell me what I've done wrong, so I can make it right. We've been together for so long. I don't want to imagine life without you.'

He knew now he'd been fooling himself about her lack of suspicion. He'd misread her as he'd lied to her. If what she wanted was a confession, he'd make it.

Anne forced a pillow into a too-small case and handed it to him to add to the mismatched sheets, garish, happily received from his mother a decade earlier.

'When the girls get back, we'll explain, and you'll leave.'

'I refuse to believe that that's what you want,' John replied.

'Why not? You'd rather believe that what I really want is to spend the rest of my life with a man who won't stop cheating on me?' she demanded, leaving the room.

John gripped the pillow with both hands against his stomach. He could see her waiting for a denial, for him to defend himself, and he fought the urge to lie.

Anne continued. 'No matter what I've done for you, no matter what I've given up, no matter that I keep telling myself that it can't be true…' Anne trailed off. 'I thought I was losing my mind, your lies were so good. To make things worse, you keep up this sham about how much you love me and the girls.'

'It's not a sham,' John shouted then quieted himself. 'I'm sorry, I didn't mean to yell. Think anything you want about me, but I love you and our daughters unequivocally.'

He threw the pillow on the floor and came to stand in front of her. 'Please, Anne, don't leave me. All those things I've done, they'll end here.'

'I'm not going to talk about it anymore. There's no point,' she said and turned her back to him, hand on the doorknob.

'It's Edmund,' John called to her. 'You want Edmund, don't you?'

She stopped. 'That's so pathetic, John.' She sighed heavily. 'I don't want anyone. I've had enough of liars.'

41

Anne closed the door firmly between them. She walked down the landing to what would no longer be their bedroom. Once he was gone, she'd redecorate. She'd take some of the money she'd been saving for her daughters' room and give herself the urban sanctuary she'd envisioned. She'd create a room, and eventually a house that was all about her and her taste. She picked up her iPad and scrolled through her blog – the one John had never seen and, she knew, he'd never have liked. She logged in and switched to edit mode.

Anne lives in London with her two daughters and is training to be an interior decorator.

Too simple, she thought, but she decided it would suffice for that night.

She'd call or text Ovidia and Holly and offer her friendship on her own terms and not as John's appendage.

She caught her breath, covering her mouth with a balled hand. She'd been happy, but her happiness had been predicated on her continuing to turn a blind eye to his infidelity and the subtle ways he steered her life in the direction he wanted.

'Go on, cry,' she said aloud, as her eyes moistened like she expected them to. She knew this would not be easy.

She heard a shuffling outside the bedroom door.

'Go away, John,' she said loudly. 'You're never sleeping beside me again.'

The shuffling quietened.

She got into bed with all her clothes on and thought about how wonderful it would be to not sleep beside a man wondering if he'd been with anyone else before coming home to her. She'd never lie close to him, trying to catch a scent or tell-tale glimpse of lipstick, or touch the nape of his neck and wonder if some other woman had touched him there.

42

Alone in their flat, Jasper threw himself on the sofa, jacket and shoes still on. He'd looked at his hands all the way home, rolling them into fists and unfurling them. He could see the bruises forming on his knuckles, and his fingers ached. The last time he'd ever hit someone, he'd been nine years old. Never once, in all the times Ovidia had been violent towards him, had Jasper ever hit Ovidia back.

Holly had refused to come home with him at first, but he begged, weeping, and she acquiesced. John and Anne had watched, but Anne had insisted that they part, that this was a situation that Holly and Jasper needed to resolve without them.

In the lounge, Holly remained standing and wrapped her sweater tightly around herself. 'You have to explain today to me, please. How could you accuse her of killing her own child? And Edmund, he basically agreed?'

Jasper opened his mouth and then shut it again.

'Jasper, you have to tell me now. If I'm left to imagine all the possibilities myself, I'll definitely leave. How am I supposed to get in bed with a man who might punch me in the face? How am I supposed to sleep at night worrying?'

'I can give you some pointers.' He meant it to be funny.

'Jasper!' Holly shrieked. 'This is not funny!' Then she frowned.

Jasper saw the notion begin to unfurl in her mind. He watched as she began to understand.

'You used to hit her?' Holly said, breathlessly, looking fearful. She took a step back.

'What?' he replied. 'No. How could you think that?'

'But that's what an abuser would say. What am I supposed to believe?' Holly wiped her eyes. 'I don't know. I've always believed you when you've said you loved me. I'd never have thought that of you last night. But now...'

She sat down, hesitating as she went, straightening her culottes and pulling at her top.

'Are you going to tell me what really happened between you two, or do I keep guessing until it drives me mad?' she pleaded.

'Please don't make me tell you...' He looked at her sadly. 'You're right. I'm not over what happened. Sometimes when I think about it, I just fall apart... well, you know better than anyone. You're always there for me,' Jasper said.

Holly closed her eyes. 'If I'm going to keep being there for you, I have to know the truth.'

It seemed a little easier this time, perhaps because he'd already told John. 'Ovidia was...' He still had to steel himself. 'She emotionally and physically abused me.'

Holly was aghast – her eyes wide and jaw slack. Her mouth moved as if she was trying to speak. For a moment, she stared at the floor, then she cleared her throat.

'You're lying,' Holly said.

Jasper recoiled at her response.

'I'm going to my mum and dad's,' she said, standing up.

Stunned, Jasper watched her leave.

When Holly was gone, Jasper slithered from the sofa onto the floor. A leftover bottle of celebratory wine was still standing unopened on the coffee table. Ignoring the sets of wine and champagne glasses they kept in the kitchen, he forced it open and drank from the bottle. He fumbled for the remote control, digging it out from between the sofa cushions, turned on the TV, and let the sounds of late-night television engulf him.

43

Holly shuddered when she closed the front door. She'd had enough, she said to herself, enough of having to look after a man who gave her too little in return to justify what he put her through.

And he *lied*; she took a deep breath to ease the tension in her chest. How could he say such a mean and evil thing about a woman he'd hit? She covered her mouth, replaying the punch in her memory. The sight of Ovidia on the floor, barely conscious. Holly was going to report him to the police for hitting Ovidia. She had to. He'd committed a crime. No, she wasn't, she shook her head, as she marched down the stairs. No one would believe her: the other witnesses were all his friends and his family and would lie for him.

Edmund's response mystified her though. But the suggestion was ridiculous. Women didn't kill babies, unless they were on drugs, and they didn't hit men either, unless they'd been drinking. Edmund was deceitful anyway, she scoffed, a man who dated his brother's ex-girlfriend.

All that didn't matter, she wailed inside her head. How could she have been so wrong about Jasper?

She paced, contemplating whether to call a taxi, just so she could have something to think about for a few moments.

She stood in a corner of the corridor and cried for a while. He could at least have tried running after her and begging her to come back to the flat and to talk to him. *That's what men in love do, isn't it?* How was she supposed to stop loving him? She asked herself how she'd get her life back, what she would do on her own in the evenings, and she mourned the time they spent together.

It was gone. The future that the two of them were meant to build, the wedding, the babies, the love that one day would allow Jasper to heal completely. She would have to come back and collect her furniture, her books, the mementos that the two of them had collected together. *He would have to build his own life,* she mused and then reprimanded herself for still caring what happened to him.

She opened the front door and started the journey to her parents' house, trying to imagine what she'd tell them.

44

Ovidia woke on the grey sofa. Her hysterics had left her exhausted. She'd begun after the others had left. Edmund had protested when she struggled off the sofa to use the toilet. As she'd dragged herself back from the bathroom, she'd seen that it was nearly midnight. The image of Oliver, dead, flashed through her mind, and she fell apart.

Now, she watched the clock on the wall. The numbers were in focus, but she still couldn't take them in with her face throbbing with pain. Her skin was clammy, and she trembled with an imagined chill.

Edmund had tucked the grey blanket around her. This time she'd assented, earlier she'd kicked it away screaming. He sat beside her on the floor, scrolling through his phone. She couldn't see what he was doing, but she was glad he was awake with her.

Ovidia had refused to go to bed, and they remained where their guests had left them hours earlier. Anne had overseen her care, checking her for concussion, asking her questions to make sure she was lucid. Edmund had stood behind her, repeatedly asking if Ovidia was all right, if he should call an ambulance. Every other minute, Anne had glanced at the door through which John had dragged Jasper, John shouting incomprehensibly, and Jasper too stunned to answer.

When, finally, Edmund had helped Anne get Ovidia onto the sofa, Anne had said, 'I should go. I'll call you tomorrow to see if you're okay?' She had turned away too quickly, showing her discomfort in their presence.

Ovidia hadn't heard what everyone had been talking about, the conversation in which Jasper had charged at her, but she didn't ask. She could guess the reason he'd hit her, and if she was wrong, she said to herself, it didn't matter. He'd hit her, and she wondered if he was as filled with conflict and guilt as when she'd first hit him. She wanted to talk to him, to tell him it was too easy to never stop.

'This is all my fault,' she said.

Edmund looked up, surprised to find her awake. 'Not all of it,' he replied.

'Could you have imagined a year ago that we'd be planning our baby's funeral?' she asked.

He shook his head and held her hand.

'Please stay with me,' she began to blubber. 'What am I supposed to do without you?'

He squeezed her hand tighter, 'What about Jasper? I can't imagine the rest of my life without him. If I'd been more attentive…'

'If you hadn't been with me,' Ovidia said.

'Maybe, but I can't make the same mistake again.'

Ovidia was silent, looking at the floor, letting the flow of pain free. She winced. Edmund put his arm around her.

'When I saw him go for you, I couldn't believe it. I couldn't stop him. What if you'd been seriously injured?' He slumped a little, his phone sliding on to the floor.

'You're texting your mum at this time of night?' she asked, seeing the profile on the screen.

'And my dad, and John, and our cousin Margret. Jasper won't answer his phone,' he replied. 'I didn't want to disturb you.'

Ovidia struggled to sit up. 'What if he?' she trailed off. 'You have to make sure he's all right. You have to go over there.'

'According to John, *"He's finished off two bottles of wine and is vomiting in the loo"*,' Edmund read from his texts.

She pulled the grey blanket around herself and forced herself to remember.

She had nearly pried the insole out of her running shoe.

'Ovidia! Stop mucking around with that shoe and take care of Oliver!'

Ovidia had erupted at his words. She leapt to her feet and, in a few steps, was on the landing.

'Ovidia! Call an ambulance!'

Had a second passed? Or a minute? Her hand was empty where it had held a running shoe.

Edmund had been dazed, trying to get to his feet.

She remembered not being able to move. She'd stood frozen in place, her eyes fixed on Oliver at the bottom of the stairs – inert – silent.

Edmund had been a few steps below her, holding his head where it had struck the wall on his way down. He'd pulled himself up. He'd snatched his phone from where it had fallen and stumbled down to their baby.

The details were nebulous. Her memory of the incident clouded by misery and guilt. She'd launched the shoe at Edmund. But, only at Edmund, she'd told herself. She didn't see Oliver through her rage. Had she assumed he'd already put him down? Had she even thought?

Edmund had dialled for an ambulance, crying as he begged for help to come as quickly as it could. 'He's not moving. Please help.' He'd put his head against the wall, being sentient enough not to touch the damaged child. He'd wept.

Ovidia had watched everything from the top of the stairs, trying to understand what she'd done.

45

Edmund touched Ovidia's face, and she flinched again. He could see bruises forming, blue and black on her tender, swollen brown skin. Tomorrow, if Ovidia were to walk out in public, strangers would look at her and assume that he'd hit her. She would be swollen, the victim of a domestic altercation. He could imagine what her family, or his, would think if they saw her.

He tried to identify what he was feeling inside. It was emptiness. He'd stayed beside her after Jasper's attack, taking care of her once again.

'I'll make an appointment for you for Monday with a counsellor,' he said.

'Monday's too soon,' she turned away from him, facing the back of the sofa.

'I won't stay with you unless you see one,' Edmund said, and she stiffened. 'There's no future for us without help. I should have insisted right from the start, but I wanted to believe love is all you need and that sort of nonsense.' He shifted where he sat. 'I'm not naïve. I didn't believe that I'd saved you or that that part of you was gone. But I let myself become complacent. I was sure you'd never hurt Oliver, and it's only because I know you didn't mean to hurt him that I'm still with you.'

Her eyes filled up with tears, but they didn't move him. He wouldn't be the first man to make ultimatums to his partner. He wouldn't be the first man to declare that it would be over if she didn't do as he said.

Jasper.

Holly was gone, from what John had been able to garner from the situation. She hadn't believed Jasper when he'd told her about Ovidia – what Ovidia had done to him. Edmund could no longer keep Ovidia away from the damage she'd wrought upon his brother.

He stared at the wall and realised that despite planning to leave, he hadn't so far taken any practical action to find a new place. And now, when he envisioned the future – Jasper getting better, Ovidia seeking help – he saw it in this house.

If he could have even a modicum of that joy they'd shared before, it would be enough. Edmund told himself he was making a conscious decision to remain with Ovidia. They both had made mistakes, and, because of this, their life together would never be normal. They could never really trust each other; the naivety with which they'd launched into their relationship was gone.

He and Ovidia could have a future together, perhaps with another child. Jasper could be part of their new life, and, somehow, Jasper could be a happier man. The blanket of guilt that had shrouded Edmund would finally be lifted.

For now, there was a funeral to arrange, there was time to be taken off work, and a director to placate so he could start rebuilding his life.

He'd sent his mother a long text while Ovidia lay on the sofa.

I have a girlfriend; we've been together for four years. She hurt Jasper very badly.

It was juvenile yet strategic. Hopefully, by the time they'd see him next, his parents' anger would have dissipated. He'd signed off, telling his mother not to phone him.

His phone beeped, a reply from his mother.

I swear you'll never here the end of this! it said.

Why didn't you tell me? The second message beeped.

Then the phone rang. His mother's moniker blinking.

Edmund, for the first time in many years, deliberately switched his phone off.

'It's never going to be just us again,' he said to Ovidia.

She nodded.

'Oliver will always be with us,' he continued, choking over Oliver's name. 'And there's Jasper, and our parents, your sister.'

Ovidia snatched her hand away from his.

He looked at her.

'We won't tell them all about Oliver. We'll come up with our own version of what happened – some things will have to remain between us,' he said, and she took his hand again.

Edmund stroked Ovidia's forehead, knowing he'd failed to accomplish what he'd hoped for – he wasn't leaving her.

ACKNOWLEDGEMENTS

I'd like to thank

Samuli and Joona – my boys.

Anne Johnson and Trui Meyns, for being my first readers and for their friendship.

To Sam and Peyton, for helping turn my manuscript into a real novel.

And especially

Baba, Auntie Luo and Lord Lewis, it hurts that you'll never read this book.

But most of all to Jo – I did it, just like you said I could. I just wish you were here to read it.